A long stretched hour it was;
Nothing undone
Remained; the early seeds
All safely sown.

Sowing
Edward Thomas

20/9/25

NOTHING UNDONE REMAINED

An evocative and charming Edwardian family saga

DOMINIC LUKE

The Brannans Family Trilogy Book 2

JOFFE BOOKS

Revised edition 2021
Joffe Books, London
www.joffebooks.com

First published by Robert Hale in Great Britain in 2014

Cover art by Jarmila Takač

ISBN: 978-1-78931-836-4

CHAPTER ONE

Roderick Brannan leant out of the railway carriage window. The wind pummelled his face, roared in his ears. The permanent way seemed to flow like water as the train forged along the track. He stretched out his arms as far as he dared, testing himself, rising to the challenge. Was this how it felt to fly?

Scenes of home seemed to swim up towards him out of the speeding, swirling chaos below. He saw Mother, Father, sister, cousin lined up in the hallway ready for his departure. He saw the motor car on the gravel outside waiting to take him to the station. He remembered how he had twisted round on the back seat to get a last glimpse of the house. The great, grey facade had swung away as the motor turned into the drive. Trees had obscured the view. Clifton Park had faded from sight. It faded again now, receding back into the chaos from which it had come.

Flecks of soot from the labouring locomotive came spiralling out of the high blue sky. Roderick closed his eyes to protect them. At once he was plunged into a mad, tumultuous darkness. He felt as if he was teetering giddily on the edge of a bottomless void. At any moment he might lose his balance and fall.

His eyes snapped open. He gripped the window frame with all his might. He had saved himself, he felt, just in time. A viaduct had appeared in the distance and was rapidly getting nearer, a series of massive stone arches curving across the valley towards him. That was the railway line from Nottingham. Up ahead, the line he was on passed beneath it, after which the branch to Downfield veered off to the left. There was not long to go now. His journey was almost at an end.

He drew back into the empty compartment and flung himself into his seat. The scenes of home still lingered in his mind. The wrench of departure was raw. After the long summer hols he had been torn from the ground like a sapling whose roots were just taking hold. Now he was to be replanted once more in the stony ground of school. An interminable autumn term stretched ahead of him.

He groaned at the thought, sliding down to put his feet up on the opposite seat, legs bridging the gap. It was damnably hot again today. The Indian summer continued. His new uniform hung heavy. His shirt was clammy with sweat. Impatiently, he loosened his tie and took off his cap, flinging it aside. Shoving a hand in his pocket, he dug out his cigarettes and lit one.

He scowled as he smoked. What sort of sap was he, getting into such a lather over something as commonplace as going back to school? He ought to have grown a thicker skin than this at the ripe age of fourteen. He ought to be used to the day of departure. He'd had plenty of practice: all those years at prep school, and this was his fourth journey to Downfield. Autumn term 1906 was here already — which meant three terms at Downfield had come and gone. Three terms! And what did he have to show for it? Precious little, that was what.

Roderick blew out smoke, disgruntled. School wasn't everything, he tried to convince himself. The Duke of Wellington, for instance, had not been a success at school. The Duke's mother had written, 'I don't know what I shall do with my awkward son Arthur.' Yet look how he had turned out!

But hang it all! Roderick didn't want to wait until he was middle-aged to make a name for himself! He wanted to be someone here and now! He'd been someone at his prep school. Not to start with, it was true: he'd struggled to start with. But he'd got there in the end. He'd been quite the celebrity. Which made it all the more galling having to begin all over again at Downfield.

He'd tried to explain this to Father as they walked round and round the walled garden at home. A little light exercise was good for Father's health, the doctor said. 'A lot of fuss over nothing,' was Father's view. But he liked to show willing, for Mother's sake.

Father was a down-to-earth sort of chap. He had a knack for putting his finger on things. But that afternoon about a week ago he'd been, for once, a let-down. All his talk about big fish and little ponds had not really helped.

'Where did *you* go to school, Father?' Roderick had hoped to jog the old chap's memory as to what school was really like. When one was as old as sixty, one's school days must seem as remote as the flood.

'Ah. Well. Now.' Father had smoothed his moustache in that way he had, had looked sidelong at Roderick. 'I never had your advantages, my boy. There were no Education Acts in my day. I *learned by doing*, as my old man used to say.'

Father, it turned out, knew nothing even of prep school, let alone a place of the calibre of Downfield. It shouldn't have come as a surprise: it was just that he seemed so at home at Clifton these days that one was apt to overlook the fact that he'd been born somewhere in the back streets of Coventry. Father's father had been a watchmaker who'd gone into business on his own account and made quite a success of it. But even in the good years, it seemed, the family had not exactly lived in the lap of luxury.

'When I was your age, my boy, I was already at work.'

Slumped in his seat in the swaying carriage, Roderick wondered what it would have been like to follow in Father's footsteps and be at work now instead of at school. He couldn't begin to imagine. All he knew was the life he had. The footsteps he was actually following were Uncle Fred's. That was why Mother had insisted on Downfield. The same school, the same house — Ransom's — as Uncle Fred: that paragon Uncle Fred. But if Ransom's had been pre-eminent in Uncle Fred's day, it had fallen low since then. It was now the beastliest house in the school.

'If only I was in Harcourt's instead of Ransom's!'

'Why? What's so special about Harcourt's?' his cousin Dorothea had asked.

'Oh, nothing! They've only won the Cricket Cup two years running! They only make up half of the First Fifteen and more than half of the Eleven!'

'There's no need to be sarcastic.'

'But Harcourt's men are the lions of Downfield!'

'They are *boys*, Roddy, not *men*. And I can't see why you're complaining. Your house wins most of the school prizes. What could be better than that?'

'Only *scholars* win prizes.'

'You are all meant to be scholars.'

'We call chaps who spend too much time swotting *scholars*. No one thinks much of scholars. It's the inter-house cups that matter! It's the school teams!'

'*Games*, you mean.'

'You needn't take that tone! There's nothing wrong with games! But I shouldn't expect *you* to understand. Girls have no idea about the world.'

'And boys like to make mountains out of molehills. Instead of grumbling, you should count yourself lucky that you get the chance to go to school at all. When I lived in Stepnall Street—'

'Yes, yes, I know all about it: there was only bread and water to eat and children were sent up chimneys from birth. I don't believe it was half as bad as you make out!'

But as he drew on his cigarette in the railway carriage, Roderick had to admit that Dorothea was not prone to exaggeration, that Stepnall Street had probably been — if anything — *worse* than she made out. Father might have come from somewhat humble origins, but it was nothing compared to the places where Dorothea had lived as a little kid. Fortunately for her, she had been brought from the slums of London by her father and dumped without ceremony at Clifton Park. From all that one gathered, it was the only worthwhile thing her father had ever done. This had been years ago. One tended to forget these days that Dorothea had not been around forever.

'You should stop and think how lucky you are, Roddy!' she'd repeated, insistent. As if he'd been born with a silver spoon, as if he was spoiled and pampered, as if going to Downfield was like having a rest cure! 'There are almost no boys of your age in the village who are still at school.' Was that *his* fault? Why should *he* care about the village, dreary old Hayton? 'Nibs Carter,' she'd added: 'Nibs Carter—'

Roderick pulled a face in the train, watching the ash crumble and fall from the end of his cigarette. Mentioning Nibs Carter had been a ploy on her part, he was sure of it. She'd done it to rile him. Nibs Carter was the most objectionable of all the good-for-nothing village boys and just happened to be Roderick's age-old enemy, too. Nibs Carter was a peasant. He probably didn't even know what a school was. But up until this summer there'd been no avoiding him. He'd worked at Clifton as assistant to the decrepit old gardener Becket. Then, in June, he'd been caught stealing vegetables and dismissed. Dorothea had been upset. She had an inexplicable soft spot for the little rat: inexplicable but only too typical. She simply refused to see the bad in anyone. At her age — she was actually a few months older than Roderick — she ought to know better.

Roderick rolled the dwindling cigarette between his fingers. It was a waste of time trying to convince her that Nibs Carter (or anyone else) was a bad egg. It was a waste of time trying to explain about school. She just couldn't see how important it was. How could it not be, when a chap spent more than half his time there? Any chap worth his salt would want to get on, make a name for himself.

Uncle Fred would have understood. He'd been through it. But peerless Uncle Fred had breathed his last years ago. One had never got the chance to know him. A pity, really. If only he'd still been around! Why did he have to die? *How* had he died, for that matter? It had never really been made clear. He couldn't have been all that old. He'd been eight years older than Mother, it was true, but Mother was hardly on her last legs even now. Mother was — well, she was a brick for one thing, an absolute brick. No weeping and wailing for *her* when term time came round again, no scenes of dreadful desolation as her darling boy set forth once more. Just a calm and measured smile and, 'Goodbye, Roderick. *Do* have a good term.' Mother in another age might easily have passed for Boadicea. Or maybe Good Queen Bess. Yes, that was it! One could just imagine Mother spouting all that 'weak and feeble woman' stuff! Mother had the heart and stomach of a king, if anyone did!

But now the train was toiling up the final incline and it was time to thrust aside all thoughts of home. As he tossed the last of his cigarette out of the window — as he brushed ash off his trousers and pulled on his cap and straightened his school tie — Roderick could not help but feel that the *real* business of life was about to begin once more.

* * *

He picked out Harrington-Shaw's podgy face in the melee on the platform. As usual, H-S had arrived on an earlier train. As usual, he had waited for Roderick. He was nothing if not predictable.

Roderick elbowed his way through the crowd. 'What-ho, H-S! This is a beastly scrum! Who are these small fry I keep stepping on?'

'New boys, Branners.'

'A contemptible collection! I'd swear *we* were never so puny! Let's leave them to it.'

They sauntered out of the station, old hands after three terms, superior. Their route took them past the railway workers' cottages on Station Lane and then rather grander houses on the climb up Grey Hill Road.

The little market town of Downfield was built on an escarpment. The railway was at the bottom of the slope, the main square at the top where also the fourteenth century church was situated with its slender spire, along with some shops and the White Hart Inn. The school buildings were mostly situated to the west of the main square. Almost half the town was taken up with the school — the most important half at that. But as Roderick passed the church and turned into Market Street, H-S trotting beside him, he was not thinking of the importance of the school, he was mulling over the relative insignificance of Ransom's and his own obscurity within it.

'Something must be done!' he burst out. 'Something to shake up the house! A *grand gesture*. But what?'

'I *do* wish you wouldn't talk like that, Branners. You'll cause the most awful stink. No one will thank you for it, least of all Martineau.'

'Martineau is an ass.'

'Martineau is head boy.'

'He doesn't deserve to be.'

'If he didn't deserve to be head of house, then he wouldn't be head of house.'

Roderick sighed. H-S could be maddeningly obtuse. Why couldn't he see that it was only in a house like Ransom's that such a boy as Martineau could hope to prosper? Ransom's was a house where the natural order of things had been turned on its head. In any normal house, games were held in high regard and the bloods ruled the roost. In Ransom's, the bloods were kept in check by a pack of frowsty scholars, like elephants spooked by mice. Martineau was the chief of the scholars and the housemaster's favourite.

'Raynes should be head boy,' said Roderick. 'Raynes is the one who *deserves* it.' Raynes Major was so illustrious a figure that he actually played for the school Eleven. But the housemaster, Mr Moxon, looked down on sporting prowess and set more store by Martineau's supposed *brains*.

'Raynes is junior to Martineau,' H-S pointed out pedantically. 'Perhaps he'll be head of house next year.'

'He's the finest chap in the school! He should be head of house *now*! Why must we wait?'

'You're always in such a hurry, Branners. You want everything straight away.'

Was it any wonder, with the world the measly place that it was? How had it got to be so dull? Things had been different a hundred years ago, with Nelson at Trafalgar and Wellington setting off for Spain. Life had been worth living back then.

Roderick had a brief but glorious vision of himself as Wellington setting his sword into that Napoleon-like scoundrel Martineau.

'Don't you ever feel, H-S, that you want to *do* something, *be* someone? Like Wellington or Nelson — or even General Gordon at a pinch.'

But H-S said no, he could honestly say that he'd never felt like that in his whole life. In any case, hadn't Nelson and General Gordon both been killed in battle? Who'd want to be like *them*? It was better to do nothing, be no one: at least that way one stayed alive.

This was exactly the sort of craven attitude that had brought Ransom's low. It was why a grand gesture was so desperately needed, to lead the way, to show what was possible. But Roderick didn't explain this to H-S. He didn't want to hurt H-S's feelings. One had a certain duty towards H-S, like a knight with his squire. It was none of the squire's fault if he lacked the lofty ambitions of his master.

There was no time for further thought. They had reached the far end of Market Street. Here were the two old and much-extended grey stone cottages which formed the core of the Ransom's buildings: a rather ad hoc, ramshackle sort of place, nothing heroic about it.

They stepped over the threshold to be engulfed in the first-day mayhem. The summer holidays were well and truly behind them now.

* * *

Lights-out had been ages ago but Roderick was still awake trying to get used to the dorm again, to sleeping in an attic full of boys after the luxury of his own room at Clifton. Homesickness often lay in wait at such moments. One never knew quite when it would strike. He was thinking about his new puppy and how he'd barely had time to start training it. By the time the Christmas hols came round, it would have forgotten all about him. He remembered how it had felt, warm and wriggling in his arms. He remembered its doleful eyes looking up at him. He remembered its wet tongue on his face.

His lip trembled in the dark. He bit down on it fiercely, spurning insidious homesickness. He bit rather too hard and tasted blood. He was just exploring the wound with his tongue when inspiration struck. He suddenly knew what he had to do.

He would walk on the Jitty.

As an idea it was deceptively simple. As a grand gesture, it was perfect.

It would create a sensation, of course. Tradition dictated that only Conway's men could use the Jitty, a narrow alley connecting North Street to one of the school playing fields, the Upper. Conway's was pre-eminent amongst the houses, second only to Harcourt's in pride and prowess. In days gone by, it was said, boys from other houses had dared to test the exclusivity of Conway's Jitty. On occasion, pitched battles had been fought over it. But that was in a remote and lawless past. In these more enlightened — and boring — times, no one bothered much now about the Jitty — but no one trespassed on it, either. If he set foot on the sacred alley, he'd make a name for himself and raise Ransom's reputation in one go. A kid like him, only in his fourth term: even in the old lawless days it would have been unthinkable. Only senior boys had taken the risk.

That was what made his plan so perfect.

* * *

Heading down at the double to the basement with his towel draped round his neck, Roderick on the stairs seized the chance for a quick word with H-S.

'Walk on the Jitty?' cried H-S. 'You can't! You mustn't! Honestly, Branners, I wish you wouldn't!'

This was hardly encouraging. But H-S was an inveterate sheep. Of course he'd be appalled at the very idea of walking on the Jitty. Nonetheless, as Roderick splashed himself in a glacial bath, his teeth chattering, he was beset by sudden doubts. He remembered how he'd felt yesterday, hanging out of the train with his eyes shut, teetering on the edge of a giddy fall into nothingness. This was exactly the same. The whole project was fraught with danger. Not just the physical danger of being set upon by a pack of Conway's bloods; there was the risk he was taking, too, of going against tradition. Traditions were sacred at Downfield. When — if — he walked on the Jitty, would the school applaud his courage or condemn his act of sacrilege?

The hand bell was ringing. Boys began leaping out of baths on every side, their bare feet slapping on the flagstones. Roderick was swept along in the mad stampede. Still shivering, he took his place in chapel. As the first hymn began, he looked down at the hymn book, trying to find his place on the page. But was it the right page, even? He was all at sixes and sevens.

The hymn came to an end, leaving an echoing silence in the chapel. With much shuffling, bumping and coughing, they all sat down. The soporific voice of the chaplain started up. Hitching himself forward, Roderick let his hand slide along the underside of the shelf in front of him. His fingers found the carved initials. He read them like Braille: *H.F.A.R.*, and a date, *1871*.

He'd come across them by accident last term, bored during one of old Methuselah's endless sermons (the chaplain's sermons were notorious). There could be little doubt about it: they had to be the initials of Uncle Fred whose first name — never used — had been Henry, after his father. It was Roderick's middle name, too: a connection of sorts, a tenuous link with his prodigious uncle. Thirty-five years ago, Uncle Fred must have sat in this very spot carving the wood: no doubt singing the same hymns, perhaps even listening to the same sermon (Lord only knew what old Methuselah was going on about today — and probably even the Lord wasn't interested). This morning Roderick felt as if the initials had been carved there on purpose, for just such a moment as this. Uncle Fred was reaching across the years to give his young nephew the fillip he needed.

It was time for the next hymn. Everyone got to their feet. Roderick jumped up, puffed out his chest, sang with gusto. He might be afraid but he wouldn't let that stop him. Had Wellington ever given in to fear, or Nelson? As for tradition — well, one couldn't blindly follow tradition forever. If nothing ever changed, the world would still have been living in the dark ages.

So this was it! *Jacta est alea*! In memory of Uncle Fred. For the honour of Ransom's. And to the greater glory of Roderick Henry Brannan!

* * *

A knot of boys had gathered in the golden afternoon sunshine in North Street near the entrance of the Jitty. H-S, trusty squire, was prominent amongst them. He had not failed to spread the word. It wouldn't have done for Roderick's great undertaking to go unnoticed. But now it had come to the point, Roderick found his feet dragging. The temptation to turn and run was all but overpowering.

'Screw your courage to the sticking place,' he muttered. Now, who was it had said that? Oh, yes: Lady Macbeth. *Screw your courage to the sticking place and we'll not fail.* His cousin Dorothea had, for some reason, a morbid dislike of Lady Macbeth but Roderick rather admired her. All that business about bashing babies' brains out was first-class stuff. But — funnily enough — as he walked on the cobbles of

North Street in the autumn sunshine, it was the thought of Dorothea rather than Lady Macbeth which steadied him and stiffened his spine. Just about now Dorothea would be taking her afternoon walk in the gardens at Clifton, a habit she had got into during the era of her Frog governess. It was almost as if he could see her, strolling along the cinder paths, stopping to turn and look at him, shading her eyes with her hand.

'All this fuss over a little alleyway!' She would have used the same tone of voice that she used when talking about games. 'Boys are so *silly* about such things.'

Silly, was it, walking on the Jitty? That was all *she* knew!

He squared his shoulders, forced himself to think about honour, glory, all that stuff — not to mention the sacred memory of Uncle Fred. Counting helped. He counted each step in his head. It distracted him and stopped him going at it in an unseemly rush.

One . . . two . . . three . . .

There it was, the entrance to the Jitty, a narrow slot between two large buildings: the half-timbered School House to the left, and brick-built Conway's on the right.

. . . eight . . . nine . . . screw your courage . . . screw your courage . . . twelve . . . thirteen . . .

There was an audible and very encouraging gasp when he actually stepped onto the forbidden path. He would have liked to have whistled a nonchalant tune but couldn't trust himself to pull it off. He concentrated on his counting instead; he concentrated on putting one foot firmly in front of the other. The walls closed in. He was walking in a deep and sunless abyss.

. . . twenty-two . . . twenty-three . . .

He rounded a dog-leg in the alley. His audience was lost to him now. He felt like Livingstone alone in darkest Africa, off the edge of the map.

Except that he wasn't alone.

His heart did a somersault as he caught sight of two Conway's men ahead: two brutish, brawny-looking boys walking side-by-side towards him, blocking his way. Roderick focused on the middle distance, kept going forward. He sensed rather than saw the two Conway's boys slow up and look at each other in consternation.

. . . *thirty-nine* . . . *forty* . . .

He couldn't breathe. His heart was trying to fight its way out of his chest. And the Conway's boys had stopped dead, were waiting for him. Glory, honour, the sacred memory of Uncle Fred: they seemed such flimsy straws to cling to out here in the wilds of the Jitty.

And then something unexpected — unbelievable — happened. The two boys stepped aside. One of them made an elaborate gesture, indicating that Roderick was free to pass. He felt their breath on him as he walked between them.

It wasn't long before he'd left them behind. He broke into a run. It didn't matter about being nonchalant now. He'd lost count in any case. The high buildings fell away. There was just a low brick wall on one side, a clipped hedge on the other, and ahead a glimmer of green: the Upper!

He felt grass under his feet. He'd made it! He'd done it! He was back from darkest Africa, back in the gentle golden sunshine of England — and there was even a welcoming party to hand! H-S and the others must have run like the wind to have got here before him. He was glad they had. As they cheered and clapped and slapped him on the back, he all but fell into their arms, his legs giving way. They hoisted him up and carried him. Slowly, boisterously, they snaked across the playing field and down Little Lane, making their way back to Ransom's. Roderick felt like a hero from one of those adventure books of old. Dorothea would have laughed at him but at that moment not even Dorothea's laughter could have dented his sense of triumph.

* * *

By evening prep it was all round the house; indeed, half the school was said to be talking about it. The other boys in Roderick's dorm were cock-a-hoop. His heroism, they felt, reflected particularly brightly on them. It was the only topic of conversation after lights-out.

'It was the bravest thing I ever saw!' H-S enthused.

'Brave? Or stupid?' The dissenting voice was Westaway's. He was known as something of an individual. It was not meant as a compliment.

'Of course it was brave, Westaway!' H-S insisted. 'It was pure pluck!'

'If you say so. But we haven't heard the last of it, I know that much.'

Westaway proved to be right. Next morning after first school and before breakfast, Roderick was summoned to see the head of house. He prepared himself for one of Martineau's tedious monologues about *doing the right thing* and *keeping one's head down*.

'Shut the door. I shall be with you in a moment.'

Martineau was writing at his desk, did not look up. The sound of his pen scratching across the paper was loud in the quiet of the study. Roderick recognised this keep-you-waiting ruse. Mother Moxon used it to throw boys off guard. No doubt Martineau modelled himself on the fussy, bespectacled housemaster whose soubriquet *Mother* suited him perfectly.

Roderick wrinkled his nose, rocked on his heels, bored. In lieu of anything more interesting to do, he began to catalogue the items on Martineau's desk. There was a blotter, an inkwell, a well-thumbed dictionary, a tidy pile of essays. To the left of the essays was a little wooden marquetry box with the lid not quite shut. Something was poking out, something metal. Roderick tilted his head first one way, then the other, trying to work out what it was. A key, maybe? Too small to be a door key. It might perhaps be the key to a desk drawer.

'Ah, it's you, Brannan.' Martineau took notice at last. Putting his pen aside, he sat back, placing his hands on the desk. It was all done with such great precision — the movements, the facial expression, the tone of voice — that Roderick wondered if Martineau practised in front of a mirror.

'I hear you made quite an ass of yourself yesterday, Brannan.'

'Rather not, I think, Martineau.' Yesterday had been a triumph, but of course Martineau was far too small-minded to see it.

'I don't know who you think you are, swaggering about the place. Just what did you hope to achieve by walking on Conway's Jitty? I wish you'd enlighten me.'

Roderick felt bold enough to look Martineau in the eye. 'I wanted to show that not *all* Ransom's men are measly saps.'

Martineau flushed at this but did not break eye contact. 'Very noble of you, Brannan, I'm sure. But it won't do. It won't do at all. It's time you were put in your place. School traditions can't be flouted just because you want to make yourself look big. Traditions are what make a place — though perhaps it's too much to expect of a boy like you, to understand about tradition.' He paused, then said slowly, 'Your father's in trade, isn't he?'

Roderick felt his cheeks burning. He was dismayed. It must look as if he was *ashamed* of Father! He wasn't, he truly wasn't. But he could feel Martineau's mocking eyes on him and he realised that the fact that Father was successful and had gone up in the world counted for nothing. What mattered was one's name, one's pedigree, one's bloodline. Father could never alter the fact that he came from the back streets of Coventry. People would always look down on Father, just as they would always look down on him, Roderick Brannan, the tradesman's son. Boys like Martineau with his well-connected clergyman father always had the advantage.

Roderick grimaced. The injustice of it all goaded him. He blurted out, 'Keeping off the Jitty has nothing to do with tradition, Martineau. It's . . . it's *cowardice*. Pure funk.'

Martineau's mouth contorted. 'You odious little tick! What gives you the right to brand the whole house cowards?'

'Not the whole house, just—'

'Don't interrupt! Don't *ever* interrupt *me*!'

Roderick clamped his lips together, stood silent. He watched the fingers of Martineau's right hand twitching on the desk. After a moment Martineau became aware of this too and moved his left hand to cover his right.

'This is what's going to happen, Brannan. You will go to Conway's and you will apologise for trespassing on the Jitty. You will beg their forgiveness. You will *beg*: do I make myself clear?'

'Apologise? I don't think so, Martineau.'

Roderick braced himself. Open defiance of the head of house was worth a beating at the very least. But to his complete surprise, Martineau merely shrugged and picked up his pen.

'Then there's nothing more I can do for you. You may go.'

Roderick hesitated in the corridor, closing the door slowly behind him. Why had Martineau backed down? There could only be one explanation. The head boy must be even more of a weakling than anyone had imagined.

Roderick broke into a grin. First the grand gesture, now Martineau licked. Even that prodigy Uncle Fred could never have achieved so much in the space of two days.

He was on his way at last. He was finally making a name for himself.

* * *

They came at him from behind, threw a sack over his head on Ransom's very doorstep. Strong arms restrained him. He objected, put up a fight, but there were too many of them, he was powerless. Pushed and half-dragged along the street, he didn't need to ask where he was being taken. It would be the first time he had ever set foot in Conway's.

He was ushered up a flight of stairs and along endless corridors before being marched into a room. A door closed. The strong arms were removed. He stood motionless. What next?

After a long minute, the sack was pulled away. He blinked and looked round. He was in a large study, wood panels on the walls, books stacked on shelves. Either side of him were two burly fellows, like prison warders. In front was a wide desk. Behind it sat three boys, watching him gravely. No one spoke.

'What do you want?' he asked at last, trying to keep his voice level.

He was answered by a blow from the right which sent him reeling, made his head spin. He slowly straightened, gritting his teeth, blinking away a few treacherous tears.

'Speak only when you are spoken to, otherwise keep silent.' The middle boy at the desk spoke coldly, distinctly, acting out a role. 'I am the Chief Inquisitor. This court martial is now in session. What is the charge?'

The boy on his left spoke up. 'This Ransom's man, er . . .' The boy looked down at a piece of paper, then up again. 'What's the blighter's name? I've completely forgotten.'

'You!' barked the middle boy, the Chief Inquisitor. 'What's your name?'

'Brannan.'

'Brannan, *sir*. Well? *SAY IT*!'

Roderick stayed silent. Another blow was his reward. This time it knocked him off his feet. He got up bit by bit, hanging his head until he was in full control of his face.

The Inquisitor raised an eyebrow. 'Well?'

'My name is Brannan. Sir.'

'Good. You will show due deference to the Court at all times. Let us continue. The charge, please.'

The other boy spoke up again. 'This Ransom's riff-raff by the name of Brannan is accused of defiling the sacred flagstones of the Jitty with his filthy, heretical feet. His guilt is established beyond doubt. Twenty-seven eyewitness statements have been submitted to the court.'

'Very well.' The Inquisitor fixed his eyes on Roderick. 'What have you to say for yourself? Anything in mitigation?' He paused, waiting. 'Nothing?'

Roderick, though acutely aware of the clenched fists poised either side of him, could not stop himself saying, 'This is a farce! You have no jurisdiction over me, a Ransom's man! And the Jitty is a public lane!'

'Wrong!' snapped the Inquisitor. 'The Jitty belongs to Conway's under the laws of use and custom. It is forbidden to men of other houses. Do you understand? Well?'

Roderick moved his head. It might have been a nod — but then again, it might not.

'Good. Let us proceed. The court will now deliberate.'

The three boys leant together and talked in whispers. Roderick scowled, watching them through narrowed eyes. The shock of the unexpected abduction was at last wearing off. He was beginning to feel defiant. What was the worst they could do to him? Hit him again? He could take it. He wasn't a milksop. It was time Ransom's men showed some backbone in their dealings with other houses.

The deliberation was over. The Inquisitor said, 'As this is your first offence, the court is inclined to be lenient. We will, this once, overlook the grave insult that you have directed to this most august and venerable house — provided that you beg the court's forgiveness.'

The burly fellow to his left gave Roderick a shove. 'On your knees!'

Roderick weighed his options. Might discretion be the better part of valour? After all, there was no one to witness his humiliation except these Conway's vermin — and they didn't count.

'What? Reluctant?' The boy who'd announced the charge was grinning. 'I thought that if there was one thing Ransom's men were good at, it was grovelling.' He laughed.

Roderick glared at him. Discretion be blowed. This was now a point of honour. He could hear Martineau's voice in his head: *you will beg their forgiveness* . . . Well, he wouldn't.

He took a deep breath. 'I will walk on your rotten Jitty whenever I choose and there's nothing you can do to stop me!'

The boy stopped laughing. The Inquisitor's eyes widened in disbelief. 'So that's your attitude, is it? Insolence! Well, it won't be tolerated. It certainly won't be tolerated from Ransom's scum!' He glanced left, then right. The other boys nodded. 'We repeal our previous judgment. You are sentenced to the firing squad. Five rounds. To be carried out immediately. Court dismissed.'

Quick as a flash, the sack was back over Roderick's head and his arms were pinioned at his sides. He heard the scraping of chairs, sensed that the three boys who had been sitting behind the desk were now leaving the room. There was a pause and then, roughly, his two guards turned him round and they all set off.

He was taken to a larger, airier room. A murmur of voices alerted him to the presence of an audience. It was to be a public spectacle, then, his punishment by firing squad — whatever that might entail.

He was taken to one side of the room, positioned facing the wall. They made him bend over. His fingers slid down the wooden panels, found the chair rail. He gripped it, waited. The room had fallen silent. There was an air of expectancy. Fear clenched his bowels.

He heard running footsteps coming towards him; then, without warning, something slammed into him from behind. It felt like being hit by a train. He lost his grip on the chair rail and his head cracked against the wall. An excruciating pain exploded in his buttocks and spread up his spine like fire.

So this was what it was all about: flying kicks. And there were four more to come. He groped around in blind agony but could not find the wall to brace himself — and already the running footsteps were approaching again . . .

* * *

They thrust him out into the street, only then removing the sack. He blinked in the sudden brightness, using his arm to shield his eyes, feeling horribly conspicuous — although North Street was mercifully quiet at this time of the afternoon. He was sure they had crippled him, that he would end up deformed, bedridden, like that wreck of a boy Richard, his late cousin. Just then he felt he'd be better off dead like Richard too. His short-lived triumph seemed a world away now.

He hobbled off, bent over like an old man. He wanted a corner to curl up in, somewhere to lick his wounds: not easy to find in the teeming precincts of Ransom's. Opening doors at random, he suddenly found himself in the housemaster's study. This was a door that was usually kept locked unless Moxon was there. Roderick turned away, wary of encroaching. Then it occurred to him that Moxon must be teaching. No one would disturb the peace of the study for a good hour or so. He would be safe here.

He closed the door. He was too sore to sit down. He lay on his front instead, on the rug by the fireplace. Pain ravaged him. He gritted his teeth against it. This, for a while, took all the strength he had.

After a time, a knot of anger grew inside him. He clenched his fists. They had no right, those Conway's boys, to treat him the way they had! He'd make them pay!

Oh, but what was the use? It was not as if anyone would listen. He was nobody, he had no standing in the house. He could have gone to the beaks, of course, but they wouldn't be interested. The boys were supposed to deal with such petty matters of discipline amongst themselves. They could be trusted to do what was right, being young gentlemen. But the beaks had no idea. They were completely oblivious to what really went on.

All his wild schemes for revenge melted away. He became aware of the measured ticking of a clock. How much time had passed while he'd been lying here? He ought to think about moving. Moxon might come back at any moment.

He scrambled to his knees, taking a proper look round as he did so. The walls were lined with floor-to-ceiling book cases, the window shrouded with net curtains. There was a big desk with neat piles of paper. There was a mantelpiece with the ticking clock and a daguerreotype of Moxon in a cap and a gown. But Roderick's eye was caught by a tall wooden cabinet with many drawers. As he stared at it, he wondered if there was any truth in the story of Moxon's *secret files*? It was rumoured that Moxon had an exhaustive dossier on every boy in the house. He was certainly the sort of stickler who *would* have files. But did they actually exist?

Curiosity overrode pain. Shuffling forward, Roderick reached out a hand to tug at one of the drawers. To his surprise, it opened. It was packed with folders.

He glanced at the clock. Had he time? Did he dare? But what did it matter if he was caught! What did anything matter after today!

There was one folder sticking up above the others, a name in neat writing on the flap, a name beginning with 'W'. Slowly, carefully, Roderick eased it out and opened it up. He would take a quick look, just to satisfy his curiosity. He would take a quick look, then he would go.

* * *

He'd missed afternoon school. It had not gone unnoticed. He was summoned once more to see Martineau. With barely disguised relish, Martineau recited the growing list of Roderick's misdemeanours: skipping lessons, flouting school traditions, showing insolence to the head of house. 'Need I go on? You have left me no choice, I'm afraid, Brannan.' He smiled.

The beating was administered before prep and in public. Martineau never did his own dirty work. Raynes was appointed from amongst the prefects to whack Roderick: six strokes.

'Is this really necessary, Martineau? An apology would suffice, surely, on this occasion?'

'Just get on with it, Raynes. Yours is not to reason why.'

Raynes did not hold back. He couldn't, with Martineau standing over him and the whole house watching. Roderick dug into his deepest reserves, managed to get through it without blubbing or crying out. When it was over, he shook Raynes's hand in the approved manner. He really did bear Raynes no grudge. All his loathing was reserved for Martineau.

Lying prostrate and sleepless in the dormitory, Roderick had to admit that Martineau had been very clever. Sap he might be, but he was no fool. It was obvious now that he'd known all along about the likelihood of a Conway's court martial. That was why he'd been so casual over the matter of an apology. He'd *wanted* Roderick to refuse because he'd *wanted* him to face the court martial. Bitterly, Roderick realised he'd walked right into Martineau's trap. What an idiot he'd been! What a hopeless little scug! So full of himself, blinded by his own daring, like Icarus flying too close to the sun. Instead of becoming a hero, he'd been made to look a fool, he'd been made an example of, both by Martineau and by the Conway's boys: they'd lost no time in spreading word of the court martial, to discourage other fortune hunters. The grand gesture seemed pointless now, a reckless act of empty bravado.

What would Uncle Fred think of him now? What would Dorothea think, Father too? And Mother? *I don't know what I shall do with my awkward son Roderick* . . . Perhaps it would be better if they didn't think of him at all. They were so far away. There was nothing they could do for him. He was all alone.

Pain gnawed him, pain like fire, burning. In the limbo between waking and sleep, he imagined he could see two shadowy figures standing over him, Admiral Nelson in a tricorn hat, the Duke of Wellington tall and stern. He felt their admonishing eyes on him, he heard their words echoing: *England expects every man to do his duty . . . up, Guards, and at 'em!*

He ground his teeth, his eyelids flickering. He'd show them! He'd show them if he was beaten! He'd show them all!

His eyelids flickered and then were still.

CHAPTER TWO

Roderick shivered, blowing into his hands and rubbing them briskly together as he peered into the mist on the Upper, watching Ransom's Fifteen being demolished by Harcourt's. The players were lumbering around on the boggy pitch, most of them covered head-to-toe in mud. It was grey, it was cold. The stand of oaks on the far side of the field was barely visible. Everything beyond was blanked out entirely. Lent term might be two-thirds over but February had not yet run its course and winter still had them in its grip. There had been frost on the pavements that morning as he made his way to first school.

He'd lost track of the score, could not bring himself to ask H-S or Kennedy who were standing beside him. Ransom's had yet to get a point, he knew that much. It filled him with a sense of despair. Barely half the house had traipsed up here to watch this rout. Maybe the ones who hadn't come had the right idea.

A groan broke from his lips. 'Oh lord! How much more of this is there?'

Kennedy patted his waistcoat pocket. He was an amiable sort of chap, nearly a year older than Roderick. The fact that he'd been in the house Eleven last summer gave him a certain glamour that he might otherwise have lacked.

He pulled a face. 'Damn and blast! I'd quite forgotten! I couldn't find my watch this morning.'

'Your watch is missing?' said H-S. 'I say, do you think it's the Petty Pilferer? It must be!'

'That's not in his line, is it, pocket watches?' said Kennedy. 'I thought the so-called Petty Pilferer only took books and sports kit and common property of that sort?'

'He's moved on since then,' said H-S, growing animated. There was nothing he liked more than house gossip. 'He took Lewis's pen last week.'

'Are you sure it was the Pilferer?' asked Kennedy.

'What other explanation can there be? We turned the dorm upside down looking for that pen. And Branners's tie pin has disappeared too.'

'Is that true, Branners? Have you had your tie pin stolen? I must say, you don't seem much bothered!'

'Oh, I'm mad as hell, Kennedy,' said Roderick mildly, keeping his eyes on the match as Raynes made a forlorn attempt to get out of the Ransom's half. 'But what can I do about it? Nobody listens to a nonentity like me.'

'But this is past a joke!' cried Kennedy. 'Lewis's pen, your tie pin, and now my watch! It was a present from my guv'nor, too! Something needs to be done!'

'That's up to Martineau,' said Roderick. 'He's head boy. He'll have to go cap in hand to Mother Moxon and confess that he can't keep order in the house. He's got no choice. He'll look such a fool!'

'If I know Martineau,' said Kennedy darkly, 'he'll think of something a lot more devious than that,'

But, after the events of last term, Roderick knew more than enough about Martineau's deviousness. He preferred not to talk about it.

The self-assured voices of the Harcourt's Fifteen rang out in the misty air, calling to each other, offering encouragement. Another try looked likely. Roderick watched glumly, huddled in his coat. He shoved his hands deeper in his pockets, fingered a letter that he found there, the latest from his cousin

Dorothea. When he came to write his reply, it might be best not to mention today's rugger match. She would only make some clever remark. He'd made the mistake in a previous letter of trying to interest her in the match that Harcourt's had played against Grayson's. Grayson's was a rather small, rather new and rather hopeless sort of house that had never won a match in all six years of its existence. But in the opening game of the Rugger Cup, Grayson's Fifteen had, in the first half, run rings round Harcourt's. At the interval, against all expectation, the scores had been level pegging. 'It was the most thrilling thing I have seen in life!' he'd gushed on the page.

Needless to say, Harcourt's had gone on to win the match by a country mile. Roderick hadn't mentioned that in the letter. It rather spoiled the story. He'd added instead a P.S. 'Have you asked Mother yet about my new cricket bat? I will need it for the summer term!'

'You forget to mention,' Dorothea had written back, 'which team won the match in the end. I expect it was Harcourt's. It always is, from what you've told me. Why don't you just give them the trophy or cup or whatever it is from the outset and save yourselves a lot of bother? But never mind about that. I have some real news!'

What she termed *real news* was a lot of drivel about Timms falling down the basement stairs and breaking his arm. 'Timms is the footman, in case you've forgotten, which you probably have: you take so little interest in what happens at home, it's as if we don't matter!' There'd also been 'news' about Nanny, who had given notice. 'Her constitution is worn down, she needs sea air, she is going to live with her sister in Great Yarmouth. I can't believe it! Nanny has *always* been here. The nursery won't seem the same without her.' This 'real news' had taken priority over helping with the new cricket bat. 'P.S. Why don't you ask Aunt Eloise yourself? I'm sure she'd be glad to receive another letter from you after waiting for so long.'

Roderick in high dudgeon had written by return of post: 'Hand over the Rugger Cup without a fight! Honestly, Doro,

I've never heard such rot! If everyone took that attitude, Wellington would have surrendered at Waterloo rather than wait for the Prussians, and Nelson outnumbered at Trafalgar would have sailed for home at once. As for Timms, he is such a clumsy clodpole I'm surprised he hasn't broken his neck before now, never mind his arm. P.S. I did ask Mother in the Christmas hols about my cricket bat, but all she said was, "What, *another* new cricket bat, Roderick?" I thought you might have more luck with her. She listens to you. But you could try Father instead if you like.'

'You seem to have got in a bit of a muddle,' Dorothea had replied (this reply was the letter in his pocket). 'Waterloo and Trafalgar were big battles in history, not boys playing games. It's no wonder you get delusions of grandeur! Timms is *not* a clodpole, he is really rather nice, but you wouldn't understand about that, you always heap scorn on nice people. P.S. I'm sure Uncle Albert would prefer to hear about the cricket bat from you. You could write to him, it wouldn't hurt. While you are at it, you could explain why it is you have developed this sudden interest in cricket.'

But it was a bit late in the day, thought Roderick as he stood in the mist on the edge of the Upper, to start writing to Father *now*. How would one even begin? What would one say? Father didn't suffer fools, he could be rather daunting. One would hate to put a foot wrong.

Why couldn't Dorothea do this one small favour for him and help secure the cricket bat? Why did she write reams of nonsense instead? As if anyone would be interested in Timms! Mother called Timms *John*: it was tradition, she said, to call the footman John. Roderick wrinkled his nose at tradition. Father had no truck with all that. He called a spade, a spade; and he called Timms, Timms. Dorothea no doubt called Timms by his Christian name, but she was like that. As for Nanny, Roderick didn't give a fig about her. She was an absolute beast, it was good riddance. The only thing that had made prep school bearable in the early days had been to get away from Nanny. All that gumph about her constitution, it was absolute rubbish. Nanny had always been as strong as an ox — had looked like an ox, too, for that matter. *The nursery won't be the same without her.* One could almost hear Dorothea's wistful voice, see the tears in her eyes. But only Dorothea — a girl — could weep over Nanny. What a rum lot they were, girls!

Her attitude to cricket was typical of a girl, too.

'One boy throws a ball. Another hits it with a stick. What's so wonderful about that?'

Why wouldn't she open her eyes? Cricket was — oh, all sorts of things: bravery and brilliance, artistry and adventure, more important sometimes than life.

'More important than life? You *do* exaggerate, Roddy!'

But cricket was something he was good at, something he was proud of. People admired him for his cricket. If she was going to pour scorn even on the best bits of a boy, then what was the point?

She was being deliberately contrary when she talked about his *sudden interest* in cricket. He'd played cricket for as long as he could remember. His tutor had taught him. Later, he'd got up those games in Row Meadow with the village boys. Dorothea must remember that. Or had it been before her time? Possibly, quite possibly. The tutor had most definitely had. Now he came to think of it, Roderick realised that he'd already started at prep school by the time Dorothea arrived at Clifton.

Most of the village boys, it went without saying, were good for nothing, always had been. Many were cronies of his enemy Nibs Carter. But there's always been one or two worth the effort. Turner, for one, who was now the stableboy at Clifton. And Harry Keech, the younger of the carpenter's sons, who hated Carter on principle, to goad his older brother, Carter's trusty sidekick. Was the older brother, Nolly Keech, still thick with Carter? One could ask Dorothea, she'd know. But one did not want to give the impression that one was *interested* in the village.

Harry Keech, to be honest, had not been up to much when it came to cricket, but Turner had been a decent batsman, and Lambell, the village headmaster's son, had shown promise. How one had envied Lambell! When the time came to go off to prep school, Lambell had been sent instead to a day school in Lawham and went home every afternoon.

Roderick was surprised to feel nostalgia for those afternoons spent in Row Meadow. But this, here and now, was as far from Row Meadow in high summer as it was possible to get. This was the Upper on a dank and misty February afternoon. It was a scene of considerable carnage. Raynes was doing his best but he had about him today the air of General Gordon at Khartoum.

The final whistle blew. The match, such as it was, was over. Roderick turned away. He couldn't bear to watch the Harcourt's boys strutting round like kings.

Making their way back to Ransom's, Roderick trailed behind H-S and Kennedy down Little Lane, still fingering the letter in his pocket.

Waterloo and Trafalgar were big battles in history, not boys playing games. No wonder you get delusions of grandeur.

Delusions of grandeur, was it? Such brass-necked cheek! What about the fact that Waterloo had been won on the playing fields of Eton? Wellington himself had said as much. But Dorothea didn't see the connection, didn't even *try* to understand. She was such a *girl*. What were girls actually *for*? Why had God even bothered? They were nothing but a measly spare rib, more trouble than they were worth.

But perhaps it would be better not to put *that* in his reply either.

* * *

During prep that evening, when Raynes and some others of the Fifteen walked into the busy day room, Martineau and his coterie got to their feet and gave them an ironic round of applause. Roderick's heart burned to see a chap of Raynes's calibre being treated in this way.

'Look on the bright side,' said H-S behind the rampart of open books they had propped on the desk to conceal their chess board. 'Martineau will be leaving at the end of the summer term.'

But that was an age away. It was no comfort, either, to think of Martineau walking off without getting his comeuppance. Perhaps the Petty Pilferer would change all that. Roderick smiled grimly as he checkmated H-S. The Petty Pilferer was making a name for himself this term, there could be no doubt about that.

The supper bell rang. H-S began packing away the chess board, disconsolate at losing yet again. Roderick demolished the rampart of books. He hadn't done a stroke of work this evening. But no one who was anyone ever did. There'd be plenty of time between prayers and lights-out — twenty minutes at least — to scramble through whatever was needed for tomorrow. After all, he didn't want anyone to think he was a *scholar*.

* * *

The great advantage of Lench's Latin class was that one could sit at the back and safely take a nap. Lench didn't mind a boy sleeping. It was noise he objected to. He liked a nice quiet classroom, only one person speaking at a time. He was funny like that, old Lenchy.

The church bell had just chimed midday, the sound carrying faintly from the main square. Still half an hour of old Lenchy to go, and a whole hour to wait until dinner. A chap might starve to death in a place like this, were it not for the tuck shop.

Roderick yawned, settled himself more comfortably at his desk near the back, closed his eyes. Rain pattered on the windows. Gaffney Major's voice droned on, translating Virgil. Roderick tried to empty his mind, relax, but as so often happened he found himself picking at old sores and making them bleed. He remembered with rancour Martineau's hour of triumph last term. He remembered too what an idiot he'd been in Martineau's study, blushing at the mention of Father. *Your Father's in trade*, Martineau had said. *In trade*: such an old-fashioned phrase, out-of-date in the twentieth century. But it was just the sort of phrase a mealy-mouthed clergyman's son *would* use.

Martineau didn't know what he was talking about. Father wasn't *in trade*. He was an *industrialist*. He owned factories in Coventry, two factories. He made bicycles and motor cars and the bits and pieces which went to making a motor car: *components*, those bits and pieces were called, a twentieth century sort of word which a stuffy, hidebound article like Martineau wouldn't have a clue about. Father had more or less built up these businesses with his own hands, a heroic endeavour. Father, in fact, was rather heroic all round, like a modern-day Hercules labouring to achieve the impossible. *Modern* was just the word, too. For all his advancing years, Father was a very *modern* sort of fellow.

He was sixty — or was it sixty-one now? That took one back to the mid-1840s. One struggled to imagine a world as remote as the 1840s. It made Father sound even older than he really was. But he must in truth have been getting on a bit when he married Mother. A simple calculation proved it. This meant there had to be forty years or so of Father's life which even Mother would not be able to shed much light on. All one knew were the things that Father had let slip over the years. Not that he ever talked much about the past. He was always focused on the future: next autumn's Motor Show, or a new and more up-to-date model of the BFS motor car. Mother was different. She liked nothing better than tales of long ago: her childhood, her father, the slow, unending story of Clifton Park. She could recite a list of ancestors as long as her arm. There'd been baronets amongst them. Martineau had no right to cast aspersions when one's forefathers had been baronets and when one had an uncle who'd attended this very school (*HEAR, 1871*).

Mother was rooted in Clifton Park whereas Father was a Coventry man. One was a Coventry man oneself, for that matter. One had been born there.

Roderick opened one eye, half-expecting to see everyone staring, as if suddenly he had *Made in Coventry* stamped on his forehead. But the class was steeped in soporific indifference, heads nodding at most of the desks in all the rows in front of him. Gaffney Major was still droning on. Lench was listening to him with a beatific smile on his face as if congratulating himself on Gaffney's fluency. But from where Roderick was sitting it was clear to see that Gaffney had an English translation of Virgil secreted inside his text book.

Roderick closed his eye again, picked up the skeins of his thoughts. Impossible as it was to imagine — one could only ever picture her at Clifton — Mother too had lived in Coventry for a time after she was first married — which must have been in the early 1890s, Roderick calculated, given that he was born in 1892. Mother's father had died around that time and Uncle Fred had inherited Clifton.

Mother's father, thought Roderick, had been the last of his grandparents. He'd never known any of them. He'd felt rather aggrieved as a kid, listening to other boys boasting of doting grandmothers, munificent grandfathers. Harry Keech the carpenter's son had been able to boast of a *great* grandmother although he'd never mentioned that she was either doting or munificent. She looked in fact like a toothless old witch — not that one had ever said so: not to Keech and certainly not to Dorothea, especially after the witch's house had burned down. Thinking about it now, Roderick realised that the deaths of all his grandparents had closed yet another door on Father's past and made Mother's tales seem even more dim and distant.

Uncle Fred had not held Clifton for long. He had soon met his untimely end (the one thing Mother *didn't* talk about: would one dare ask?). His sickly son Richard had succeeded. Mother and Father had come from Coventry to act as guardians. Then Richard too had shuffled off, leaving Mother as mistress of Clifton. It was impossible now to think of any other outcome. Mother *had* to inherit Clifton. It was fate, destiny, God's will. Mother and Clifton were inextricably linked. But Mother was not immortal. Inconceivable as it seemed, one day in the distant future she would die and Clifton would pass to her only son.

This was obvious. It was beyond question. It was a fact of life that Roderick had known ever since his cousin Richard had died of diphtheria in 1904. But sitting in Lench's Latin class, Roderick found himself turning this fact over in his mind with the same sense of wonder as when he stumbled on a correct answer in algebra. Given that *y* followed *x*, and all other things being equal, there could be no doubt that Clifton Park would one day be his.

To *own* Clifton Park. To be *master*. It was an extraordinary thought. It wasn't any old house, either, that he'd be master of. Clifton was a house with a history. He'd be the latest in a long line of masters, heir to the Massingham baronets Mother so lauded. This, in effect, was what all Mother's tales amounted to. They culminated in him: Roderick Henry Brannan. He was the offshoot of all that history.

A pity about the lost baronetcy. That would have been the icing on the cake. *Sir* Roderick Brannan had a nice ring to it. But what was in a name? Clifton Park itself was a misnomer, there being no park to speak of, the landscaping never finished (another of Mother's tales). That didn't make Clifton any less of a house. And not being a *sir* would not make him any less of a man.

He grinned, slouched in his chair. Dorothea would have had a thing or two to say if she could have read his mind right now. *Delusions of grandeur* would be the least of it. But give a chap some leeway! How could it not go to one's head when one was the offshoot of history, the boy who would be master?

Roderick's pleasant reverie was interrupted by an elbow in the ribs.

'Do you mind, H-S? I'm trying to sleep!'

'But Branners! The Petty Pilferer has struck again! Gaffney Major has had eighteen shillings taken from his drawer! That's the third thing this week after Kennedy's pocket watch and Simpson's postal order!'

It never ceased to amaze Roderick how H-S contrived to learn all the latest news even in the middle of a lesson. Had Gaffney somehow managed to slip the revelation about his eighteen shillings into his droning translation of Virgil?

'Martineau is making himself look no end of a juggins!' Roderick said savagely. 'Why doesn't he go to Moxon and admit he's failed? That would make an end to it then.'

'I hardly think Martineau will—'

But H-S was abruptly silenced as Lench's Latin dictionary came hurtling through the air, nearly taking his head off. Lench had his own inimitable way of keeping his class in order. He was — it bore repeating — funny like that.

* * *

Martineau got to his feet at the beginning of evening prep.

'Pens down, books closed. I have something to say.'

A collective shudder ran round the day room. They were used to Martineau's homilies. There was something about the way he delivered them that set one's teeth on edge. It cost an effort to listen, too, and the house slackers — the majority — were not used to making any sort of effort during prep.

As he looked round, Roderick realised that even the Sixth had crammed into the day room this evening: normally they'd have been in their studies. Something was going to happen. But what?

It didn't take long to find out. Martineau, it emerged, had finally decided to take action against the Petty Pilferer.

'I intend to put an end to this affair once and for all. I intend to put an end to it *now*. I offer the culprit one last chance to turn himself in before I take matters into my own hands.'

There was silence. The Petty Pilferer was obviously not in confessional mood. Roderick smirked. Was this the best that Martineau could do?

'Very well,' Martineau continued briskly, looking suspiciously pleased with himself. 'The prefects and I will now conduct a thorough search of all studies, cupboards, desks and lockers, of all bags, boxes and hidey-holes. While the search is under way, everyone else will stay here and turn out the contents of their pockets for Raynes to inspect.'

Raynes looked rather surprised about this and not entirely happy. He'd obviously not been consulted beforehand. This was not exactly surprising as Raynes had never been amongst Martineau's inner circle. All the same, he was a prefect, and it was a prefect's duty to stand by the head of house. Raynes was the last man on earth to shirk his responsibilities.

He stepped forward briskly, raising his voice above the groundswell of muttering about *defamation of character* and *innocent until proven guilty*.

'Now, now, chaps. All we are interested in is finding the thief, nothing more. We'll turn a blind eye to your stash of cribs, Boyson, and to your filthy postcards, Verney.'

A roar of laughter greeted these remarks, diffusing the tension. Raynes was a match for any situation. But as he watched Martineau carefully, Roderick realised that — whatever Raynes might say — cribs and filthy postcards were exactly the sort of thing the head boy hoped to uncover. No doubt he planned to gather enough incriminating evidence to hold half the house to ransom. That was precisely the sort of sneaky, underhand way that Martineau went about things. It was the only way he knew how to uphold his authority.

'I say, Raynes, if everyone is to be a suspect, oughtn't that to include the prefects too? Shouldn't their studies be searched as well?' This was Gaffney Major, punctilious about fair play — except when translating Virgil (but hoodwinking the masters was not only expected, it was an unwritten law).

The general consensus was that Gaffney had a good point. It fell to Raynes to smooth things over once more.

For form's sake, the prefects' studies would be searched first, he announced. Anticipating Gaffney's next point of order, he added that half a dozen non-prefects would be taken along as observers to ensure that everything was above board. 'If that meets with your approval, of course, Gaffney?'

'By all means, Raynes old chap: by all means.'

Roderick was chosen as one of the observers. He hung back, looking on with satisfaction as Martineau's scheme for a thorough-going scourge of the house rapidly descended to the level of a farce. Raynes, right-minded chap that he was, had naturally assumed that all his fellow prefects matched his own exacting standards of probity. He little thought how even a token search of their studies might uncover all manner of skeletons in any number of cupboards. The nervous prefects were well aware of this — as were the observers, who soon began to enjoy themselves enormously as they trooped from one study to the next.

'What about that cupboard there?'

'Don't forget to look under the desk!'

'Have you checked the pockets of his jacket?'

'I don't think you got *this* book from the school library, Baylis!'

'I say, Farquharson, is that a Bohn hidden under your mattress?'

Martineau's study was the last to be searched.

'There's a locked drawer here, chaps.' The judicial watchdog, Gaffney, was seated on Martineau's desk happily picking holes in a blotter.

'Well, Martineau?' Raynes held out a perfunctory hand. 'The key?'

'This is an absolute travesty!' Martineau raged. Nonetheless, he reached for a little wooden marquetry box and took out a small key. 'There's nothing in that drawer. I haven't used it in months.'

Raynes was prepared to take this on trust. He opened the drawer without looking inside, was on the point of closing it again when Kennedy suddenly piped up.

'I say! My pocket watch!'

Raynes gave him a withering look. 'Very amusing, Kennedy. But perhaps we can continue the search *without* the clever remarks.'

'But Raynes! It *is* my watch, it really is! It's inscribed if you don't believe me!'

Raynes turned a deathly pale, picking the watch out of the drawer. As he did so, a chorus of voices broke out around him.

'Look, there's Lewis's pen!'

'And that must be Simpson's postal order!'

'What about my eighteen shillings? Is that there too?'

Roderick was at the back of the group. Gaffney turned to him with something in his hand. 'Here, Brannan, isn't this your tie pin?'

Roderick held it up to the light as if making sure. 'I do believe you're right, Gaffers. Well, well, I never thought I'd see *this* again!'

He closed it in his fist. He thought back to last term. Martineau had gloated over him. *You've left me no choice I'm afraid, Brannan*, he'd said as he condemned Roderick to a beating from Raynes. Roderick since then had often wondered how it would feel if the tables were turned. But this was much more. A storm had broken in the house that no one could have expected — least of all the Petty Pilferer.

Gripping the tie pin so that it dug into his palm, Roderick was perturbed to find that at this critical moment he could not bring himself to study the expression on Martineau's face.

* * *

Roderick came in late to breakfast. He'd been kept back after first school to receive an imposition for acting up in class — his second imposition in as many days.

'You'll be writing lines in your sleep,' Kennedy had remarked after yesterday's penalty. 'How many impots is that now for the term?'

'Couldn't possibly tell you. I've rather lost count.'

Now he had another to add to the score. He just couldn't help himself.

Taking his place at one of the long, scrubbed tables in the refectory, he realized that the place was abuzz. Silence was usually the order of the day when it came to the serious business of breakfast. He looked round, on edge.

'Haven't you heard, Branners?' H-S was breathless with the news. 'Martineau's got the sack!'

'He's . . . he's *what*? Are you sure, H-S?'

'Quite sure. I got it from Lewis who—'

'But I never thought — I didn't expect . . .'

'What is it Branners? What didn't you expect?'

'Nothing. It doesn't matter. I rather thought that Mother Moxon would move heaven and earth to protect his favourite, that's all.'

'I'm sure he did his best, but once the Big Man got involved—'

'Moxon went to the headmaster? Why did he do that?'

'He had no choice, surely you can see that? This was too serious a business to deal with in house. He *had* to take Martineau to the Big Man. And Lewis said that Dobbs said that Martineau denied everything, and the Big Man was *furious*: you know what the Big Man's like about playing the game and acting like a gentleman.'

'W-w-what if Martineau was telling the truth? What if he *didn't* do it?'

'But it *had* to be him, Branners! All the stolen articles were in his desk and he was the only one who knew where the key was. What I can't understand in all this is why he took all those things in the first place. What did he want with them?'

'Don't ask me, H-S. How would I know?'

'Well, Lewis said that Dobbs said—' H-S broke off, peering at Roderick across the table. 'I say, Branners, are you feeling alright? Grayson didn't whack you, did he, for playing up in class? You've gone rather green about the gills and you haven't touched your porridge. I'll find a home for it if you don't want it.'

'What? What did you say? Oh, my porridge. Yes, I'm eating it. Look, this is me, eating.' The porridge stuck in his throat. He had to swallow hard to force it down.

'Word is that Raynes will be promoted to head of house,' H-S continued. 'Funny, when you think about it. You've always hated Martineau, and you've always sung paeans about Raynes. And now Martineau has gone and Raynes is head boy. It couldn't have worked out any better if you'd planned it.'

'If someone had . . . if they'd planned it all—'

'I wasn't being serious, Branners. How could anyone have planned all this?'

'But if they *had* . . . They'd have done the house a massive favour, getting rid of Martineau. It wasn't just me who hated him. He held the place back. Now he's gone . . . well, we should be grateful — if that's what happened, if someone planned it. He'd need to be a damned clever fellow to pull this off.'

'Clever? He'd be an absolute swine, I would say! But that's all rot. No one in the house would be as underhand as all that.'

'Yes, yes, there's no need to go on! You're quite right. No one could possibly be such a swine. Now for pity's sake let a chap eat his brekker in peace!'

* * *

'Damned weather!' Squatting in the shelter of an old apple tree, Roderick turned up the collar of his blazer while drawing on a cigarette. March rain was pouring down on the unkempt garden. Occasional drips, collecting on the branches above, landed splat on his nose or slid stickily down the back of his neck.

Strictly speaking, this garden was out of bounds. It was at the back of the old cottage which formed Moxon's private apartments. Up near the cottage itself, an effort had been made to bring some order, but down here by the hedge the place had long been neglected. This spot beneath the apple tree was a refuge used by smokers. There was a wooden door set in the hedge, falling to pieces and half hidden by long tendrils. It opened onto a footpath which led from the back of the Ransom's buildings down to the Lower, the second of the school playing fields.

Roderick was not enjoying his cigarette. It left a nasty taste, somehow. He sighed, threw it down to join all the other butt-ends in the trampled grass. Getting to his feet, he stepped out into the rain — and immediately ducked back again, flattening himself against the tree. He'd seen something, a flicker of movement; but as he peered out at the overgrown garden he realised there was no pressing danger: he was still alone.

What, then, had he seen? Not anything in the garden. It had been further off, he decided, in one of the upper windows of the cottage. Was he being watched?

He stared at the window. Nothing. No one there. Then—

His heart skipped a beat. There was another flicker of movement. White lace, pale skin (a bare arm, was it?), and dark hair tumbling loose, as dishevelled as the garden. He held his breath, pulling the branches aside to get a better view. But the window was now blank again, reflecting the dull grey sky.

All the same, there could be no doubt about it: he must have caught a glimpse of Mrs Moxon, the housemaster's seldom-seen wife.

Mrs Moxon was a lot younger than her husband — not a wrinkled old matron like Mrs Grayson, for instance. The few times one ever got to see her, she was swathed in high-collared dresses with long sleeves, her hands encased in elegant gloves. To get a glimpse of her in different guise was somehow disturbing, like stumbling on a secret. Had he *really* just seen her bare arm, her loose hair? But so what if he had, why should it matter? She was a measly spare rib, God shouldn't have bothered. Except . . . except . . . well, what *was* it about her that stuck in one's head?

He waited in the rain, eyes fixed on the cottage. Would she come to the window again? He wished she would! Only to set his mind at rest, of course, so he could be sure of what he'd seen. What was she doing up there? Anything. She could be doing anything. She might be getting changed, she might be dishabille.

He was shivering, his heart racing. He couldn't understand it. It wasn't as cold as all that. But it *was* wet. He was getting soaked. It was madness to go on standing here.

Perhaps one more cigarette. If she hadn't reappeared by then . . .

But when he glanced at his pocket watch, he saw that it was later than he'd thought. He'd have to run to get to half-past-four school on time. There was no point waiting, in any case. Ten to one it hadn't been Mrs Moxon at all, just a trick of the light.

He hauled the wooden door open, slipped through, yanked it shut again. The rain began to come down even heavier as, hunched up and still shivering all over, he ran along the footpath towards Ransom's courtyard.

* * *

'Ah, it's you, Brannan.'

The very words Martineau had used all those months ago. But it wasn't Martineau sitting behind the head of house's desk, it was Raynes. The desk was still scrupulously tidy but the marquetry box had gone.

'Now look here, Brannan.' Raynes didn't keep a chap waiting. He didn't need clever tricks like that. 'You were late for afternoon school yesterday, Mr Rimmer informs me, and when you did show up you looked like a drowned rat.'

'Sorry, Raynes, I—'

'Never mind about that. I haven't hauled you in here to slap your wrists for bad timekeeping.'

Then what? Disconcertingly, Roderick felt blood throbbing in his cheeks and flushing up his neck. There was something about Raynes's clear and penetrating gaze that made one feel like a rotten swine — as if one's darkest secrets had come floating to the surface. There'd once been a mad king of France who'd thought he was made of glass. That was exactly what it felt like being scrutinised by Raynes: that he could see right through you.

'I like you, Brannan. You've always shown a lot of promise. I wanted for nothing when you were fagging for me, I know that much. But these last couple of terms you've done nothing but slack off and play the fool.'

'But everyone slacks off, Raynes! Everyone does as little work as possible. We all crib like Hades and lie to the beaks and get by as best we can — except for a few frowsty scholars like Westaway.'

'Westaway makes a show of it, I'll give you that. But I think you'll find there are others who work just as hard though you'd never know. You have to learn the rules, Brannan: the rules of the game.'

'What game?'

Raynes sidestepped the question. 'That business over the Jitty last term: what sort of tomfoolery was that? I may say, I didn't like having to whack you that time one little bit, but I told myself you deserved it, for being such an ass as to get in that fix. Do you see?'

'Yes, Raynes. Sorry, Raynes.'

'Don't be sorry. Learn the lesson. Unless you're irremediably fond of getting swished.'

'No, Raynes.'

'You want to look big, I suppose. You want to make a name for yourself. But that's no way to go about it, acting like a damned idiot. Play to your strengths. Cricket, for instance. You want to make the house Eleven, I assume?'

'Oh, rather!' He wasn't going to pretend that it was beyond his wildest dreams but it often seemed too much to hope for. He wasn't even sure if he was good enough. Running rings round the village boys was one thing, to compete with the Downfield virtuosos quite another. Yet Raynes seemed to be suggesting . . . was Raynes actually saying . . . ?

But having raised Roderick's hopes, Raynes promptly dashed them. 'Don't think for one moment that you'll be in the Eleven next term, Brannan. You're too young, too green, in too much of a hurry. Talent isn't everything. You need to prove you're worthy. Think about that. Think about everything I've said. There's the makings of a jolly decent chap somewhere inside you. It's time you started to let us see him.'

Roderick closed the study door behind him. Raynes! Who did he think he was? God Almighty? Making his way down to the courtyard, Roderick was in a filthy temper. He didn't appreciate being called a fool. He didn't appreciate having the house Eleven dangled in front of him only to have it snatched away. What would be the point of a new cricket bat now?

But what if Raynes was right? An ass. A damned fool. In too much of a hurry. That was what Raynes thought of him. Dorothea would probably agree. Roderick had lost count of the number of names she had called him over the years.

'I can't help who I am, Doro. It's in my nature. It's the way I'm made. Slugs and snails and puppy dogs' tails.'

'That's what you'd like people to think, Roddy. But it's not true. Underneath it all, you're nice.'

Nice? To be called 'nice' was an affront. But as he turned out of the courtyard and walked disconsolately along the alley between Ransom's extension and the school library, it occurred to him that Raynes had said something similar, something about there being a decent chap inside him. A compliment from Raynes was worth all the gold in the world. Talent had been mentioned too, and the house Eleven not ruled out forever. Perhaps there was still hope.

The house Eleven! Imagine that!

Round the back of the buildings, the footpath that led to the Lower turned sharp right. But there was another footpath that went straight on, over a stile in a hedge and down the grassy slopes of the escarpment, away from the town, away from the school, fading into the fields. Roderick climbed up onto the stile and sat there looking out at the lowlands. The wind gusted in his face. The white clouds glowed with the sun behind them.

As he sat there he suddenly experienced a deep and ardent longing to see Clifton. Not homesickness: something more elemental than that, like the pull of gravity. He ached to be walking up the drive, to see the familiar facade, to open the front door, to step onto the black and white tiles of the hall. But Clifton was lost in the vast and hazy distance, so far away one could scarcely believe in it.

Dark clouds were scudding across the sky. The brightness faded. A shadow fell across the lowlands. The March wind had a nip in it. But Roderick felt buoyed up. He would look forward, like Father. He had hopes of the house Eleven, real hopes. But that was next year. All manner of things would happen between now and then. The Easter hols were coming up to be followed by the junior matches next term in which he'd be sure to shine. He'd have the whole summer at home to spend as he liked. Then, come autumn, he'd be back here again, older, wiser, undaunted. This time next year he'd be ready, he'd make sure of it. He'd earn himself a place on the house Eleven or die in the attempt.

He jumped down from the stile. Whistling tunelessly, his hands in his pockets, his head held high, he made his way towards the day room to while away the hours until tea.

CHAPTER THREE

Roderick sat four-square on the wooden steps of the cricket pavilion, staring out at the green and empty Upper and having a quiet smoke. A Downfield veteran now, he knew, with first-day chaos prevailing, he'd not be missed for a good while yet. He'd felt the need for some calm reflection before he joined the fray. This, after all, was set to be the most important term of his career.

It was beastly cold for April. Looked like rain, too. Hardly an auspicious start. Dorothea, had she been here, might have passed some comment about the sun only shining on the righteous. Raynes, had he overheard, might have agreed. But in all the months since his awkward interview with Raynes in the head of house's study, Roderick had done his best to be the sort of chap that Raynes expected him to be. At least, he'd done his best when Raynes was around; no one could be virtuous *all* the time, Roderick defied anyone to prove otherwise.

He put the cigarette to his lips. A year. A whole year since that interview with Raynes. Back then he'd vowed to be ready when the time came; it was the house Eleven or nothing. And now—

Well, it was H-S who had put it most succinctly. 'I suppose you will be in the house Eleven this term, Branners. Everyone says you will.'

Flicking ash impatiently from the end of his cigarette, Roderick couldn't get over how unutterably gloomy H-S had been earlier when they met as usual on the platform of Downfield station.

'You might as least *try* to be pleased for me, H-S.'

'I am, Branners, truly, congratters and all that. It's just . . . well . . . we'll have even *less* time together, this term.'

'What can I do? However much I'd like to spend more time with you—' Throw the dog a bone. '—I can't shirk my duty to the house — *if* I'm selected, that is.'

Roderick crossed his fingers. He didn't want to tempt fate. Everyone might be saying he was a certainty for the house Eleven but he wouldn't really believe it until he saw his name down in black and white. The Eleven was everything. Nothing else mattered. Mr Shackleton might think his measly boat trip to the Antarctic worthy of note but if a chap wanted true adventure this summer he'd only find it in the cut-throat competition for the Cricket Cup. Having Raynes as head boy only added to a growing sense of expectancy. There'd been a real change in the house since Raynes had taken charge. The house Fifteen had acquitted themselves admirably last term, beating Rimmer's before losing to Harcourt's for the second year in a row. Now it was time for the Eleven to shine. And if . . . if . . .

But spots of rain were beginning to fall. It was time to take shelter.

Roderick got to his feet, grinding his cigarette under his heel. As he made his way across the Upper, the rain began to come down in earnest. He broke into a run, swooping down Little Lane and into Market Street as the rain sighed out of a sodden April sky.

* * *

‘Raynes will be captain,’ said Kennedy in the refectory, stating the obvious as only Kennedy could. Dinner was in full swing. He had to raise his voice above the din to make himself heard. ‘There’s Hills, too. Hills is bound to be in.’

‘What about Branners?’ H-S, faithful squire, spoke up on cue. ‘Don’t forget Branners!’

‘Well, obviously Branners,’ said Kennedy. ‘That’s a foregone conclusion. Branners is the most promising young cricketer in the house.’ This was gratifying but then he rather spoiled things by adding, ‘Apart from Scotson, of course.’

‘I don’t think much of Scotson,’ said H-S. ‘He’s all show.’

‘The small fry worship the ground he walks on,’ said Kennedy.

‘Like I said,’ H-S insisted stoutly, ‘all show. I think he’s—’

Roderick interrupted. H-S was loyal to a fault, but there was no denying that Scotson was idolized by the younger boys. But this couldn’t be held against him, especially when — and this couldn’t be denied either — he was a half-decent cricketer. He was needed in the Eleven. And nothing was more important than the Eleven.

‘Eat your pudding, H-S, and leave the thinking to Kennedy and me.’

‘But Branners—’

‘What is it now?’

‘I was only going to say about Howlett. Lewis told me that Howlett won the match for them single-handedly when C dorm played E on the Lower yesterday.’

‘Howlett *is* rather good, I’ve heard,’ said Kennedy. ‘But there’s one small problem: he hasn’t passed his shooting test. It’s a farcical rule, I know, that a chap can’t play in the house teams unless he’s passed his shooting test, but with the Big Man being so hot on the Corps, there are no exceptions, ever.’

Roderick shook his head in wonder. ‘How is it possible *not* to pass the shooting test?’

Kennedy shrugged. ‘It must be congenital. All I know is that Howlett is a positive menace on the range.’

H-S looked up from his steamed pudding. 'If only Howlett could shoot like Westaway.'

'Oh, thanks for that, H-S!' Kennedy was crushing.

Roderick, however, held up his hand. 'No, wait. H-S might be on to something. Westaway has represented the school at Bisley, he must have passed the shooting test with his eyes closed.'

'That helps us how?'

'Think about it. Howlett and Westaway just happen to be very similar in build.'

'You mean . . . ?' Kennedy eyed Roderick speculatively. 'No. It would never work. Old Grayson would spot it a mile off.'

'He would if he had his spectacles on. But he's blind as a bat without them.'

Kennedy broke into a slow grin. 'Grayson is forever taking his spectacles off in class. It would be the work of a moment to hook them off his desk when his back was turned. And then—'

'Then Westaway could take the shooting test pretending to be Howlett and Grayson would be none the wiser.'

'You're a cunning devil, Brannan. But what will Raynes say? He'll never approve of a devious scheme like that.'

'Raynes does not need to know.'

'We lie to him?'

'We simply don't tell him. That's not lying. What we would be doing would be done for the good of the house. Raynes would appreciate that. But we can't expect him to compromise his position by *agreeing* to it.'

'I suppose you're right, Brannan. All the same, I can't see how we can pull it off. Westaway won't cooperate, for a start. He's the one person in the whole house who doesn't give a damn about the Cricket Cup. It won't matter to him whether Howlett is in the Eleven or not.'

'You leave Westaway to me, Kennedy. I'll make sure he does as he's told.'

'And how will you manage that?'

Roderick gave him a placid smile. 'I have my methods,' he said.

* * *

'It's very good of you to do this, Westaway.'

'I had no choice in the matter, Brannan, as well you know. Machiavelli would be proud of you.'

'Machia — who?'

'Look him up. Though I don't suppose there's much he can teach a chap like you.'

They were on their way to the range, had stopped to allow Westaway to adjust his scarf and pull his cap down. Old Grayson had been informed that Howlett had laryngitis which would account for the scarf and explain why 'Howlett' did not sound much like Howlett.

'You really have no compunction, do you, Brannan.' Westaway's reproachful brown eyes regarded Roderick from the gap between scarf and cap. 'You are, in fact, a complete scoundrel.'

Roderick sighed. 'Not you as well, Westaway. Why is everyone so quick to tell me what a rotter I am?

'Perhaps because it's true. You always were something of an insufferable prig but just lately you've become a positive fiend. You do realise that this is blackmail?'

'Call it what you like, just as long as you do your bit for the house.'

'And what's the house ever done for me?'

'Heresy! No wonder you get persecuted, asking questions like that! Why do you feel the need to theorize about everything? Some things are quite straightforward — loyalty to one's house being a case in point. Oh, and I'm not a *complete* scoundrel. If I was, I'd have threatened your life. As it is, I've merely used some gentle persuasion. Come on, now. Shake my paw, and no hard feelings.'

'No hard feelings? Like I said, it's blackmail. I want to know where you got your information. I've never told a soul about my . . . about the . . .'

'I have my sources, Westaway, and if you'd like me to keep quiet, you'll do this one thing for the house. By the way, you might want to make your voice a bit gruffer when you talk to Grayson. You're supposed to have laryngitis, remember?'

'Thanks, Brannan, but I don't need any advice from you. Let's just get this charade over with, shall we?'

* * *

Roderick made haste to write home as soon as the line-up of the house Eleven was known — as soon, that was to say, as he was able to tear himself away from staring at the notice board in a daze of exultation. To see his name on the list was the pinnacle of his existence.

How nice for you, Mother wrote back. *Nice*, under the circumstances, seemed rather inadequate. But Dorothea was not much better. She was *glad*. Would Father have more of an idea? Insofar as anyone at home took an interest in cricket, it was Father. He'd even taken Roderick to the Oval last summer. Perhaps now, thought Roderick, was the time to write that letter he'd always been meaning to write. This was, after all, momentous news. It could not fail to make Father proud.

But there was such a bedlam in the day room in the half hour before dinner that it was impossible to think let alone write. Roderick took himself across the street to the New Hall where he could get some peace and quiet. The New Hall had been built half a dozen years ago to host school concerts and double up as a gym. It was deserted at this time of day. It was gloomy, too. The windows were high and narrow, the ceiling lost in shadow.

Sitting in the semi-dark, Roderick found himself thinking about the week he had spent with Father in London during the hols last summer. It had been Father's suggestion. He had business in town, he'd said: something to do with the BFS motor showroom on the Edgware Road. Why didn't Roderick come too? It wouldn't be all work. They'd probably have time to take a gander at the Test Match. And there'd be no bother about hotels. They could stay at Essex Square.

Roderick had accepted with alacrity. And so they'd travelled to London (by train, not motor) and installed themselves at number twenty-eight Essex Square, Father's town house in South Kensington, a property he'd bought four years ago in a moment of uncharacteristic profligacy. Dorothea had a theory that Father had bought number twenty-eight because he wanted somewhere that was entirely his — Clifton Park, of course, being Mother's inheritance. As was usual with Dorothea's theories, she had not a shred of evidence to back it up. Intuition, she called it. One scoffed. One would have scoffed longer and louder had she not so often been right.

'We don't use this place anywhere near as often as we should,' Father had said on the first evening, making a tour of the rooms, inspecting his investment. 'Next summer—' Well, what they weren't going to do next summer wasn't worth knowing about. That was typical Father. Always making plans. Always looking ahead.

They had gone to the Test Match, England versus South Africa, on the Monday, the opening day. It had rained. It would rain. God was a rotter, there was no other way of looking at it. But to see the Oval — a mythical place, previously only a name in the newspaper — had sent a shiver up Roderick's spine even in the wet. And the day had not been a complete wash-out: there'd been some play in the end. England had won the toss and chosen to bat. It had been a shaky start, Hayward out first ball and then Tyldesley clean-bowled in the sixth over. C B Fry had come in to bat. He'd been the man for the occasion. He'd put in a measured, almost dogged, performance. It had been thrilling to watch.

Father, of course, was not exactly up on cricket. One had found it necessary to explain the finer points. He'd listened patiently. 'You certainly know your onions, my boy!' There was something about the way Father said *my boy* that made one feel awfully bucked up.

Sitting in the gloom of New Hall, Roderick could recall every detail of that day, a treasured memory. England's total had been almost respectable at close of play, with C B Fry on 108 not out. Leaving the Oval, Father had taken Roderick to dinner at a restaurant on the Strand. There'd been muted lighting, murmured conversations, the scrape of cutlery, the soft and sophisticated sound of a piano. Father had held his menu at arm's length, peering at it. 'Now then. What do we have here?' Roderick had chosen mutton in a piquant sauce. Eating it, sitting man-to-man with Father in such decorous surroundings, he had felt a different person: grown up, worldly wise.

The meal over, they had taken a motor cab from the Strand back to Essex Square. Father, in characteristic fashion, had struck up a conversation with the taxi man. Were motor cabs popular in London? What was the ratio between motorised and horse-drawn? What did the taxi man think of his own particular vehicle? Was it everything he had hoped for?

'I may have missed a trick here, my boy,' Father had said in an aside, smoothing his moustache. In those unfamiliar surroundings, Roderick had noticed there was a lot more grey in Father's moustache these days. 'There's obviously a ready market amongst London cab men. Can't think why it never crossed my mind before.'

Roderick grinned in the deep silence of New Hall. Good old Father! He'd talk to anyone! He was like Dorothea in that respect — except that Father never suffered fools, wasn't taken in. But he was a bit like Raynes, too, a match for any situation, never at a loss. One had felt that strongly in London. One had seen a new side to Father. One had felt somehow closer to him.

Roderick remembered the lighted streets of London swirling past the taxi window. Fashionably dressed people had been promenading on the pavements of Piccadilly against the dark backdrop of Green Park. He had thought about Dorothea, who came from those parts. Or, well, perhaps not quite those parts, the Strand and Piccadilly and Hyde Park Corner. Her London was a different London.

Where on earth *was* Stepnall Street, for that matter? One hadn't the foggiest.

Dorothea had not accompanied them last summer. *Cricket*, she had said, turning up her nose.

'You take cricket far too seriously, Roddy. I don't see why it *matters* so much. I don't see why it matters to *you*. You're not even in any of your precious house teams!'

She certainly knew how to hit a chap where it hurt. Last summer he had still been sore about missing out on the house Eleven. He had felt that time was ticking by. He had just turned fifteen — *fifteen!* — and had still yet to make any sort of mark on the world. But that was last summer. Now Dorothea could eat her words. His name was on the list, he was in the Eleven: R H Brannan.

In the shadows of the empty Hall, his eyes picked out the words inscribed on the end wall: *caesorum comitum memores*. Of course. This new building had been dedicated to the memory of the Old Downfieldians who had fallen in the South African War. Their memorial was etched in stone. What would his memorial be?

A chap like him — a chap with ancestors, a chap who would be master — couldn't afford to sit around doing nothing. And he wouldn't. He had dreams. He had ambitions. How they burned inside him! How he ached for glory! She wouldn't understand, a girl like Dorothea, a girl with no ancestors at all, a girl from that den of depravity Stepnall Street — wherever that was.

To be Ransom's very own C B Fry: why not? It could happen. It *must* happen. But how to explain all this in a letter to Father? It was impossible. So perhaps the letter could wait. It *would* get written, but later, another time.

Roderick got to his feet. The dinner bell must be ringing now in Ransom's. And after dinner there was a whole afternoon given over to cricket. After all, even C B Fry must have to practise sometimes.

* * *

'Well you fellows,' said Raynes in his study, the Eleven all around him, standing, sitting, squatting on the floor. 'Tomorrow is the big day: the biggest day that Ransom's has known for many a term.'

Roderick had to pinch himself. That he should be in Ransom's Eleven, that Ransom's Eleven should have reached the semi-finals of the Cricket Cup: it was nothing short of miraculous. It would have seemed much too much to hope for a few short weeks ago when he'd sat on the pavilion steps at the beginning of term.

They had gathered for a council of war on the eve of battle. Tomorrow they were facing Conway's. Expert opinion throughout the school summed up Ransom's prospects in two short words: *no hope*. Or, as Kennedy put it, 'Conway's will hammer us, then in the final Harcourt's will hammer Conway's.' The experts agreed that a third successive Harcourt's-Conway's final was a foregone conclusion.

Roderick had listened to such predictions over the last few days with growing indignation. He remembered Dorothea's scathing words: *why don't you just give them the trophy or cup or whatever it is at the outset and save yourselves the bother?*

'We have to *believe* we can win, or else what's the point?' he insisted now in Raynes's study.

Raynes laughed. 'Good old Brannan! You keep it up! Keep telling us we can do it and you might even convince us in the end! But we need to bat first tomorrow. It's our best chance of making a match of it. If Hills, Howlett and I can knock up a decent score, it might give Conway's pause for thought. Batting first is vital, though, with bowling our Achilles' heel. Anyway, you fellows, there's not much more we can say. It's time to turn in. We all need a good sleep tonight. I'll see you bright and early!'

But it was one thing to need sleep, quite another to find it. Roderick in the dark of the dorm tossed and turned in bed as long, slow minutes crawled by. He felt like flotsam washed up on a forgotten beach. If he could just find something soothing to think about he might settle down. Something, something — anything — Mrs Moxon—

No, no, no! Not Mrs Moxon! What was Mrs Moxon doing in his head? Thoughts of Mrs Moxon weren't soothing. They were, if anything, positively unsettling.

He groaned and rolled over, stuffed his pillow into his ears, tried to block out Mrs Moxon, to block out the whole dorm with its rows of beds receding endlessly into the measureless dark. But even through the pillow he could hear the sound of boys breathing, resounding to the rafters. Someone was whimpering in his sleep, someone else was snoring and snorting. There was a stink of soap and hair oil and feet. There was something else, too, some indescribable odour, as if the residue of a hundred thousand other boys on a hundred thousand other nights, through all of Downfield's long and illustrious history, was oozing from the whitewashed walls and unvarnished floor.

Roderick flung his pillow aside, turned over once more, growling with irritation. Staring up at the great drifts of inky darkness between the beams of the sloping ceiling, he surrendered control, gave his galloping thoughts free rein. Some higher part of him looked down, sneering at those thoughts, the way his mind was running like a credulous junior's on some of the absurd stories that circulated about Mrs Moxon. That she'd been an actress, for instance, and that Moxon had seen her on stage and fallen passionately in love with her — as if a dry old stick like Moxon could be passionate about *anything*. Another version had it that Mrs Moxon was an actress still, that she made secret forays to appear on the London stage under an assumed name. But there were more lurid stories even than these. One had it that Moxon was so insanely jealous (Mother Moxon, insanely jealous?) that he kept his young and pretty wife under lock and key. Roderick pictured her, manacled to a wall. He pictured himself, a knight in armour, riding to her rescue. Or maybe it would be better if he was a dashing cavalier. But no, that wouldn't do either. He wiped the scene from his mind, replaced it with another.

Mrs Moxon not manacled but locked in her room, the one at the back of the private apartments. And he not a knight but the swashbuckling hero of the Eleven in his cricket whites, fresh from some stupendous victory. He would fight his way through the overgrown garden, she would let her hair down like Rapunzel, he would climb up and say . . . and say . . . well, he'd say something, he'd come back to that bit later. He would speak and she would reply.

But things got a bit hazy here. One had so little to go on: a glimpse of bare arm, of dark hair tumbled loose. One wasn't even sure what her voice sounded like. If only it was possible to see her again as he'd glimpsed her that day in the garden! But no matter how often he went back, in all the months and months since that first sighting there'd never been anything but blank windows, not even the merest hint of Mrs Moxon in her boudoir.

Her *boudoir*. His lips formed the word in the glutinous dark of the dorm, lying flat on his back with his hands behind his head. Her *boudoir*. Her *bedroom*. Her *bed*!

. . . the rank sweat of an unseamèd bed, stewed in corruption . . .

Why did that stick in one's head? It was rather foul: *stewed in corruption*. Rather foul and yet somehow . . . somehow . . .

But at least the King and Queen in old Shakespeare's play had known what they wanted and had left no stone unturned, whereas Hamlet — Lord, what a prize sap, wandering round and making a debate of everything! He'd be no good in the Eleven, a shilly-shallying chap like that!

Roderick yawned. He'd be no good himself at this rate. Sleep. A little sleep. Was it really too much to ask?

But when he did finally drop off, he found himself in the most uncomfortable dream. He was at home, he'd been summoned to Mother's parlour, he had to try and explain to her why he'd been such a failure in the semi-final of the Cricket Cup.

'There was nothing I could do, Mother. I was caught at cover point and—'

She looked him over with infinite contempt. 'Cover point, Roderick? What on earth is cover point?'

* * *

Cold, dismal April was forgotten. Summer had arrived in full panoply. The verdant Upper sparkled with dew. The long shadows of the poplars at its eastern edge were rapidly shrinking as the blazing sun climbed into a cloudless sky. The tall, tapering spire of the church was etched against the blue. But the church seemed remote, the town not worth bothering with. Today the Upper was the centre of the world.

The gods were on their side, it seemed. Conway's won the toss but put Ransom's in to bat just as Raynes had hoped. But it did not take long for the gilt to be knocked off the day. Hills went for a duck. Soon after, Raynes himself was caught in the slips for a measly seven.

'That's torn it,' said Roderick looking on, utterly wretched. 'It will all be over by the time I get in to bat.'

'Bah humbug!' said Kennedy. 'Where's the Brannan braggadocio? It's early days yet.'

But even Kennedy's optimism was shaken when two more wickets fell in quick succession.

'Four for nineteen!' he groaned. 'It's a debacle, a complete debacle! Well, it's you next, Branners. Chin up!'

It was a long walk to the crease. His legs felt leaden. He was sweating. His canvas shirt was stuck to him. Was it really this hot so early in the day? To think there'd been snow on the ground only a matter of weeks ago!

But why was he blithering on about snow? Anyone would think he was nervous. Anyone would think he was a novice at all this. He wasn't.

He adjusted his cap, tapped his bat on the turf. He was ready.

All sound ceased as the bowler readied his next delivery. Roderick, in the silence, could hear his heart thudding. And then — everything happened in a rush. The ball was on him before he knew it. He mistimed the easiest of long hops — and suddenly his dream from last night was becoming a reality. The biggest match of his life — a Cricket Cup semi-final — and he'd made an absolute pig's ear of it. He'd have a hard time explaining this to Mother — or anyone else.

But when he looked round he could scarcely believe his eyes. Conway's fielders had contrived to drop the catch. Were they still half asleep? What other explanation could there be? He'd survived by the skin of his teeth.

There was no time to pull himself together. The next ball was on its way. He took a swing at it that turned out to be more of a panicky stab. Somehow he got a run off it. Now Howlett was back on strike. Good old Howlett, the only one of them today to have played his part. Not just today, either. He'd been in tremendous form all term. Roderick had congratulated himself on more than one occasion that he'd arranged for Howlett to 'pass' the shooting test. Surely it proved that sometimes the ends *did* justify the means?

Crack! Howlett pulled the ball past square leg. A four. He made it look so easy. Whereas Roderick found that his hands were shaking. They were shaking so much he could barely hold his bat. How could he face Conway's demon bowler in this state? Pathetic. That was the word. That was the brutal truth. A desperately poor show from the auspicious heir of the Massinghams. Uncle Fred in the afterlife must be shaking his head in disbelief.

Roderick's heart sank as Howlett gave the ball another good whack and began to run. Lashing himself into action, Roderick set off on wobbly legs. He'd soon be back in the firing line. Well, there was only one thing for it. He would give the ball a good wallop and see what happened. Hit and hope. If he came a cropper, so be it. It would be better than a long, slow death.

It seemed to work. He scored a two, another two, and then a single. His hand stopped shaking. But no sooner had he settled than Howlett contrived to be caught at third slip.

Gloom descended once more. Things looked pretty hopeless now.

Scotson took Howlett's place. A fine cricketer, Scotson, everyone said so. But he had a tendency to lethargy in all that he did. It was because things came so easy to him. Not just games, but everything. Most chaps, for instance, had to flog the juniors before they'd warm the seats in the latrines. Not Scotson. They queued up to do it when it was Scotson. Well, Roderick was in no mood to pander to Scotson's majesty today. He gave the older boy a hard stare, to remind him of his responsibilities.

The sun climbed into the bleached-blue sky. The dew vanished. The air was breathlessly still. Conway's demon bowler started to fade. So soon? But when Roderick glanced at the scoreboard, he was amazed. They'd added more than eighty runs to Ransom's total, him and Scotson — yet it had seemed so easy! How much more could they manage?

* * *

There was a buzz in the air all through lunch that Roderick could not ignore. 195 all out. Quite a decent show. Ransom's had displayed a lot of pluck. And a century from that chap Brannan: a performance almost worthy of the First Eleven. But there was no point getting carried away. Conway's were notoriously difficult to beat, everyone knew that. 195 was good but probably not good enough — especially as Ransom's had no bowlers to speak of. It was difficult to see how they could do any real damage to the Conway's batting order. A pity, really. It would have been gratifying to see an upset. This Harcourt's-Conway's duopoly was getting to be a bore. Facts, however, had to be faced. Cream always rose to the top.

* * *

Ransom's started brightly after lunch, taking two early wickets thanks to their one decent bowler, Finch. The Ransom's contingent amongst the onlookers were biting their nails. This was ripping stuff! But how much longer could it last?

'What's Raynes doing now, the silly idiot?'

'He's resting Finch. It won't do to overplay him. Raynes is a decent bowler himself. He's not in the First Eleven for nothing.'

'Decent bowler, is he? Then what do you call that, ten runs off his first over? Conway's are making hay. It should be Finch and only Finch.'

'We'll never win with Finch alone.'

'Then we'll never win. But we could at least give it a try!'

In the outfield, Raynes jogged across for a word with Roderick. He was showing no signs of panic. One expected nothing less of Raynes.

'It's not my day, Branners. I can't get my eye in. Why don't you have a spell? You were super with the bat earlier. Let's see what you can do with the ball. Here, catch!'

There was a hollow feeling in the pit of Roderick's stomach. He was always able to dredge up some sort of performance when he was batting, even on a bad day. His bowling was much more hit-and-miss. When he was off, he was off by miles.

His arm felt stiff. His nerves were jangling. Who'd remember his century earlier if he made a hash of this? And the waiting Conway's batsman looked so calm, so casual, as if he knew there was nothing Ransom's could do to hurt him.

Roderick looked at the batsman again. Surely the face struck a chord?

It came to him just as he was throwing the ball. The Conway's court martial nearly two years ago. The humiliation of the firing squad. That chap waiting at the popping crease was none other than the boy who'd called himself the Chief Inquisitor.

Roderick's arm jerked. His aim was spoiled. The ball swung wide. The batsman reached for it, missed, gave a little shrug. Their eyes met. Roderick felt himself flushing. But the Conway's man turned away, not the slightest glimmer of recognition on his face.

Roderick weighed the ball in his hand as he walked back. An icy determination took hold of him. Gone were his anxieties about putting in a good performance. He thought of the bullies at prep school and how he'd eventually got the better of them. He thought of Nibs Carter, of Martineau: they too had got what they deserved. Now it was the Chief Inquisitor's turn.

He knew the moment the ball left his hand that he'd got it spot on. He watched with a sense of detachment as it bounced off the turf, pitching up unexpectedly high now that the ground was drying out. Caught by surprise, the Conway's batsman was forced to change his stroke mid-action. The ball fizzed off the edge of his bat. It reared up into the cloudless sky. Then slowly it fell — straight into Raynes's outstretched hands.

The Chief Inquisitor, dismissed for nought. He looked around in bewilderment, seeking the bowler who'd encompassed his doom. Roderick met his eyes once more and then, after a heartbeat, turned away — turned his back.

The Ransom's contingent were jumping up and down with excitement. 'Good old Brannan! That's the stuff! Raynes knows what he's doing, didn't we tell you? Finch is still fresh, too. We'll see some fireworks now!'

* * *

The Upper was a different place in the dark, wild and uncharted, as if wiped clean. The momentous match already seemed as remote as Agincourt. Roderick was sitting on the pavilion steps in the exact same spot where he'd sat all those weeks ago at the beginning of term, when his place in the Eleven had been in doubt and a victory over Conway's the stuff of dreams. It still seemed incredible. That was why he'd come here. That was why he was sitting alone in the dark. He was trying to convince himself that it was real.

The dismissal of the Chief Inquisitor had ushered in an extraordinary hour or so yesterday. Conway's order had crumbled. It had seemed no time at all before Scotson brought the innings to a close with a magnificent clean bowl which brought gasps of admiration from the onlookers. The gasps had died away. A stunned silence had followed. Conway's all out for forty-nine. It was more than unprecedented. It was, quite frankly, absurd.

There'd been no doubts in Roderick's mind after that. Conway's had blustered. Lightning didn't strike twice, they'd said. Tomorrow would be different. But Roderick had slept like a log, unperturbed, and today had been an effortless procession to victory. But why did that victory now seem so unreal?

Stars glimmered in the dark sky. The lights of town faded in and out as the poplars swayed in the breeze, the sound of their rustling leaves laid thinly over a deep and expansive silence. Nearer at hand, lights also showed in the back windows of Conway's where they'd be licking their wounds tonight, still wondering what had hit them. R H Brannan would be a name on everyone's lips.

But—

But what? Mile upon mile away through the empty night, Mother, Father, Dorothea would be going about their unchanging routine at Clifton, completely unaware of his triumph. And even if they knew, would they have understood? Mother never remembered about cover point no matter how many times one explained it to her. Dorothea was more excited by motor cars than she was by cricket. As for Father — well, what *did* one talk about with Father?

Dorothea had asked this very question back in the Easter holidays. 'I've always wondered what men talk about after dinner when the ladies leave the room.'

'Oh, I don't know. It's all rot, mostly.'

'What sort of rot?'

'I can't remember half of it. Last night — let's see — Father was rattling on about Shelsley Walsh and Lippets Hill, whoever they are.'

'They are places, not people. They are places where motor races are held: *hill climbs*, the races are called. Henry has made quite a name for himself, driving BFS machines.'

'Isn't he a bit old for that sort of thing?'

'At least he is doing something useful, getting BFS motors in the limelight.'

Roderick scowled, staring out at the dark Upper. *At least he is doing something useful.* What was *that* supposed to mean? But he should have known better than to pass comment on her precious Henry Fitzwilliam. The son of a neighbour back home, Henry Fitzwilliam was also a junior partner in Father's motor business — and a complete duffer to boot. One was ashamed to share a name with him, even if it was only one's middle name. Driving at speed up the side of a hill: how difficult could that be?

'Whereas I,' said Roderick, addressing the myriad stars, 'I—'

He sighed. Was this what victory tasted like? Except it wasn't victory. There was the final to come, Harcourt's standing between Ransom's and the Cricket Cup.

Win or lose, Dorothea wouldn't be impressed either way. She didn't think the Cricket Cup *useful.* For everyone at Downfield, however — everyone except a few obstinate individualists like Westaway — the Cricket Cup meant everything. Who was right? Dorothea or the school? They couldn't *both* be right, could they?

Roderick became aware of a shadowy figure emerging out of the dark: a shadowy figure crossing the Upper in a meandering line like a restless ghost. The ghost drew nearer. It was unsteady on its feet and had a bottle in its hand. Roderick thought he recognised it.

'Ash, is that you?'

Scotson during the course of the Conway's match had become Ashley or Ash, just as Raynes had become Tommy and Kennedy Cyril. Nothing was taboo for Ransom's heroic Eleven, even the arcane mystery of a chap's first name.

'Damn it, Ash, I thought you were a ghost! You're stinking drunk, you swine!'

'No. No. Not drunk. Tipsy.' Scotson seemed to like the sound of this word, repeated it slowly. '*Tipsy.*' He manoeuvred clumsily to sit on the wooden steps next to Roderick. The smell of beer wafted under Roderick's nose. 'I've been looking for you, Rod. I've been looking all over. You're a damned fine fellow, you know. A damned fine fellow. I wanted to tell you.'

Roderick laughed. 'So are you, Ash. So are we all.'

'No, no, listen, you don't understand! It was that look you gave me, Rod: that look you gave me when I came in to bat. That's what fired me up. I knew I couldn't let you down after that.' He hiccupped.

'Not me, Ash. The house. The team.'

'The house, the team — *hic* — yes.'

Roderick for a split second had a vision of Scotson as he'd been in the match, tall and slender in his whites, golden hair shining in the sun: almost god-like. It had seemed obvious at that moment why the small fry worshipped him, why they followed him round and aped him. One had watched them on the sidelines taking off their caps and mopping their brows in self-conscious imitation of their hero. And here now was their hero, drunk and shambolic on the Upper. One had heard rumours now and again of Scotson's drinking. But rumours so often turned out to be rubbish, complete fiction, that one had never really taken much notice.

'You're drunk,' Roderick repeated, grinning. It did seem rather a rag just then. What a roué he was, Ash Scotson! But there was something else, a feeling of unease that Roderick could not quite put his finger on.

'Where's — *hic* — where's — *hic* — where's my bottle?'

'It's here, you silly ass, right at your feet. But it's empty. All gone. Come on. Up you get. It's time to go. I'll walk you back.'

Roderick began to laugh again as they left the Upper and struck out down Little Lane. He had questioned the great victory as he sat in the dark, alone. It had seemed remote; it had seemed almost pointless. Now it began to shine again. They had beaten Conway's! Not just beaten: trounced, thrashed, annihilated! It was the talk of the school. It would pass into legend.

So this was what it felt like to be someone. As if one was as drunk as Scotson. But drunk on glory, not beer.

His heart swelled. If only this moment could last. If only he could capture it and pin it on a board as he used to pin butterflies.

'We few—' he began and Scotson joined in. 'We few, we happy few, we band of brothers!' Ransom's Eleven of 1908: had a finer body of men ever existed?

'We few, we happy few—' Their voices echoed in the silent street, their boots rang on the cobbles, and they swung arm-in-arm into Market Street where the glowing windows of Ransom's were waiting for them.

CHAPTER FOUR

Blue sky glimmered between the leaf-laden branches of the oaks. Faint sounds of cricket drifted through the air. Recumbent in the long grass at the edge of the Upper, Roderick yawned and stretched, languid as a sated lion. The whole afternoon stretched empty ahead of him. There was nothing until tea.

He'd lost interest in the cricket. It was only a junior match in any case. That didn't mean, of course, that it wasn't a gladiatorial contest every bit as fierce and brutal as any senior game. But the batting side was decidedly average. Seven wickets had fallen already. The little knot of spectators were impatient for more, chanting, 'We want eight and we won't wait!' The heavy air blunted the fervour of their youthful voices.

Roderick flattened the grass with long sweeps of his outstretched arms. Beneath the layers of his lethargy was a burning impatience, a feeling of suppressed excitement. Once the junior matches were out of the way, it would be time once more for the main event, the Cricket Cup. After last year's heroics, hopes were running high in the house, bolstered by a splendid performance by the Fifteen last term — a performance in which Roderick had for the first time played a part.

The Fifteen had reached the semi-finals of the Rugger Cup. Even greater things were expected of the Eleven. They were without their talisman Raynes this year, of course: he was now at Oxford. Scotson too was missing — but that was another story. The men who remained, however, had grown in stature and the team had been infused with new blood. Was it too much to hope? Dare one dream?

But what was he saying? He'd done nothing *but* dream, for weeks and months, ever since last summer. For all the glory of the Conway's match, it had been Harcourt's who'd won the Cricket Cup, crushing Ransom's in a one-sided final. That was all that would be remembered in years to come, all that would be written on the roll of honour: *1908, Harcourt's*. A fourth consecutive victory. Unheard-of domination.

Roderick sighed. Harcourt's. Always Harcourt's. Harcourt's was the bane of his life. And what swells Harcourt's men were becoming! They had started to boast now that the whole of the rest of the school was just a sort of a colony of their own great house. Would anyone — *anyone* — ever get the better of Harcourt's?

A shadow fell across him. Propping himself on his elbows, Roderick squinted up at the boy standing there. For a split second, dazzled by the bright sunlight, Roderick thought it was Tommy Raynes risen like King Arthur in Ransom's hour of need. But it wasn't Raynes. It was Raynes's littlest brother, red-faced and panting. He wore a conscientious look.

Roderick regarded him with customary irritation. 'Yes? What is it?'

'Please, Brannan. Mother Moxon wants to see you in his study.'

'That's *Mister* Moxon to you, you worm. What does the old buffer want, do you know?'

'No, I don't, I'm sorry, Brannan.' The boy waited, hopping from one foot to the other, anxious. 'He did say *at once*, please, Brannan.'

'Yes, yes. Just let me watch the end of this over.' Roderick pretended to a sudden interest in the cricket. It didn't do to go dashing off at the behest of a little maggot like Raynes the Third.

'Please, Brannan—'

'What? Are you still here?' Roderick yawned, stretched, got lazily to his feet. As he did so, there was another burst of cheering. The eighth wicket had fallen at last. 'Here, you — what's your name, you little tick?' One never admitted to knowing the names of the small fry.

'I'm Raynes, please, Brannan.'

'Well, Raynes, I don't suppose you happen to know who it is that's bowling?'

'It's Cawley, I think, Brannan.'

'He's half way decent for a junior. Five wickets already.'

'Cawley's uncle plays for Surrey.'

'Does he, indeed? Quite a mine of information, aren't you! Well, off you go. You can tell Mother Moxon I'm on my way. Go on! Shoo! Shoo!'

Raynes the Third went lumbering off, puffing and panting. Roderick followed at a more dignified pace, sauntering round the edge of the field before pausing at the gate to see the fall of yet another wicket. As he turned into Little Lane, he wondered what Moxon wanted. Something trivial, no doubt. It usually was. But at least it would help pass the time until tea.

Outside Moxon's study he adjusted his tie before knocking.

'Enter . . . Ah, Roderick, it's you.'

Roderick was instantly on his guard. For Moxon to use a boy's Christian name was almost unknown. This was obviously something more serious than one of the old duffer's pep talks.

Moxon pushed his spectacles up his nose. 'Sit down, won't you . . . I'm afraid it's . . . er . . . bad news. The wire came just after lunch.' He cleared his throat, looked shifty. 'Most awfully sorry but I have to tell you that . . .'

Moxon's voice seemed to fade in and out. Roderick struggled to understand the disjointed words.

'. . . quite sudden, I understand . . .there is an hour before the next train . . . here, sip this . . .'

Roderick looked down. He had a glass of brandy in his hand. He was quite at a loss to explain how it had got there. With a great effort he raised his head, met Moxon's eye. 'Dead? My governor is dead?'

Moxon looked away. 'Most awfully sorry. Quite sudden.'

Roderick blinked three times then stood up, putting the untouched brandy on the desk. 'Thank you, sir. Will that be all?'

Out in the courtyard he walked in circles, dazed. There seemed to be lots of jigsaw pieces in his head that wouldn't quite fit together. Father, dead? But when? How?

He came to a halt, looked around and suddenly realised that he hadn't been walking in circles at all. He was back on the Upper with the hot sunshine and the smell of pollen. The junior match was still in progress. That kid — the one who's uncle played for Surrey — was bowling again, causing all sorts of havoc; but most of his good work was coming to nothing, because the fielding was hopeless, placed all wrong. Someone should—

'Rodders . . .'

'H-S. What are you doing here?'

'Mother Moxon said I should . . . I've been looking everywhere. It's jolly rotten luck, about your . . . your—'

'Do you have a cigarette, H-S? I need a cigarette.'

'No, I'm sorry, I don't. I wish I did.'

'This bowler's rather good. I've forgotten his name.'

'Rodders—'

'A few more terms and he'll be ripe for the Eleven.'

'Your train, Rodders—'

'Oh, yes, the train. I ought to catch it, I suppose.'

'Yes, you ought. I'll take you to the station. This way.'

'It's alright, H-S, I can find my own way. I'm quite compos mentis.'

It seemed only seconds before he was on the platform at Downfield station, searching along the carriages for an empty compartment. Running footsteps sounded behind him.

'I got you these.' Gasping for breath, H-S pressed a packet of Woodbines into his hand.

The next moment H-S was getting smaller and smaller as the train pulled out of the station. Steam billowed up, obscuring the view of the town on the hill. Roderick looked down at the cigarette packet in his hand.

Had Moxon *really* meant to say that Father was dead?

There had to be some mistake. It wasn't possible. It just wasn't.

* * *

'I'd just like to say, sir, how sorry I am.'

The young man addressing him was like a beanpole and had crooked teeth. He was dressed as a chauffeur, presumably came from Clifton. The familiar BFS saloon was parked on the concourse behind him.

'It came as a shock, sir. To us all.'

'Yes. I see. Here, take this bag. And my jacket. It's most damnably hot this evening.'

The motor purred along the Hayton Road. The countryside was bathed in the last of the day's sunshine. Roderick began to feel, of all things, increasingly nervous. What on earth was he going to say to Mother?

Jolly rotten luck, Mother. Hardly. That might have done if he was a kid but he was nearly seventeen, an adult, a man. But hang it all! It was Mother who needed to speak, to explain what had happened, how it had happened, why she had *allowed* it to happen . . .

He looked out of the window, realised they were all but home. The motor rounded the sharp turn at the head of the drive. The house came into view. His heart lurched. There was a lump in his throat. He looked up at the symmetrical grey facade, the many windows. Late sun glowed on the chimney stacks. It was odd, seeing it like this, unexpectedly, in mid-term. It was almost like seeing it for the first time. Yet it was wholly familiar, too. It was real and solid and grounded when everything else was suddenly in flux. He felt a deep reverence for the place. Almost he wanted to get down on his knees and give thanks. Ancient, enduring, unchanging, seat of the venerable Massinghams, this was the centre of the world, his home.

The motor rounded the cedar tree and pulled up by the steps. The chauffeur opened the door. Roderick stepped down.

* * *

Mother was in the drawing room. She got up from the Eugenie armchair as he came in. Her face was pinched and pale. She was dressed in mourning. Black did not suit her, diminished her in some way.

'Roderick. You're home at last.'

She grasped his hand tightly. It cost him an effort not to snatch it away. He felt as if he was being dragged down into some dark place where he did not want to go.

'It was very sudden,' Mother continued. 'His heart. Arthur Camborne says he wouldn't have suffered. Arthur has been very kind.'

Roderick wrinkled his nose. Dr Camborne, that shrivelled old gnome. He was like a parasite, feasting on misfortune, making his living from illness and death. Roderick's hand curled into a fist as he experienced an intense hatred for the village doctor.

He had to sit for a while with Mother in the drawing room. He had to sit there, pretending. Pretending to be what, he was not sure. Pretending to be Roderick Brannan, perhaps; because at that moment he did not feel as if he was anyone. The jigsaw pieces lay in an untidy heap in his head, the picture unguessed-at.

The clock ticked, shadows lengthened outside, dusk fell. The footman came to close the curtains. It was a new footman, not Timms: he was unhurried, precise, didn't fall over his own feet the way Timms had. Roderick felt affronted.

How dare things change! How dare a new footman come! One should be able to rely on home being the same!

A new footman. And Father—

But it was time to dress for dinner. Roderick retreated to his room, bathed, donned the black clothes laid out for him, then stretched on his bed, waiting for the gong.

* * *

'Mrs Brannan won't be down, sir. She said to tell you.'

Roderick paused, his hand on the handle of the dining room door. 'Very well, Ordish. In that case you might serve dinner straight away.'

Dorothea was already seated. 'We expected you earlier,' she said. 'We expected you at tea time.'

Roderick shook out his napkin. 'I missed my connexion.'

It wasn't entirely true. Standing on the platform at Rugby waiting to change trains, he'd suddenly remembered the packet of Woodbines that H-S had given him. He'd paced up and down, smoking the cigarettes one after another (his throat was still feeling the effects). Three trains at least had come and gone.

He wished he was back at Rugby now. He didn't want to be in this mausoleum, sitting silent at the mahogany table listening to the scrape of cutlery and the discreet tread of the footman, the impostor. Why had Mr Ordish not stayed to serve dinner? Did he not think them entitled? Did he think them *children*?

An entrecote appeared. Roderick attacked it. He sliced it into smaller and smaller pieces but somehow he couldn't eat it. It seemed only a moment ago since the Easter holidays. Things had been normal then. Timms had spilt the soup one evening, had broken a wine glass on another. And what about that time when he'd tripped over himself and smashed a whole decanter of whisky? Lord, that had been so funny! But that had happened ages ago, not in the Easter hols. Nor had it happened here at home. It must have happened at

Essex Square, nearly two years ago, the summer of the Test Match. He and Father had . . . he and Father—

But where was Timms now? Who was this impostor? One could hardly ask when the impostor was here in the room. Roderick asked about the chauffeur instead, also new: the little boy like a beanpole.

'Young Stan is not little boy, Roddy, he is the same age as you.'

'Young Stan? As opposed to Old Stan? And who . . . ?'

'Old Stan is his father, Mr Smith.'

'Mr Smith the motor man? Mr Smith who is—' Roderick stopped, bit his tongue. He had been about to say *Mr Smith who is Father's business partner*. But it didn't seem right, talking like that about Father, so casual.

Roderick stabbed a piece of steak with his fork, shied away from the subject of Father, thought about Mr Smith instead who was only a junior partner in the motor business but whose expertise that had gone a long way to making the BFS machines such a success. What, then, was Mr Smith's son doing, playing at servants here at Clifton?

Dorothea explained. 'Mr Smith believes his children should learn how to make their own way in life. He wants them to work their way up, as he did.'

'What rot! Why does the boy put up with it?'

'Out of respect for his father, I should think.'

Dorothea was looking at him oddly, almost as if she suspected the truth, that he wasn't the real Roderick Brannan, that the real Roderick Brannan had got lost amongst the jigsaw pieces in his head.

She put her knife and fork down. 'I should go and see if Eliza is alright.'

'But you haven't finished dinner yet!' His words echoed, rather. Why was he talking at the top of his voice? 'You shouldn't spend all your time dancing attendance on my sister, you know!' He winced. He hadn't meant to sound quite so tetchy.

'I don't mind. I like to be useful.'

'Oh, yes, Miss Goody-Goody!' *Listen to yourself! Stop being such an ass!*

'It's the least I can do when everyone has been so kind down the years, Aunt Eloise and—'

'So kind, my eye! You've only been treated as you deserve! It's kindness *owed* to you. You aren't required to pay it back!'

'There's no need to shout.' She got to her feet. The new footman hurried to open the door. She always had them fawning round her.

'He was *my* father!' Roderick yelled as the door closed. 'Mine,' he added in his normal voice, 'not yours.' He pushed his plate aside, knocking his glass of wine over as he did so.

The footman darted forward. Roderick snapped, 'Go away! I don't want you! Get out! Go!'

The footman froze for a second, then said calmly, 'Very good, sir.'

He exited without a sound.

Roderick righted his glass, poured more wine. But then he sighed, pushed the glass away to join the discarded plate. What was the point of having dinner on one's own?

He stared out across the wide, desolate table. There was silence.

* * *

Later he went looking for her, to apologise. She was in the nursery, of course.

'Doro, I—' The words stuck in his throat. He paced up and down the day room, picked toys off the shelves, put them back again. Tapping the bars of Polly's cage, he earned himself a baleful glare.

He gradually became aware that Dorothea was crying. A sense of panic gripped him.

'Oh, lord, Doro, I'm sorry, I truly am! I didn't mean to upset you, I wouldn't upset you for the world! I . . . I don't know what's got into me today. I'm just a beast.'

'It's . . . it's not you.'

'No. I see. Father.'

She shook her head. 'The . . . the semolina pudding.'

He stared at her, nonplussed. 'The semolina *pudding*?'

'We never even touched it, after Cook went to so much trouble. I feel awful. I feel . . . oh, I feel . . . oh, oh!' She was sobbing her heart out as if it was the end of the world.

'What an absurd child you are!' He tried to be bright, breezy, but he couldn't pitch his voice right, ended up sounding gruff and brusque. 'Look, Doro, Cook prepared that semolina pudding because it's her job. Whether we eat it or not doesn't signify.'

'You don't understand. I knew you wouldn't.' She turned away from him and said some things which he could not make out but which might have included the words *heartless brute* — or was that just his imagination?

He could see no alternative but to put his arms round her.

It was not so bad once he'd taken the plunge. Like the cold baths at school, it was only the thought of it beforehand that was unbearable. Once one had got over the first shock of the water — well, one could get used to anything.

'Oh Roddy!' She turned to him, flung her arms round him as he crouched by her chair, buried her head on his shoulder. He patted her back, waiting for the storm to subside. From the cage, Polly watched with a malicious glint in her eye, as if relishing his discomfiture. He'd always had his doubts about that bird.

At length Dorothea shuddered, stopped sobbing, eased herself away from him. He stood up, handed her his handkerchief.

'He's gone,' she said simply. 'He's gone and he's never coming back. He was always so kind. That time when I was ill, he sat with me every day, he sat with me for hours.'

'I . . . I don't remember. I was away at school, I suppose.' He took a deep breath. 'At least you can cry. I feel nothing, absolutely nothing. Oh God, Doro, you're right, I *am* a heartless brute!'

'But I didn't . . . I wouldn't . . .' She looked up at him. A faint, sad smile appeared, like sunshine after rain. 'It's because it was so unexpected. It hasn't sunk in yet. The numbness will wear off by and by.'

'Will it? Perhaps you're right.' He couldn't stifle a sudden yawn, realised that he was really very tired. It had been a long day. 'I'm going to turn in, I think.'

'Roddy?'

He paused by the door, looked back. 'Yes?'

'Good night, Roddy.'

'Night, Doro.'

* * *

He left the nursery, went downstairs and along the first-floor corridor. His room was on the right towards the end. Father's room was straight on, the door shut fast. Roderick stopped and looked at it. He reminded himself: *Father is dead*. But that sounded ridiculous. It couldn't be true. A man as robust and alive as Father didn't just *die*.

In his own room, Roderick tore open the curtains and threw up the sash. Leaning out, he could hear a breeze rustling in the trees hidden round the corner of the house. There was no moon, there were no stars, the countryside was folded in shadow. Far off to his left a solitary light glimmered, tiny as a pinhead. As he tried to guess at the line of the canal, faint and remote he heard the tremulous hoot of an owl, hunting perhaps in Ingleby Wood.

A sense of frustration swept over him. Presumably there'd be some sort of funeral. He'd be stuck at home for days just when the inter-house matches were about to begin.

The inter-house matches! The Cricket Cup! How odd. How peculiar. He'd completely forgotten. It was all he'd thought about for months and months, but the Cricket Cup had ceased to exist from the moment he entered Mother Moxon's study.

He shivered, drew back, closed the window. He eyed his bed with misgiving. He was dead tired but he'd never get to sleep in a million years, not with so much going on inside his head.

But against all odds he began to nod off almost as soon as his head touched the pillow. It seemed to him that the bed was rocking and rolling like a train carriage. He could hear the clickety-clack of the wheels. He could hear, too, a jumble of voices. . . . *his uncle plays for Surrey . . . I got you these . . . I'd just like to say, sir, how sorry I am . . . how sorry . . . it was so unexpected . . . I feel nothing, absolutely nothing . . .*

'Semolina pudding,' he muttered, half asleep, shifting his position, exploring with his toes the cool, crisp sheets. 'Semolina pudding.' He snorted with sudden laughter. 'My God, Doro, you're a one-off, a one—'

His laughter turned into a snore. He slept.

* * *

Next morning after breakfast he took his hat and coat and Hecate — a puppy no longer — and got out of the house. The weather had changed, the sky was a uniform grey. A cool wind gusted amongst the poplars on the summit of Rookery Hill. Roderick kicked up last year's leaves while his dog grubbed in the mould. Rooks cawed in the branches above.

From the brow of the hill he gazed down at the house where smoke was curling from the chimneys; he gazed at the village away to his left, the crenulated tower of St Adeline's rising above the trees in the churchyard. Lawham Road ran like a ribbon from the village, past the turning to Clifton, and down to the canal where it passed over the humpbacked bridge and disappeared behind the green smudge of Ingleby Wood. The canal itself, invisible last night, was clear to see from up here, a silver thread following the contours of the land. A patchwork of fields stretched as far as the eye could see. The grey rim of the horizon seemed a long way off.

A sudden violent gust of wind whipped Roderick's cap away, sent it tumbling along the ground. Hecate barked excitedly and went bouncing after it.

'Leave, Hecate! Leave it!'

The dog came to a halt, watched disappointed as Roderick retrieved the cap for himself and jammed it back on his head. Turning away, feigning indifference, Hecate began to rake up the leaves with a cautious paw, snuffling the damp earth.

'Everything's the same to you,' Roderick accused her. 'You don't care about death.'

The dog took no notice. Roderick's face crumpled, tears brimmed in his eyes. He gritted his teeth, stuck out his jaw, battened down. In less than a second he was master of himself again.

* * *

The church was full, Mother all in black and veiled, Eliza with her hand in Dorothea's. Roderick, clutching his black gloves, wearing a black frown, stared at the coffin, bedecked with white flowers. Was Father really in that ridiculous little box? Father's personality had filled any room he was in. Now he was reduced to this.

'We bring nothing into this life and we take nothing out . . .'

The vicar's words washed over him. He felt like a kid again, a kid in church on Sunday. What was that game they'd played in the old days to stave off boredom? *Who's There*: that was it. One had to remember who was sitting where in all the rows back to the door.

He tapped his gloves on his knee, applying himself. Lady Fitzwilliam was sitting directly behind them with that motor-racing milksop of a son of hers. Then came Colonel Harding with two — or was it three? — of his brood. Mrs Somersby of Brockmorton Manor was impossible to overlook, dazzling in a vast hat and a svelte black gown. After that things got hazy. Where did Mr Simcox fit in? He was Father's foreman and — one had always vaguely felt — Father's friend. And Mr Smith the motor designer who made his children play at servants: where was he sitting? Mrs Smith, of course, hadn't come. Mrs Smith never came. Had anyone ever actually seen Mrs Smith? Perhaps she was a figment, a myth.

There was an empty row between Mr Smith and the Clifton servants — or was it *two* empty rows? Roderick was tempted to look, to remind himself. But if one looked, that was cheating, one forfeited the game.

One empty row or two, and then the Clifton servants. Finally, right at the back, there was a motley collection of villagers. Only Dorothea would know all *their* names. Dorothea, in fact, had always been infuriatingly good at this game.

It was a stupid game.

At last they all filed out of the cold church. One had forgotten it was May, sitting there freezing. It was another breezy day. The sky was strewn with tattered clouds. The sun shone fitfully. Buttercups nodded in the long grass between the weathered, moss-grown gravestones. Wrens trilled. A dunnock faintly warbled.

They gathered around a freshly dug hole. The vicar started up again. '. . . sure and certain resurrection . . . everlasting life . . . he turneth the shadows of death into morning . . .' Had Father believed in all this gumph? What exactly *had* Father believed in? Why didn't one *know*? Why hadn't one *asked*?

Roderick was weighed down by a feeling of remorse. All those letters unwritten, those conversations aborted. They had sat, the two of them, having dinner in that restaurant on the Strand two years ago. And what had they talked about? The Test Match. The Motor Show. How is your mutton, how is the beef? Words, just words.

One had always assumed there was plenty of time. The letter would get written eventually, they'd sit and talk in the end. And now it was too late, Father about to have half a hundredweight of earth shovelled on top of him.

Roderick grabbed a handful of dirt and flung it resentfully, bitterly on top of the coffin.

* * *

The morning room was teeming, the buzz of conversation slowly getting louder. What were all these people doing here? Surely it wasn't the done thing to accept an invitation back to the house after a funeral? Or was that just wishful thinking?

He had kicked his heels by the lych-gate of the churchyard waiting to come home while villagers queued to offer their condolences to Mother ('Mr Brannan used to bring me ointment for my rheumatics.' 'Mr Brannan was ever so good to our Arnie.' 'We've never forgotten all that Mr Brannan did on the day of the Great Fire.'). The irony was, Father had probably had more respect for that lot in the village than for most of the people who'd fetched up at the house. Colonel Harding, for instance: there'd always been a certain formality in Father's dealings with Colonel Harding. The Colonel had an officers-versus-rankers view of life. He'd regarded Father as someone who'd risen from the ranks and was therefore not quite *comme il faut*. Then there was the village doctor, Camborne. Father had always given the impression that he thought most doctors were quacks. Camborne also had a way of ingratiating himself. Father had always seen through people of that sort.

Roderick squared his shoulders. The doctor had an unctuous smile on his lips, was edging towards Dorothea who was standing quietly looking at a painting of a racehorse. She had to be protected at all costs, Roderick felt. He stepped to her side.

'Apparently, it's a Stubbs,' he said.

'Apparently?'

'I think it's more likely to be *in the style of*.'

'Does it really matter? You either like it or you don't.'

'Father didn't like it. Do you remember? "The sport of kings?" he used to say. "The sport of spendthrifts, more like!"'

She smiled. 'Yes, he did say that, didn't he! Oh, Roddy . . . !' The smile faltered.

Oddly, it was thinking about Dr Camborne which gave Roderick sudden inspiration.

'Inque brevi spatio mutantur saecla animantum et quasi cursores vitai lampada tradunt.' Quite brilliant, he thought. It was clever, consoling and had stolen Camborne's thunder. Camborne liked nothing better than spouting Latin at people.

But Dorothea looked blank. Roderick sighed. He'd forgotten how ignorant girls were.

'It means—' he began but he was interrupted.

'It means, "The generations of living things pass in a short time and, like runners, hand on the torch of life." Lucretius, my dear.' Dr Camborne fawned his way between them.

'That's nice.' Dorothea smiled at Dr Camborne. It hardly seemed fair.

'It's nicer in Latin,' muttered Roderick.

'But I don't understand Latin, Roddy.'

'The admission does you no discredit, my dear. The fair sex has no call for Latin. As the Duke of Wellington once said to a young MP — and it might apply to others, too — "Don't quote Latin. Say what you have to say, and then sit down."'

Roderick nearly choked on his own bile. That sneaking, stooping, bald Uriah Heap had spent his entire life quoting Latin and looking smug about it. Now suddenly he was suggesting that Latin was puffed-up and puerile. Bringing Wellington into it only added insult to injury. No doubt the doctor thought himself very clever, very clever indeed. Well, he hadn't been so clever when it came to curing Father. He shouldn't be swaggering around at Father's funeral as if he had no shame.

Roderick glared at Camborne, but the old fellow's leathery hide was thicker than an elephant's.

'Well, my boy—'

Roderick ground his teeth. Only Father called him *my boy*.

'How are you bearing up? You're getting decidedly tall, I'll say that much for you. Now is the time for you to win your spurs.'

'Sir?'

'You now are the man of the house, Master Roderick: that is what I am saying. Your mother, your sister, the . . . er . . . delightful Miss Ryan: they are all under *your* protection. You are their defender, their champion — their shining knight, if I may use a medieval analogy.'

'I see, sir. A shining knight. Of course.' Honestly, what *was* the old fool babbling on about? Even Dorothea must find this a bit much.

But when Roderick turned to catch her eye, he found that she wasn't there, she had disappeared into the crowd. He grimaced. So that was how it was going to be, was it, everyone conspiring against him? He'd need a large brandy to get through this. That new footman could fetch it. It was about time he made himself useful.

* * *

Roderick woke feeling like death. What time was it? What day?

When he was finally able to drag himself out of bed, he went downstairs to find Dorothea and Eliza in the middle of luncheon. There were places set for him and Mother. Father's place, of course, was empty.

He slumped in his chair, poured himself some water. Even the *thought* of food made him queasy.

'I can't eat. I'm ill.'

'It's your own fault,' said Dorothea. 'You got drunk.'

He eyed Dorothea through a haze of suffering. 'I did not get drunk. I can't have been drunk because I even remembered to put my boots out to be cleaned.'

'That will have been Basford. He will have seen to your boots. He's efficient like that. He had to carry you upstairs, had to undress you too, I expect.'

Eliza giggled. 'Basford carried you? You must have looked like a big baby!'

Basford, thought Roderick. That must be the name of the new footman. How dare the fellow take such liberties as to undress him! Though it was lucky, perhaps, that it hadn't been Timms carrying him up to bed. Timms would probably have dropped him on his head.

Roderick glowered at his sister. 'Why aren't you in the nursery? Can't a fellow have his lunch in peace?'

'Don't pick on Eliza,' said Dorothea. 'It wasn't Eliza who got drunk and made a fool of herself.'

'What do you mean by that? In what way did I — No, on second thoughts, don't answer, I don't want to know.' He groaned again. He could not even manage his water. 'I suppose Mother . . . ?'

'Aunt Eloise was spared the worst of your depravity. She had already retired.'

Yesterday was rather hazy in his mind. He remembered being angry. He'd been angry about the hole in the ground where they'd buried Father, he'd been angry with the villagers for importuning Mother, he'd got in a towering rage with Dr Camborne for reasons that were no longer quite clear. Henry Fitzwilliam had made him angry too. He'd overheard Fitzwilliam talking to Dorothea. 'If there is anything I can do at this sad time . . . if I can be of service in any way . . . I feel I ought to call you *Miss Ryan* now you are so grown up . . .' Fitzwilliam had been looking at Dorothea in a way that reminded Roderick of Hecate: dumb, devoted eyes in a bland, chubby face. And the way Fitzwilliam spent all his time driving motors up and down hills, and round and round race tracks! What a duffer!

But Father had rather liked Fitzwilliam. It had been Fitzwilliam who'd first got Father interested in motors. Why, then, did one despise him so much?

Roderick groaned. It was all too much to cope with in his delicate state.

'Shall we ask Cook for a poultice?' Eliza suggested. 'Roddy might need a poultice.'

'A walk, I think, would be better,' said Dorothea. 'A walk will do us all good.'

'I don't want a poultice, or a walk.' Roderick got unsteadily to his feet. 'I'm going back to bed.'

* * *

He lay on his bed staring up at the ceiling. Brandy of all things! What had possessed him? He'd end up like Scotson.

Roderick shuddered, remembering Scotson on the night of the Shrove Tuesday fair less than three months ago. The Shrove Tuesday fair, held on Downfield's main square, was strictly out of bounds to boys from the school. Anyone who dared to break the embargo was considered a devil of a fellow. Roderick had felt that for a chap in his position — up-and-coming, a member of the house Eleven — the Shrove Tuesday fair was obligatory.

Scotson too had been at the fair. Roderick had not known this until, on his way back to Ransom's, he'd found Scotson bedraggled and rolling drunk lying on the pavement in Market Street right outside the Big Man's quarters.

It had been a drab night towards the end of February, cold and dank, moonless, the black sky blurred by mist. Roderick had hauled Scotson to his feet, had lugged him like a sack of potatoes along Market Street. Scotson's heels had raked along the ground as Roderick dragged him down the alley and into Ransom's courtyard. The windows of the Sixth's studies on the ground floor had from time immemorial served as the nocturnal portals for clandestine comings and goings. Their sills bore the marks of countless years of use. But Scotson, although he'd revived a little by then, had seemed incapable of climbing in.

'For pity's sake, Ash, do buck up! There'll be the most awful row if we're discovered.'

'Oh. Ohhh. I feel rotten.'

'So you should. You stink of beer. Now put your leg up here, why don't you?'

'I can't, I can't, I really can't!'

'Yes you can! Stop being such a damned fool! You'll make me wish I hadn't stopped to help you if you carry on like this. And for Hades' sake keep quiet. You'll have the whole house up!'

'Quiet. Shush.' Scotson had tried to put a finger to his lips, had missed. The finger had scraped up across his cheek and ended in his ear. He'd giggled. 'Good old Rodders! You'll look after me!'

'Get in, damn you! Let go of me and get in!'

'You're such a brick, Rodders. I'm awfully fond of you, you know. *Awfully*.'

'What are you *doing*, Ash? Get *off* me! Get *off* me, you swine! I shall lay you out if you don't stop this at once!'

'You're the best chap that ever lived, Rodders. I wish we could . . . I wish . . .'

The memory of Scotson clinging like a limpet — of Scotson's clammy fingers groping, of his hot breath and cold lips, of his wild eyes — made Roderick's gorge rise as he lay suffering on his bed. He'd had to use brute force. Scotson had gone sprawling across the flagstones. He'd lain there like a fish on a slab, a sickly smile on his face, half-seen through the mist. The sound of the church clock chiming the quarter hour had been loud in the sudden silence.

And then a light had come on in one of the windows opposite.

Roderick remembered his sense of panic. He'd been sitting on the window ledge, one foot in, one foot out. For a split second he'd hesitated. But already there'd been voices in the courtyard. He'd had to leave Scotson and save himself. There'd been nothing else he could do. He'd dived into the study, slid the window softly shut, made his way swiftly through the inky dark up to the dorm.

Scotson had refused to go quietly, the story went. Mother Moxon had appeared in the courtyard in his dressing gown. Scotson had tried to knock him for six. That had sealed his fate. He'd been given the sack.

But what was the use, Roderick asked himself: what was the use in going over it? It didn't matter anymore that Scotson wouldn't be in the Eleven. It didn't matter when he was trapped here at home. The Cricket Cup was out of reach. Everything was in pieces.

Roderick groaned and rolled over, burying his face in the pillow, blotting out the night of the Shrove Tuesday fair. The world was a rotten place. It was a rotten place all round just now.

* * *

Some old duffer, a legal type, came from Lawham on the matter of Father's will. Everything was left to Mother, of course, apart from a few odds and ends, legacies and so on. Roderick gathered that his allowance might be increased on the strength of it, which was something.

Turning the pages of some dull document to do with the motors, Mother said, 'I had no idea the business was doing so well.'

'*Both* businesses are doing well,' said the old duffer fussily: 'the motor cars on one hand, and the bicycles and components on the other.'

'Albert, of course, always made a success of anything he put his mind to,' said Mother regally. 'All the same . . .'

Roderick knew what she meant. One had always vaguely thought of Coventry as a sort of hobby, something to keep Father amused. One had always assumed that the family wealth (such as it was) came from the estate. The old duffer seemed to be implying that it was the other way round. Coventry generated a large and growing income, whereas the estate — it was intimated — barely paid its way.

What was the estate, exactly? Roderick had never given it much thought. There was the house, Clifton Park itself, but what else? All those endless acres that one could see from the summit of Rookery Hill: how much of that was attached to the house, the legacy of the lauded Massinghams? Roderick felt that he ought to know. If he was the heir, he ought to take more of an interest. But somehow it had never seemed important before. He knew one day he'd be master but *one day* was a long way off — or so it had seemed, with Father immortal and Mother unchanging and life at Clifton carrying on and on in its endless cycle. Now, suddenly, everything was different.

Coventry loomed large in the old duffer's talk. Mother, needless to say, would not be expected to take up the reins. Father in his will had suggested — and it was now agreed — that Mr Smith the designer would run the BFS Motor Manufacturing Company with the help (or hindrance) of Henry Fitzwilliam. Mr Simcox would look after what had once been the bicycle concern but which was becoming increasingly involved with making motor components — making them not just for BFS motors but for other companies too, a lucrative trade. The Brannan Bicycle Company had been renamed just before Father's death as Brannan Engineering.

Just names on a piece of paper. But they represented Father's whole life.

The old duffer finally packed his briefcase and went back into hibernation in Lawham. Dorothea wandered away. She had much to think about. Thanks to a legacy, she would be rich when she reached the age of twenty-one — richer, anyway, than she could ever have dreamed when she lived in the slums of London.

Mother gathered all the papers. She stood for a moment by the french windows — surveying her realm, as Roderick put it to himself. Slim, elegant, ageless, not a hair out of place, Mother was rather magnificent. She had a way of dealing with people, too. The old duffer had arrived, all puffed up with a sense of his own importance. Mother had effortlessly pricked his bubble, brought him down to earth. There was no messing with Mother.

'A last will and testament is such an *arid* sort of document,' she said at length without looking round. 'So much goes unsaid. Your father, of course, was very proud of you. There can be no doubt about that. Then there's Dorothea.' Mother's tone was thoughtful, as if she was weighing long years in the balance. 'When Dorothea first came here, there were holes in her boots, dirt was ingrained, she smelt. One could have been forgiven for thinking that nothing would ever come of her. Perhaps, on reflection, one might have been mistaken.'

Good old Mother! Her opinions were nothing if not measured. Here she was after nine long years finally deciding to approve of Dorothea.

Roderick grinned. It was safe to do so when Mother had her back to him. 'I think you were, Mother: mistaken, I mean.' They had all been mistaken about Dorothea, an interloper who nobody had wanted but who now they could not do without.

Mother stirred. 'Well. That's over.' She moved effortlessly across the room but paused by the door to look back. 'Don't slouch, Roderick. It's most unbecoming.'

She went away. The room lapsed into silence. Easing off his shoes, Roderick swung his legs onto the couch and stretched out. He looked along the length of his body in its black clothes — *decidedly tall*, Dr Camborne had said — and wiggled his toes inside his thick woollen socks. *Your father was very proud of you*. Mother had made a point of saying so. And Father had been an exacting sort of chap, he wasn't the type to be proud of just *anybody*. When he was proud, it meant something.

Roderick watched the clouds piling up in the sky outside. He thought of last summer. They'd been in London, making use of number twenty-eight Essex Square as Father had wanted. The Franco-British Exhibition had been on. Eliza had been entranced: the domes and fountains and waterfalls, the rides and the music and the millions of coloured lights at dusk. But best of all she had liked the palaces.

'Well, child,' Father had said, 'so you like palaces, do you? We'll have to see about taking you to the Crystal Palace. That would be just the ticket.'

Eliza's face had lit up. She had the most ridiculous of vivid imaginations. No doubt she'd been picturing the Crystal Palace as a fairy-tale concoction with battlements of spun sugar and golden pennants flying from diamond-encrusted towers. Roderick remembered that he'd caught Father's eye, that they had both laughed; that, having so recently turned sixteen, he'd felt he was now grown up, on a level with Father; that they could laugh at Eliza's imagination, understanding each other without the need for words.

And now Father was gone. He would never take Eliza to the Crystal Palace. He would never make better use of the house in Essex Square. His long story — so much of it lost in the mists of the past — had come to an abrupt end. His heart had packed up. He'd ceased to exist. All that was left was a mound of earth in Hayton churchyard, not even a crypt like the Massinghams. The flowers on the grave would be wilted by now. Would one's memories wilt too? Would one slowly forget all the details: the gruff voice, the no-nonsense manner, the way he'd smoothed his bushy moustache with his fingers? Sixty-three. It sounded so old. But Father had never *seemed* old.

'I shall *never* get old,' Roderick said through gritted teeth. 'I shall *never* die. Never, never, never.'

* * *

The days passed slowly. Roderick explored the gardens. He'd known every inch as a kid but now that he spent so much time away at school he'd rather lost track of things.

It was in the orchard that he came across his old enemy, Nibs Carter. The orchard was in the outer reaches of the gardens, a neglected place. Here, once, Roderick had discovered Carter stealing apples. They'd fought yet another battle. Roderick for once had come out on top.

But this was a different Carter, no longer a scrawny kid, though he still had the same ruffianly look about him, still wore a rag-bag of clothes: a tatty shirt with the sleeves rolled up, a shabby-looking waistcoat. There was a girl with him, one of the maids from the house. As Roderick watched unnoticed, Carter reached out and put an arm round her, carelessly, casually, as if it was nothing. He drew her close as he lounged against the twisted trunk of an apple tree and he said something to her that Roderick couldn't hear. The girl giggled. Carter smiled, that lopsided smile that made one want to punch him in the face.

'So this is where you've got to, Roddy!'

The unexpected voice made him jump. Dorothea was there. Her sudden appearance was disconcerting. He didn't want her to think he'd been spying or eavesdropping — especially on Carter, of all people.

He stepped forward. 'You, Carter. What are you doing here, trespassing?'

Carter and the girl sprang apart. The girl turned crimson. Carter, too, looked ruffled at first, but when he realised who it was his face hardened. He scowled at Roderick, savage and menacing. The tendons in his forearms stood out as he bunched his fists.

Blind rage took hold of Roderick. But before he could say or do anything else, Dorothea moved to join him, a picture of serenity.

'Hello, Susie. Good afternoon, Nibs.'

The maid went scampering past with her head down, mumbling, 'Miss Dorothea. Sir.' She couldn't get away fast enough.

Carter touched his cap to Dorothea. 'Afternoon, miss.' He glanced briefly again at Roderick then turned away, spat into the grass, sloped off.

Dorothea rounded on Roderick. 'Why couldn't you leave him alone? He wasn't doing any harm!'

'All I did was speak to him. Am I not allowed to speak? Who was that girl, anyway?'

'That's Susie Hobson.'

'Hobson, is it? Well, she's no right being out here. I shall report her to the Dreadnought.'

Dorothea's eyes flashed dangerously. 'If you do, Roddy, I shall tell Mrs Bourne what it is you call her behind her back. She might not appreciate being referred to as *the Dreadnought*.'

'Why should I care? She's only the housekeeper, I can call her whatever I like, I shall say it to her face.'

'I'd like to see you try! Even you aren't that brave.'

'I might have known you'd take *his* side,' said Roderick bitterly. 'I might have known you'd stand by Carter. I don't know what you see in that arrogant oaf.' It was monstrous, taking sides the way she did, spurning a chap who'd scored a century against Conway's, a chap who Tommy Raynes — Tommy Raynes, mark you — had said could easily make head of house one day.

'Nibs is not arrogant!' said Dorothea. 'A little proud, perhaps, but not arrogant.'

'Well, he's no right being proud, someone like him. I'm glad I got him the sack, he deserved—' Roderick bit his tongue. Too late.

Dorothea's eyes narrowed to points of flint. 'What do you mean?' she said slowly. 'What do you mean, *you* got him the sack?'

Roderick blanched. 'I . . . I caught him red-handed, that's what I mean. I caught him stealing vegetables.' He avoided her eyes but could still feel them needling him. 'Oh, alright, I might have said . . . all I said was . . . that he wouldn't dare, that he didn't have the nerve, that he was spineless. How was I to know he'd take me seriously?'

'So it was *you*, you goaded him, it was *your* fault—'

'It wasn't *me* that stole the vegetables! Anyway, it was years ago, it doesn't matter now.'

'Three years ago. Only three years. And on my birthday, too. Nibs was sacked on my birthday. Oh, Roddy, how *could* you!'

'What about *me*, what about all the things he did to *me*, what about all the times he ganged up with the village boys? I was only settling the score!'

'That's all you ever think about, revenge, revenge, revenge! It's petty, it's spiteful, you're a bully! Do you think Nelson was so small-minded, or Wellington?'

He felt himself colouring up. 'I'm sixteen, I'm not a kid! I don't care about Nelson or Wellington, not anymore! And it's not about revenge. All I do is stick up for myself. You have to show people you're not a sap or they'll come after you again and again — they'll never leave you alone!'

'Don't be silly! People aren't like that! People aren't so petty. People aren't so cruel.'

'That's what you think! You don't realise! Doro, you've no *idea*!'

'I've more idea than you! People are nice. Most of the time they are nice. It's you — you turn people against you. It's the way you treat them, the way you treat your so-called friends, poor Harrington-Shaw, for instance. You invite him here and then you *ignore* him, you don't listen to a single word he says! Sometimes you can be really . . . horrible. Well, this time you're not getting away with it. I shall talk to Aunt Eloise. I shall talk to her at once. I shall get Nibs his job back. Not that he'll *want* to come back, the way he's been treated.'

'You'll do this and you'll do that,' said Roderick nastily, unable to stop himself. 'I suppose now that Father's dead you think you *own* the place!'

He couldn't begin to imagine what made him talk like this. He couldn't think why he was so angry. It was like listening to a stranger.

Dorothea was angry too, he could tell, but she didn't give in to it. She always went through agonies of remorse afterwards if she ever spoke out in the heat of the moment. She looked all buttoned-up today in her braided dress with the high collar. She looked very grown up and superior. Turning her back on him, she swept off, her skirts trailing through the long grass. She passed through an archway in the far wall and disappeared.

He made to follow her but then came to a halt. What could he say? He'd only make things worse.

It suddenly seemed very quiet, just the humming of bees. Their hives were here, in this enclosed area like a little paddock, walled off from the orchard and from the rest of the gardens. Young nettles grew amongst the hives. There were dandelions and daisies in the grass. Butterflies flickered and flaunted. He couldn't for the life of him remember what they were called, those white ones and that yellow. Why couldn't he remember?

He was filled with anguish as he watched the butterflies rise up and up before vanishing over the top of the wall. If only he could be a kid again, the gardens his playground, no school or Cricket Cup or Scotson. If only Father wasn't dead and Timms hadn't gone. If only everything was back to normal, as it should be. Oh, to be a kid again, with a butterfly net and a spotless soul!

* * *

He mooched about the stable yard keeping out of everyone's way, feeling sorry for himself. He leaned over the half-door of a loose box trying to tempt his old pony to pass the time of day. But the pony looked down its nose at him, more interested in its oats than its master.

'Faithless beast.'

Roderick turned away. He went back outside. The stable boy was crossing the yard with a pail in each hand, hob-nail boots ringing on the cobbles. They faced one another.

'Hello, Turner.'

'How do.' The boy shifted his weight from one foot to the other, scowling down at the mucky ground.

He was not such a boy anymore. He must be getting on for twenty, not exactly tall but thickset and strong, rather dour, rather sturdy. Why was it, Roderick wondered, that everyone had grown up without his noticing? Everywhere he turned, things had changed. What was it Dorothea had once written, in some letter or other? *You take so little interest in what happens at home . . .*

'Mr Roderick, sir — about your dad and that—'

'That's alright, Turner. It can't be helped.' Roderick hesitated. What did one say to a servant? And yet once upon a time Turner had been a friend of sorts, they'd been drawn together by a mutual dislike of Nibs Carter, they'd played cricket in Row Meadow. Why now did one feel so shy of him? 'Do . . . do you still keep ferrets, Turner?' It was all Roderick could think of to say.

'Aye. I do.' Turner squinted from under his cap. 'Would you like to see, sir?'

One couldn't very well say no when one had brought up the subject in the first place.

Roderick followed Turner across the yard and up some narrow stairs to a dark little landing with two left-side doors. Turner opened the far door. It led into a small, dusty room with bare floorboards, cobwebs hanging, one grimy little window. There was a pile of straw and some blankets; a chipped basin and a jug atop some rickety old drawers; a three-legged stool. Roderick tried to recall if he'd been in this room before. He supposed he must have when he was a kid, delving into every nook and cranny, but he didn't remember. Were they above the stables here? Or — no — they must be above the generator room, the electricity generator.

Turner pointed to a crude wooden hutch. 'The ferrets, sir. Would . . . would you like to handle them?'

'That's alright, Turner, perhaps not.' Roderick again looked around the rustic billet. 'Do you sleep here, Turner? I didn't know you slept here.'

'I do, aye. Leastways, I do most nights and if it int too cold. It gets too cold sometimes, in winter. There's not much room at home and our Daisy likes her space. Very particular, our Daisy.' Turner sniffed, scornful of Daisy and her ways.

Something they had in common, thought Roderick. Turner had an annoying little sister too. But he also had an older sister, and an older brother, married. Turner was fortunate in that *his* father wasn't dead. He had a grandfather as well. Roderick wrinkled his nose, thinking that Dorothea would have been open-mouthed in astonishment had she any idea he knew all this about a mere village boy.

As Roderick stood there wondering if he'd shown enough interest in Turner for the present, he suddenly felt very light-headed, almost dizzy. What was wrong with him? It must be this place, this little room, so grubby and claustrophobic. It must be the offensive stink of ferrets and a whiff of Turner too, not to mention the all-pervading smell of horses and horse muck.

And yet it wasn't that, not exactly. He wasn't sure what it was.

Turner watched him warily. 'Sir? Anything wrong, sir?'

'I'm alright. Just a bit . . .' Roderick swallowed. 'I might sit down for a moment.' He perched on the stool, hunched over, fighting the feeling of dizziness.

'Do . . . do you want a beer, sir? A bottle of beer? It might perk you up or summat. I have a beer now and then in the evenings.'

Roderick nodded. Why not? Anything was worth a try.

Turner got a bottle out of one of the drawers. He hesitated for a second, then reached for another.

The taste of the bitter liquid made Roderick grimace. He swallowed it down. It seemed to clear his head a little but that wasn't much help. The jigsaw pieces that in the last few days had begun to slot together were now in an untidy heap once more. He'd lost his bearings so much that he couldn't even remember when and where he'd first met Turner. He ought to be able to remember that. All he could think was that Turner had appeared out of nowhere that day in the Spinney — the day he'd been ambushed by Nibs Carter and his cronies. Turner had appeared as if by magic, crashing through the trees, a black scowl on his face, swinging his fists. 'Oi, you, Carter, leave that lad alone!'

It had been a hot summer that year, back in the days of the butterfly net. Roderick had been at liberty, after his tutor bowed out and with prep school little more than a rumour. His feud with Nibs Carter had flared up again. Carter and his cronies had pursued him along the Lawham Road, had cornered him down by the canal, had rolled him in the nettles. A few days later they'd been back to ambush him in the Spinney. They'd given him a black eye. He'd given one or two of them black eyes in return. But he'd been outnumbered. They'd closed in for the kill. That was when Turner had turned up. *Billy*, he'd been back then. One had called him Billy in the days before he started work in the stables. Together they'd turned the tables on Carter and his cronies, sent them packing. Afterwards, Billy Turner had fetched his ferret and taken Roderick to hunt for rabbits in Row Meadow where later that same long summer they'd played cricket with Harry Keech and Rawdon Lambell and others. Roderick had often lost track of time. He'd been late for tea. Nanny had given him 'what for'. She'd relished it. Nanny had hated children, Roderick was convinced of it. She'd certainly hated *him*.

It must have been the summer of 1899, ten years ago now. Memories concertinaed in his mind so that he saw in quick succession a wide-eyed boy with a butterfly net; a fugitive boy being hunted by Carter's gang; a rabbit-hunting boy in Row Meadow; and finally, in the blistering heat of that August, the imperious cricketer knocking his cohort of village boys into shape.

Prep school had put an end to all that: to the feud, the rabbiting, the cricket, his nascent friendship with Billy Turner. Things had never been quite the same in later years, during holidays from school.

The butterfly boy would never have got by at prep school. Bullied and tormented by the older boys, homesick, he'd have gone under. But Roderick by then had changed. He'd been hardened and succoured by the summer just gone. He'd faced prep school with a new resolve. He'd gritted his teeth and bided his time.

All the same, the Christmas holidays had come as a deliverance. But disillusion had lain in wait. Everyone at home had been caught up with the baby, the new baby he'd not even known about. Even Mother had been preoccupied, and he'd always come first with Mother until then.

'Look, Master Roderick, look!' they'd said in the nursery. 'Isn't she a picture? Isn't she lovely? Your new sister, your little sister. What's the matter? Don't you *want* a little sister?'

Well, no, he didn't, and he'd said so.

'What a wicked thing to say! What a naughty boy you are!' Nanny had laid into him with gusto.

Afterwards, he'd lined up his toy soldiers on the big table in the day room and massacred the lot. Just so, when he was older and stronger, he would massacre Nanny and the boys at school and Nibs Carter and *everyone*.

And then, as if to add insult to injury — as if a new sister wasn't penance enough — a wretched waif had arrived out of the blue, a curly-haired, wide-eyed, most peculiar girl. She was his cousin. He'd never heard of such a cousin. He hadn't wanted her any more than he'd wanted his sister.

Now, ten years later, it was the other way round. Now it was Dorothea who didn't want anything to do with *him*.

'If you must know,' Roderick burst out, gripping his bottle of beer, 'I've had a beastly row with Doro — with Miss Dorothea. She's a . . . a . . .'

'Aye.' Turner, sitting on the straw, stared at his bottle as if it was an oracle. 'She's as nice as pie, Miss Dorothea, but she sees right *through* a chap, if you know what I mean.'

'Yes, you're right. You're absolutely right, Turner.' Fancy a fellow like Turner putting his finger on it! He lived a rum sort of life out here in the stable yard, did Turner — a different sort of life, mucking out the horses and sleeping on a bed of straw. But he was a straightforward lad. There was no mistaking him.

There was more to Turner's work, however, than met the eye. With the beer loosening his tongue, Turner began to talk about it. Since the head groom (the only groom) had given notice and gone, everything had fallen on Turner's shoulders. Not that he minded, he wasn't complaining, he liked being his own boss, having no one to answer to — no one except the master and mistress, of course: or just the mistress now (he was forgetting). But the simple truth was, there just weren't enough hours in the day — though he always made sure the horses were alright, he made a special point of that. He had a lot of time for horses. Nicer than people, they were. Nicer than most people, anyway.

Turner took pride in his work, thought Roderick, swallowing more beer. But it was deserved pride, unlike Carter, who built himself up to be something he wasn't. Roderick wondered if he could tell Turner about school, about the Cricket Cup, how he'd waited all year for this term only to have it snatched away from him. But school seemed like another world in this dusty little room and the Cricket Cup as vainglorious as those long-ago matches on Row Meadow. Turner had been a dab hand at cricket. Anyone who could play cricket like that had to be a fine fellow at heart.

And so they got the ferrets out and handled them, one each, slithering and squirming in their arms. They gripped their bottles of beer between their knees. They spoke in disjointed sentences. They avoided each other's eyes. They sat companionably in the tiny room as if nothing else mattered while, on the other side of the grimy glass, the May afternoon wore slowly away.

CHAPTER FIVE

'Dearest Roderick,' said Mrs Harrington-Shaw as they met on the stairs. 'I was so very sorry to hear about your father. How long has it been since he passed away? Two months? Three? What a horrible time for you!'

Walking down with her, Roderick squirmed with awkwardness. It was his first morning at Orsley. He had forgotten how effusive H-S's mother could be. Besides, what was one expected to say when people brought up the subject of Father? Roderick made do with muttering 'Thanks' and 'Grateful', adding a few more indecipherable grunts for good effect.

Awkwardness was alien to Mrs Harrington-Shaw. She took his arm as they reached the wood-panelled hallway, smiling beatifically.

'Shall we go through?' She led him in to breakfast.

They took their places at the table. H-S and his father were already eating. Silence, it appeared, had been the order of the day thus far but Mrs Harrington-Shaw, like nature, abhorred a vacuum.

'What shall you boys do today?' she said, pouring tea, handing a cup to Roderick.

H-S did not look up from the important business of stuffing his face. 'I haven't given it much thought, Mater.'

'Why not go riding? It's just the morning for riding. The weather, I suppose, will stay fine, Humphrey?'

Mr Harrington-Shaw cleared his throat. 'Probably cloud over. Rain, I shouldn't wonder.'

'Oh, nonsense! You are always such a pessimist!' She sipped her tea, holding the cup in both hands. Roderick, stirring sugar into his own tea, could feel her eyes on him. 'Did you sleep well, Roderick? You have your usual room.'

'I slept like a log, thanks, Mrs Harrington-Shaw.' Helping himself to bacon, Roderick wondered if she was having a sly dig, talking about his *usual room*. There'd been rather a long gap since his last visit to Orsley. This time last year he'd been in London. Raynes had been in town, Kennedy too, he'd seen both of them; he'd also spent time keeping his cousin and his sister amused, taking them to the Franco. Letters from H-S had arrived seemingly with every post. When was he coming to Orsley? But he hadn't been able to face it. Even the Franco had more going for it than Shropshire. This year, however, was different. No London. No Father. And anything was preferable to spending the whole summer at home, a house in mourning.

'Is your bacon cooked as you like, Roderick? Perhaps your eggs are over-done?'

'No, no, Mrs Harington-Shaw. It's all excellent. *As usual*.' Two could play at that game.

'Wouldn't say excellent as such,' muttered Mr Harrington-Shaw. 'The eggs are hard as iron yet again. You must have words, Aldora.'

'No one on Earth could cook eggs in a way that would please you, Humphrey.' Mrs Harrington-Shaw spoke with a twist of irritation. She took another sip of tea, dabbed at her mouth with a napkin, smoothing away her pout. Returning to her smooth and sibilant tones, she said, 'Alfie tells me you have electricity at Clifton Park now, Roderick?'

'That's right, Mrs Harrington-Shaw. For five years.'

'They have electricity, Humphrey.'

'I did hear. I am not deaf.'

‘We must seem positively medieval to you, Roderick, with our gas lamps and our candles!’

Roderick, his mouth full, could only manage a smile. He wished she would let him get on with his breakfast. Too much talk too early was liable to give one indigestion. It was just his luck she was at home. On his previous visits she had often been away, staying with relatives or shopping in London.

Mr Harrington-Shaw looked up balefully from his breakfast. ‘Electricity! Bah! New-fangled rubbish. The old ways are the best, tried and tested.’

‘Don’t be so absurd, Humphrey! One can’t shut out the modern world forever. One must move with the times or one will atrophy. For myself, I adore new inventions. I am quite besotted just now by flying machines. You must have heard, Roderick, about Monsieur Bleriot crossing the Channel. He is just the type of man I admire. Someone who embraces change. Someone who is bold and adventurous, who is not afraid of life! The young, I find, are always of that mind. But the old — how I abhor the old!’

Roderick raised an eyebrow, wondering what Mr Harrington-Shaw would make of that, but the old coot seemed not to notice, wading on through his breakfast with single-minded intent. Perhaps he didn’t think of himself as old. Perhaps he had never noticed the age gap between him and his wife. It had always been a mystery to Roderick how such a curmudgeon could have snared a (relatively) young and glamorous wife. Money probably came into it somewhere. It usually did.

* * *

‘I’m so jolly glad you’ve come, Rodders!’ H-S was walking on air as they made their way round to the stables. If he’d had a tail, he’d have been wagging it. ‘We shall have a rummy time together!’

‘If you say so, H-S.’

The groom — a brawny young man — was waiting with their horses.

'I thought you'd be here sooner, sir.' This pointed, not to say impertinent, remark was completely lost on H-S as he clambered into the saddle.

'How's her leg now, Jones? Any problems?'

'No, sir. No problems.'

The accent was Welsh, though it might have been Bengali for all the notice that H-S took. Roderick thought of Turner back home, taciturn yes but not morose — and certainly not insolent.

'He's an insolent fellow, that groom.' Roderick pointed this out as they rode through the trees, following the bridleway uphill.

'I daresay he is.' H-S had little interest in the groom. 'Probably thinks he's put-upon because he has to do the gardens as well as the stables.'

Which would explain, thought Roderick, why a large part of the gardens at Orsley resembled an impenetrable jungle. In fact, the whole place had an air of neglect, of being lost in time, like Sleeping Beauty's castle. Not that Orsley was a castle. It was a fussy red-brick building, an Elizabethan-style folly wreathed in ivy and hemmed about by secret, silent woods. A claustrophobic place. He had rather forgotten how awful it was.

Emerging at last from the dappled shade of the trees into the open, he felt he could breathe again. He urged his horse into a canter. Its hooves thudded on the turf. To his right the land rose to a high ridge with stunted trees stencilled against the blue of the sky; but to the left the ground fell away in long slopes until, far below, one caught a glint of water where the Severn rippled in its winding valley.

The thought of water was enticing. One was starting to bake in the sun. Pulling on the reins, Roderick turned his horse, waited for H-S to catch up.

'I say, H-S, shall we have a swim when we get back?'

'Oh, rather!' H-S was red-faced and sweaty. 'It is awfully hot today. The Lake will be just the ticket.'

'In that case, the last one back forfeits lunch!' Roderick dug in his heels. His horse leapt away, sped along the side of the valley.

'I say! Hey!' H-S's despairing voice was all but blown away in the wind of Roderick's speed. 'I never agreed to that! Rodders, wait!'

* * *

Returning to Orsley after being in the open countryside was like entering a green grotto. The air was still and stuffy under the thick canopy of leaves. The Lake — as it was called — was really nothing more than an ornamental pond. It had once been carefully tended, with a neat stone rim and a circular gravel walk, but had fallen into disrepair. It now had the air of a fairy tale, a place where one might expect to find frog-princes seated on lily pads. Lindens and poplars edged it round, along with rampant rhododendrons.

Roderick was already stripped and in the water when H-S came up, puffing and panting.

'No lunch for you, H-S!'

'Oh, you rotter!' H-S struggled out of his clothes. 'I'll make you pay, see if I don't!'

But H-S was no match for Roderick. He never had been. As sleek and streamlined as a fish, Roderick slithered out of H-S's revengeful grasp, flung water at him, then dived into the murky depths to grab the plump boy's ankles from below and pull him under. Why did H-S persist in these rough-and-tumble games? He always came off second best. But he was like Hecate, eager for any attention, grateful even for a clout on the snout.

H-S was vanquished. Choking and spluttering and spitting out water, he headed for dry land, floundering through the rushes like a hippo, scrambling up on to the gravel. With the pool to himself, Roderick opened up, swimming strongly from bank to bank, passing from the shade of the overhanging trees, crossing the sunlit centre, then back into the shade again.

'Ahoy, Mater!'

Halfway through a length, Roderick heard H-S's greeting and paused. H-S in his shirt and jodhpurs, his hair wet and lank, was waving across the Lake at his mother who had appeared as if from nowhere on the far bank.

'Ahoy!' she trilled. 'Did you enjoy your ride?'

'Rather! It was simply ripping! We've been swimming, Mater!'

'So I can see! What fun!' Her laughter skimmed across the surface of the Lake.

From Roderick's perspective — up to his neck in water — she seemed incredibly tall, all in white, one gloved hand holding her parasol at an angle. Dazzled by the sunlight in the centre of the Lake, it was like seeing a vision: a nymph out of the silent woods, or maybe Aphrodite herself, goddess of beauty.

Roderick squinted into the glare, waiting for her to move. The sunshine was hot on his head but the water that earlier had been welcome and refreshing now felt cold and slimy, chilling his body. He wanted to get out and get dressed but until she went away he was trapped naked where he was.

'You mustn't be late for luncheon, boys!'

At long last she turned away, disappeared into the dancing shadows beneath the trees. With a sigh of relief, Roderick swam quickly to the side of the pool, hauled himself out of the water, shook off the drips. He scouted round for his clothes where he'd flung them aside in the rhododendrons. He was just reaching for his long johns when he seemed to see something out of the corner of his eye: a shimmer of white, was it, amongst the shadows of the far bank? At the same moment he came up in goose pimples. It was as if he could *feel* someone watching him. Shading his eyes with his hand, he stared across the Lake, his long johns dangling from his fist. But there was nothing, no sign of anyone, no movement. He must have been seeing things.

He quickly got dressed then set off through the trees, chasing and harrying H-S all the way back to the house, hallooing as he went.

* * *

After luncheon, Roderick and H-S set up a game of chess in the shade of the old oak on the square of lawn at the back of the house. Roderick was sleepy. Orsley had that effect. But it didn't matter to the game. He could beat H-S with his eyes shut.

The afternoon was stifling. The surrounding trees seemed to dampen the breeze making the air thick and treacly. Waiting for H-S to make his move, Roderick became aware of someone behind him. He saw white skirts out of the corner of his eye. Mrs Harrington-Shaw. She had moved so silently across the grass that he not noticed her approach. She stood silent, watching the game.

Sweat prickled the back of Roderick's neck. His collar was choking him. And now, suddenly, H-S was making unwonted inroads into the game.

'Mater,' H-S said as he captured yet another pawn, 'it's Rodders's birthday soon: the eighth.'

'We must mark the occasion.' Her silky voice sounded very close, as if she was talking into his ear. 'And how old will you be on the eighth, Roderick?'

'S-s-seventeen,' he muttered. He fingered a knight, trying to find a way of restoring his grip on the game.

'Seventeen! So very grown up! Almost a man!'

He could feel her eyes on him. His skin came up in goose pimples. If only this stupid game was over! But he couldn't countenance the idea of letting H-S win.

Roderick made his move then loosened his collar, surveying the board. His heart stopped. He'd made a mistake, a dreadful mistake. It must be obvious even to H-S.

Panic gripped him. If they'd been alone, he'd have demanded his move again, bullied H-S into it, or else swept the whole board off the cast-iron lattice table, making the game null and void. But he couldn't do anything with *her* there, with *her* watching. Sweat ran in rivers down his back. He waited, holding his breath, for H-S's plodding brain to recognise the opening he'd been given.

He heard a rustle of skirts. What she doing now? Dare he look? Why be afraid to look? He braced himself, turned in his seat. She wasn't there. She was half way across the lawn, sashaying towards the house, hips swaying, parasol tilted, skirt trailing. She did not look back.

He turned back to the chess board. He felt angry. If only she'd waited! She'd have seen him turn the game around, snatch victory. She'd have seen—

'Rodders, are you listening?'

He looked at H-S blankly.

'It's your move, Rodders. I've told you twice already.'

Roderick wiped his palms on his trousers. There had to be a way out of his predicament. There had to be a way out and he'd find it — he'd find it and win the game, even if he melted all over the lawn in the process.

* * *

Roderick tossed and turned in bed, the sheets twisting round and round his body as he did so. It was hot and sticky tonight, the room unbearable despite the wide-open window. The darkness felt suffocating, like being wrapped in cobwebs. He wondered if H-S was suffering too. But H-S wouldn't worry about dropping off. He would just lie there doggedly counting sheep.

Counting sheep? H-S *was* a sheep! Why count sheep when there were so many more important things to count? That century against Conway's last year, for instance. His moment of glory. His perfect match.

He began reliving it ball-by-ball, got caught up, forgot the suffocating room. By the time he reached fifty he was starting to relax, he felt sleepy at last, his eyelids were flickering. Fifty-one. His muzzy brain tried to remember run number fifty-one. As he did so he slowly became aware that there was someone in the room with him, a cowled and shadowy figure over by the window, a cowled and shadowy figure reaching out a withered hand towards him—

He jerked upright, eyes snapping open, his heart racing — but there was no one there. The room was dark, silent, empty. It must have been his imagination. He must have been *dreaming*.

He lay back, breathing heavily, trembling a little. Another dream. Every night there was another dream. Every night for weeks and weeks. *Sleep like a log*? He should be so lucky! But tonight he wouldn't dream. He wouldn't, he wouldn't, he wouldn't . . .

He closed his eyes but he was restless and wide awake again now, turning over and over, winding the sheets ever tighter round his legs until he was hobbled, trapped. He began sinking, sinking deeper and deeper. Was this sleep? It felt more like being in water, hanging suspended in the fathomless green depths of the sea, gently rocked by the motion of the waves far above. It should have been soothing. Instead he felt anxious. He was in limbo, neither at the surface nor on the sea bed — neither fully asleep nor properly awake. It was torture. He writhed on the tangled bed, trying to kick his legs free. He could hear himself moaning and whimpering but could do nothing to stop it.

There was a sudden jolt. At last: solid ground. But where was he? He peered around. He was standing in some sort of gloomy dungeon. There was a slimy floor, walls of mossy stone, a ceiling dripping with condensation. The gloom seemed to lift a little. There in front of him, manacled to the wall, her diaphanous robe slipping down round her shoulders, was Mrs Moxon.

He breathed a sigh of relief. This old chestnut, a dream he'd dreamed many times before, Roderick to the rescue, the chivalrous knight in chain mail slicing with his sword through the iron manacles, setting the fair lady free.

But when he looked down at himself he found that he wasn't wearing chain mail, he was in his cricket whites instead. How would he ever cut through the manacles with only a cricket bat?

'I can't help you. I'm sorry.' He appealed to her. She must see that there was nothing he could do. But as he watched her squirming and twisting, her wrists tightly fastened, her robe slipping ever lower, her hair tumbled loose, he began to think that he did not *want* her free — not yet, not quite yet. Her skin was so smooth, so flawless. He wanted to touch it, to feel it.

He reached out a hesitant hand.

In an instant, everything changed. With the deftness of a conjuror, she somehow slipped the manacles off her own wrists and onto his. They swivelled round in a macabre dance, changing places. Now it was he who was manacled to the wall and all he had on was his night shirt. His bare feet were paddling in slime. Slime oozed down the wall at his back. Slime dripped inside his collar, slid stickily down his body. He tugged desperately at the manacles but they held him fast. There was no escape.

Mrs Moxon smiled a Mona Lisa smile. She stroked his cheek. But now her face was blurring and shifting. It wasn't Mrs Moxon at all. Then who?

He shut his eyes, squeezed them tight. He didn't want to know.

'Master Roderick . . .'

A voice he recognised. A hated voice. 'No, no, you've gone, you're not here!'

'You naughty, wicked boy! I'm going to take you across my knee. I'm going to give you what for. You see if I don't!'

'Please, Nanny! Please! You're hurting me . . . it hurts . . . please don't . . . please . . .'

But what was he saying? It wasn't Nanny. He stiffened, feeling long clammy fingers groping the back of his neck, hot breath on his face.

His eyes snapped open. He found himself staring into feverish blue eyes with the cold moonlight in them: feverish blue eyes in a pale, cadaverous face. Scotson. It was Scotson.

And he was entirely at Scotson's mercy. There would be no fighting him off this time.

'Oh, Rodders, you're the best chap, the best . . .'

'Get off me! Get off!'

'Rodders . . . mmm . . . mmm . . .'

'No! No, no, no, no—'

* * *

He was suddenly wide awake and thrashing about in bed, yelling his head off. He clamped his lips together. He looked all round, wide-eyed. No dungeon walls, no iron manacles — no Scotson. He lay still, getting his breath back, getting his bearings. Slowly he realised where he was. Orsley. The guest room at Orsley. And it was morning. The curtains were glowing with the light of the early sun. So he'd slept after all. He'd slept the night away. But he'd wrecked the bed in the process.

He sat up. Sheets were tangled and twisted round his legs. He tried to free himself. He tugged and tugged, finally gave a hard yank which made him lose his balance. He rolled over and without warning felt himself falling off the edge of the bed. He landed in a heap on the floor, jolting every bone. As he lay there winded, there was a knock on the door.

The maid with his water.

He scrambled to his feet, dived onto the bed, pulled the tangled covers up to his chin.

He took a deep breath. 'Come in,' he said.

* * *

Mrs Harrington-Shaw at breakfast was conspicuous by her absence. She had gone off early, H-S explained, shopping in Worcester or visiting friends or something like that.

'She'll be back later, I suppose?' said Roderick.

'Probably be away a week or more,' said H-S, helping himself to another egg.

A week, thought Roderick: how could anyone spend *a week* shopping? What about his birthday? What about her promise to 'mark the occasion'?

H-S was blithely indifferent to his mother's absence, nor did Mr Harrington-Shaw seem much concerned, muttering about 'that cad, that bounder' Lloyd George who'd made yet another speech against the House of Lords.

Roderick stabbed his egg morosely. He watched the yolk run then slowly congeal. He sighed deeply.

* * *

Days passed. Mrs Harrington-Shaw did not return. Sunday came, the day of Roderick's birthday. At luncheon, Mr Harrington-Shaw suddenly roused himself and began to talk about wine. It was the first time Roderick had seen the old duffer get excited about anything other than Lloyd George.

'I'm an oenophile, my boy: an oenophile. Look it up in the dictionary!'

I am not an ignoramus, said Roderick silently. *I do not need to look it up.*

'Champagne and claret are all very well, but tonight we shall be a little more adventurous. A Chateau Lafite, I think, is called for. And maybe a bottle of . . .'

Roderick stifled a yawn.

After lunch, Mr Harrington-Shaw and his son both nodded off, snoring in unison in the drawing room. Roderick watched them sleeping, dreading the thought of dinner. What a birthday this was turning out to be!

He jumped up. He had to get out, get away, anywhere. He crossed the little lawn behind the house and ventured under the trees. Silence reigned. Not a breath of wind stirred. It was like walking in a forest that had lain undisturbed since the dawn of time. This idea pleased him. Next moment, however, the effect was rather spoiled as he came to a clearing and found a dilapidated old summerhouse: a round building with a pointed roof, rotting timbers and grimy windows, obviously long neglected. He circled round it. It seemed somehow sinister. Or was he getting it mixed up with some old fairy tale told in front of the nursery fire? The summerhouse could easily have passed for the witch's cottage in *Hansel and Gretel*. No doubt Nanny would have been more sympathetic towards the witch than the straying children.

But what was he thinking? Nanny had never told stories. He was inventing a past that had never happened. And yet . . . and yet . . . *someone* had told him the story of *Hansel and Gretel*. Who? He seemed to remember being cradled in someone's arms, listening to a soothing voice, watching moving lips, sucking his thumb. Some long-lost nursery maid, perhaps? It must have been years and years ago, before Nanny, because once Nanny came he'd soon stopped sucking his thumb.

He shuddered, remembering some foul-tasting substance she'd put on his fingers, remembering too the way she had strapped his arms up at night to break him of his 'naughty, wicked' habit.

A twig snapped, as loud as a gunshot in the silence. He spun round, his heart hammering.

His eyes grew wide. At last he found his voice. 'Mrs Harrington-Shaw! You're back!'

She smiled. 'Of course. I couldn't miss your birthday.'

She'd remembered! She'd come back especially! Her hair shone like polished wood, her eyes glinted, her pale skin had a delicate sheen to it. Something stirred in his memory, the half-forgotten dream from days ago. He wondered now if it hadn't been Mrs Harrington-Shaw manacled to the dungeon wall and not Mrs Moxon. Not that they were very similar to look at, but there was something sphinx-like and fascinating about both, and they were both married to ageing, boring husbands. He wasn't sure exactly how old Mrs Moxon was, but H-S had told him that Mrs Harrington-Shaw was thirty-eight. He would never have guessed. She seemed much younger in the way she acted, the way she carried herself.

As if reading his mind, she said with a little laugh, 'I do wish, Roderick, that you wouldn't call me Mrs Harrington-Shaw. It makes me sound so old!'

What, then, should he call her? She gave him no clues. Her first name was Aldora. H-S had told him that, too. But it would have seemed like impertinence to call her Aldora.

Blood throbbed up his neck, burned in his cheeks. He smoothed his hair, tried to smooth away at the same time a feeling of confusion that he couldn't account for.

'Shall we walk back together?'

'Y-y-yes. If you l-like.'

'Perhaps you'll give me your arm? The ground is so uneven, the tree roots treacherous, I should hate to trip.'

He had to walk at her pace, threading slowly between the trees. He could feel through the fabric of his jacket and the cotton of his shirt her fingers gripping his arm. He was a head taller than she was and he felt rather solemn and splendid in his mourning black. His heart swelled at the thought of being her protector — even if he was only protecting her from some old tree roots.

They emerged from the wood. The house loomed ahead, somnolent in the late afternoon sunshine. As they crossed the lawn, H-S came out onto the terrace.

'Mater! Ahoy! I didn't hear you arrive!'

'Alfie darling! Here I am at last, back from Aunt Prudence. You were sleeping when I looked in, you and your father.'

She detached her arm from Roderick's and he was left standing as she walked on. As he watched mother and son heading to the house together, he could not smother the sudden thought that the way she had laughed just them must have been exactly how the witch in the story had laughed, catching sight of Hansel and Gretel straying in the forest.

* * *

Mr Harrington-Shaw had chosen a selection of wines to have with dinner. He knew more about wine, he said, than any wine merchant. The local wine merchant in particular was an arrant fool. Roderick tried to be as abstemious as possible, mindful of what had happened on the day of Father's funeral less than three months ago.

Mr Harrington-Shaw finally dried up during the cheese course. H-S took over. On this auspicious occasion — *auspicious* was rather an ambitious word to attempt in his condition, he had been far from abstemious — he would like to propose a toast to his great chum Roderick Brannan. A jolly fine fellow, everyone said so. Well, perhaps not *everyone*, but why listen to the cynics and scoffers: they might say that Rodders was full of himself and contumel — contu — what was the word? But hang it all, what did they know? At least one knew where one stood with Rodders, he didn't beat around the bush, he didn't suffer fools. He took after his pater in this respect. Lord, what a terrifying old chap Mr Brannan had been, one had quaked in one's boots! All the same it was rotten luck that he'd—

'Alfie,' said Mrs Harrington-Shaw softly. 'That's enough, I think.'

'But Mater, I haven't mentioned cricket! I can't propose a toast to Rodders with no mention of cricket!'

'To Roderick.' Mrs Harrington-Shaw raised her glass. 'Dearest Roderick. Boon companion and greatest of friends, charming, clever, popular, a most gifted cricketer — and so splendidly handsome too!'

'To Rodders!'

'To young Brannan. Many happy . . . er . . . yes, yes.'

Mrs Harrington-Shaw's eyes sparkled. Roderick was immensely grateful to her. H-S was well-meaning, but an ass. To mention cricket of all things, too. Roderick stabbed a lump of cheese on his plate, tortured by thoughts of the Cricket Cup, of missing out. Ransom's Eleven had lost to Rimmer's in his absence. Harcourt's had triumphed for an unprecedented fifth year in a row. H-S had reported the negative thinking now all too prevalent at Downfield. Cynics were even suggesting that Harcourt's be excluded from inter-house matches because they were unbeatable. Such abject defeatism! But Mrs Harrington-Shaw had saved him from hearing all this again by interrupting H-S just in time.

'This calls for another bottle!' cried Mr Harrington-Shaw, struggling to sit up.

'I think we've had enough wine for one evening, Humphrey. The boys are not old enough for dissipation on your scale.'

'Nonsense! Of course they're old enough! Boy there's seventeen! Wine! More wine! Bring me the — the—'

The dinner dragged on. Roderick was aware of Mrs Harrington-Shaw's growing displeasure, as palpable as a draught of cold air. Was she annoyed about the wine, or was it something else? Her husband and son, stolid and thick-skinned, seemed oblivious to her mood. It was like being caught between a hammer and an anvil.

At long last the evening came to an end. H-S and his father stumbled off to bed. Mrs Harrington-Shaw seemed to vanish into thin air. As he made his way to the guest room, Roderick promised himself that he would never, *never* come to Orsley again.

He flung off his jacket, his waistcoat, his tie, in a temper, tore out his cuff links, kicked off his boots, unfastened his collar. But as he shed these clothes he seemed to shed his bad mood too. Instead, he began to feel quite ridiculously buoyed up. He was wide awake and tingling all over. He'd brought a cigar with him from downstairs. He lit it, pulled back the curtains, opened the window wide, leaned on the sill, exhaled smoke and then breathed in, filling his lungs with fragrant night air. There was a faint glimmer of starlight on the lawn. The old oak cast a thin shadow. The cast-iron table where he'd played chess with H-S gleamed white and spectral. The trees beyond were like a wall of darkness.

He puffed out his chest. The cotton of his shirt was cool against his skin. He wanted to run, to ride, to soar like an eagle; to brave the silent, empty night; to range through the dark woods, to breast the silhouetted hills, to swim in the secret, silver waters of the Severn. Anything. He could do anything. His heart throbbed within him.

The world's mine oyster, which I with a sword will open . . . How sweet that world was, how ripe and beautiful, ready for him, waiting for him. How far he'd come, too. To think what a hopeless kid he'd been back in the days of the butterfly net, back in that long, hot summer ten years ago! He'd known nothing of school, had never heard of Downfield or the Cricket Cup, he'd yet to meet Dorothea. And now — well, what were the words she'd used? *Charming, clever, popular* . . . But this was just the beginning. He was seventeen. Only just turned seventeen. On the cusp, barely started. Downfield was just a prelude, the Cricket Cup a mere stepping stone: he could see that clearly now, here, tonight. There was so much more to life: the vast empty night, the world his oyster. What came next? Well, that was still hidden, that still lay in wait. But if he'd come so far already, made such progress, just imagine how he'd be in another ten years' time, in far-off 1919, a man of twenty-seven. Yet even that would only be a beginning. He would go on and on, birthday after birthday, year upon year. He would never get old. He would never die. How could he, when he was so full of life? He had so much life inside him — burning inside him.

He flicked away the last of his cigar, watched the glowing fragment spin away into the dark. At the same moment, he caught sight of a white and wraithlike figure gliding out across the starlit lawn. He held his breath, tense, motionless. But this was no ghost or phantom. This was no wicked witch of the woods. In a long, flowing gown, her hair tumbled loose, Mrs Harrington-Shaw — Aldora — ran lightly across the grass to pause by the wizened oak where, briefly, she looked back: looked back at the house, looked up at his window, looked directly at *him* — or so he felt.

He crouched down from instinct, his heart lurching. Quickly he steadied himself. He was seventeen, a man, the world his oyster; he had nothing to fear. He stood up boldly.

But when he looked down, the lawn was empty. It was as if she'd never been there.

But she *had* been there. He hadn't imagined it, he *hadn't*.

What was she doing out at this time? Where was she going? He had to know.

The door to his room squeaked as he opened it. The floorboards creaked as he made his way along the corridor. He could hear faintly Mr Harrington-Shaw's reverberating snores. All else was quiet. Holding his breath again, Roderick slipped downstairs.

Doors were never locked at Orsley. He let himself out onto the terrace, made his way down to the lawn. Stars glinted diamond-hard in the black vault of the sky. Crossing the grass was easy but he was blind in the dark under the trees. Thorns tugged at him, tendrils brushed his face. He came to a halt. This was a fool's errand. Moments ago he'd been picturing himself as a giant striding across the Shropshire hills. Now he couldn't even find his way through a small wood. And he had no idea where Mrs Harrington-Shaw might have gone.

He was about to turn back when he became aware of a glimmer of light barely visible through the trees. He was drawn towards it. He stepped out from the thicket. He was in the little clearing he'd found earlier. And there in the middle of it was the old summerhouse. The light was coming from inside.

He approached silently, peered through the miry window. She was there, sitting on a cross-bench with an oil lamp beside her: Mrs Harrington-Shaw. She had her back to him and — slowly, sensuously — she was brushing her hair. She looked like a woman in a painting, poised, posed, dishevelled yet flawless, her frock unfastened, her shoulders bare, her loose hair shining like polished wood in the light of the lamp.

He put his hand to the door. He felt he had no choice. The door scraped on the uneven floor as he opened it. She looked round, startled, raising a hand to her mouth, her eyes wide.

They looked at each other for a moment; then she laughed, a light, girlish laugh.

'So you've discovered my sanctum! I should have known you would. I can't keep anything from *you*. I come here sometimes when I can't sleep. So often I can't sleep.' She patted the bench beside her. 'Sit down.'

He obeyed. He couldn't take his eyes off her. She looked so very different. The memory of the buttoned-up woman glaring at her oenophile husband over dinner was completely erased.

'You have come with no shoes! Scandalous! And your shirt is torn. There is a hole big enough for my finger: look!'

She nudged the hole with the tip of her finger. For a split second he felt her touching him, his bare skin. The shock of it seemed to spread through his whole body. He trembled.

'There's a twig in your hair,' she said. She reached up to remove it, then began twisting locks of his hair between her fingers. 'Such nice hair. Dark like a raven — or like the night itself. How I adore black hair! How I detest grey!'

Grey, he thought. His mind was working sluggishly, lumpishly. *Grey: like Humphrey.*

'Humphrey,' she murmured as if on cue.

A spark ran up his spine. She must be able to read his mind. He had no defence against her. She would see him for what he was.

'Humphrey is so old.' Her hand slid round, her fingers stroked up the hairs on the nape of his neck, making him shiver. 'Humphrey is dried-up, worn out. I grow ever more weary of him. I expect you wonder why I married such an old, old man. I may tell you one day. But not now. Not now.' Her hand fell away. She sighed. 'You must think that I am old, too. I must seem terribly old to you. Do I?'

He tried to speak, couldn't. He shook his head instead, vehemently. She wasn't old. She was forever youthful, like an enchantress.

Without warning, she leaned forward, cupped his chin in her hands, kissed him, lips to lips.

He was stunned, his head spinning. Had it really happened?

Her hand went to her mouth again. 'Oh dear! What have I done? So impetuous! So foolish! What must you think of me?'

Her look of dismay spurred him to respond. He had to reassure her — he must. 'I . . . I don't mind. I don't mind at all, honestly I don't. I'm . . . glad . . . you did it.'

'Are you? Are you really?' She leant forward again, her eyes searching his face. He couldn't meet her gaze, hung his head. 'Yes. Yes. I thought you had the look of a man about you. I was right. All the same, that kiss, it was wrong.'

'No,' he muttered. 'No. I—' But she put a finger on his lips, silencing him.

'I shouldn't have kissed you but somehow I couldn't help myself. That's how it is in my sanctum. Sometimes I think that anything is possible here: *anything*.' She looked at him intently. There was no escaping her eyes. He felt the colour rise in his cheeks. 'Do you understand?' she asked him, insistent. 'Do you *see*?'

He nodded. He didn't really understand at all but he was ready to play any part she allotted him. He squared his shoulders. He was a man. She'd said he had the look of a man. But he felt like a mess. Sweat running down his chest, his hair all tangled, his shirt torn, the collar missing, the cuffs hanging loose. How could he hope to play his part in a state like this?

Slowly she got to her feet. He gazed up at her, open-mouthed. What next?

She seemed to release some hidden fastening. Her gown slipped and slithered down her body. She stepped out of it, leaving it a tumbled pile on the dusty, gritty floor. His eyes grew wide, gorging on her, so tall and shapely and statuesque: the curves of her bodice, her shimmering underskirt, the unblemished skin of her arms.

Covet, said a voice in his head. *Thou shalt not covet.* But here in the dark of the woods, in the dead of night, hidden in her sanctum where anything was possible; here, in the lamplight, amid the dust and the cobwebs; here—

'This corset . . .' A look of discomfort crossed her face. She picked at the offending garment. 'Like shackles, binding me. I can't breathe. I can't *breathe*. Help me.'

She sat down again, presenting her back to him. His hands shook. His fingers fumbled with the fastenings.

The last of the straps came loose. The corset fell to the floor to join her discarded dress in the dust.

'To be set loose at last!' She turned towards him, her bosom heaving, her eyes shut, her face ecstatic. 'To be set loose! To be free! You have no idea how it feels!' Her eyes opened. They sparkled in the lamplight. Reaching up, she gently stroked his face. 'So handsome. So very handsome.' She caressed his hair, fondled the back of his neck, slid a hand down inside his shirt.

Suddenly, out of nowhere, the memory of his dream of a week ago rose up like a foetid smell, choking him. He tensed up, remembering the way Mrs Moxon had beguiled him, slipping the manacles from her wrists to his, and the way Scotson had pawed at him—

'What is it? What's wrong? You must tell me!'

'I . . . I don't know.' He made an effort to thrust the dream aside. 'It's nothing.' He fully met her gaze for the first time, driving himself on, reckless and savage.

'Remember,' she whispered, looking deep into his eyes, 'anything is possible here.' She took his hands, guiding them. '*Anything*,' she repeated, her breath tickling his ear.

He felt warm, yielding flesh beneath his fingertips. Everything else was blotted out. Just this remained.

'Touch me,' she breathed. '*Touch me*!'

* * *

There was no Aldora at breakfast, just H-S and his father intent on their food, a little green about the gills after all the wine last night. Roderick sat hunched in his chair, waiting for them to notice, to pass comment. They couldn't fail to see how altered he was.

But when the conversation finally got going it ran on the usual lines: the weather (this fine spell wouldn't last, there'd be storms), the prospects for the Test Match (Australia ahead in the series, what was the world coming to?), and Lloyd George (that cad, that bounder).

So it wasn't obvious, thought Roderick. There was no outward sign. It was only inside that he'd changed.

He relaxed. He began to smile. He started to look forward to lunch.

But there was no Aldora at lunch either.

H-S shrugged. 'I expect Mater is under the weather. She often is. She'll be right as rain in a day or two.'

The afternoon dragged. The house dozed in the sun. All was quiet, mundane, dreary. Roderick began to doubt what had happened. Had it all been a dream, yet another dream?

But as he was dressing for dinner, he noticed bruises on his upper arm, the imprints of her fingers where she'd gripped him in her ardour. He touched the marks reverently. His heart was fit to burst. It was real. It had happened. Everything else paled in comparison.

I am Horatio Nelson, he said to his reflection, *and she is Lady Hamilton.*

He straightened his tie. He pulled his shirt cuffs an inch below the sleeve of his jacket. He smoothed his hair one last time. He was ready.

She came down to dinner. It was intoxicating to look at her. She shimmered in the light of the gas lamps like a jewel. He couldn't take his eyes off her, had no interest in anything else. Eating seemed a paltry thing to do. She didn't speak to him. He wasn't sure that she even looked at him. That didn't matter. He was Nelson, she Lady Hamilton. He trembled with expectation.

Lying on his bed fully dressed, he checked his pocket watch every half a minute. When at last the house was quiet, everybody in bed, he crept downstairs as before in his shirt sleeves and shoeless. In the summerhouse he lit the lantern and sat down to wait.

He waited. But she did not come.

* * *

'That's the third time you've yawned in a minute.' H-S wore a worried frown as they lay after lunch on their backs on the lawn watching the clouds.

'I'm tired. Everyone yawns when they are tired.'

'Tired of Orsley? Tired of . . . of me?'

'Don't be such an ass, H-S.'

'I can't help worrying, Rodders. You *do* drop people. You dropped Scotson.'

'Did I?'

'You know you did.'

But Scotson had ceased to matter, didn't even seem real. The suffocating dream — nightmare — from over a week ago had faded to nothing. 'Look, H-S, I'm tired because I haven't been sleeping. That's all it is. Now do stop gassing.'

He closed his eyes. He was in torment. Night after night he waited for her. Night after night she didn't come. Every day he hoped for a look, a smile. He was rewarded with nothing. What could he do? If, like Nelson, he lost an arm, if he got blinded in one eye — would she notice him then? But there was no call for acts of reckless heroism in the sleepy backwaters of Shropshire. He would have to think of a different plan.

* * *

He dressed for dinner in a rush, slipped out of his room, edged along the corridor. Outside her door he smoothed his hair, took a deep breath, tapped very lightly, went in without waiting for an answer. He closed the door softly behind him.

She was at her dressing table with her back to him. She had a blue dress on, was holding a string of pearls at her throat. Their eyes met in the mirror. Her face was blank.

He propped himself against the door, unsteady on his feet like a newborn foal. His heart was pounding inside his chest, pounding and pounding, wearing itself away.

'W-why haven't you come? I've waited every night, but you never come!'

The vacant eyes in the mirror regarded him a little longer, then she looked away. She replaced the pearls in a little casket, began sorting through a pile of other jewellery.

At last she spoke, calm, measured. 'We were rather foolish that night. We got carried away.'

'But it was . . . glorious, the . . . the best thing . . . I . . . I . . .'

She held up a necklace, inspecting it. The gold glinted in the gaslight. Her hair shone. But there was a smudge of darkness in the hollow of her throat.

'I wonder,' she said as if addressing the necklace, or nobody. 'I wonder if I can be sure of you?'

He jumped at this opening. 'You can, you really can. I'd do anything for you!'

She put the necklace aside, turned on her stool, fixed her eyes on him. 'Then you must stop staring. You stare at me. It's not nice.'

'I . . . I can't help it.'

'You must help it. You must stop.' She looked into his eyes. Her face softened. There was almost a smile. 'When we are alone, *then* you can look.'

'When we are alone? Tonight? Can we be alone tonight, like last time?'

'Perhaps. Perhaps.' The nascent smile played on her lips but as she turned back to the mirror it faded and a look of disquiet came into her eyes. 'Do I look old to you?' She touched her face with the tips of her fingers. 'There are lines. Wrinkles.'

'I think you're perfect. *Perfect*.'

She looked at him in the mirror once more, held his gaze. His knees trembled. 'You like me, I think. You truly like me.'

'I do. More than anything. More than *anything*.'

Her smile blossomed. 'How fierce you look!'

Fierce, not afraid: she thought him fierce!

'And so handsome! I've never seen such a handsome boy. Tonight, then. You can tell me how much you like me tonight. But now go. Go. Quickly.'

Out in the corridor he took a deep shuddering breath. He pulled down his cuffs, smoothed his hair. As he made his way downstairs, he broke into a grin. He had faced his Trafalgar, he had come out victorious. She would be waiting for him tonight.

* * *

They stayed late in the summerhouse that night, returning in the clammy dawn. Aldora ran lightly across the lawn, her skirts dragging through the dewy grass. Roderick, trailing behind, looked up anxiously at the windows of the house. The danger of being seen seemed to excite Aldora. She laughed, putting her hand to her mouth to stifle the noise. This was a different Aldora, wild, free. He had to run to keep up with her.

In the shadows of the hallway she kissed him recklessly one last time, caressing his face. Then she sent him up to bed. She stood watching as he climbed the stairs.

He knew he wouldn't sleep so he didn't bother trying. He lay in bed looking up at the cracks in the ceiling. After a time he heard her light footfall in the corridor outside, the click of her bedroom door as it closed. Only seconds later, or so it seemed, the servants began to stir. He heard muted voices from downstairs, the muffled sound of furniture being moved.

In no time, the maid was knocking on his door with his water. It was time to get up again.

* * *

He slowly buttoned his shirt, watching himself yawn in the cheval mirror. He looked pale, there were bags under his eyes, everything was such an effort, he was tired, so tired.

He was dressing for dinner once more. But this was the last time, his last day, his last evening. He sank down onto the edge of the bed, holding his head in his hands. How could he leave Orsley? How could he leave *her*?

It was another oppressive, sultry evening, all the windows wide, not a breath of air. Mr Harrington-Shaw had his best wines out again. He quickly grew garrulous, talking of south-facing slopes, this grape, that grape, the valley of the Garonne. H-S was glum and silent, like Hecate at the end of the holidays.

Aldora retired early. She had a headache. It was the weather, she said. Despite his promise, Roderick followed her with his eyes as she left the room, looking for a sign, but she didn't look back. He wanted to run after her. Of course he didn't. She'd be there at the summerhouse later, wouldn't she? Wouldn't she?

At last, at long last, it was time for bed. He waited with his ear pressed against the bedroom door, listening. As soon as it seemed safe, he made haste to get out of the house. The stairs creaked. There was still a light showing in the drawing room. He didn't care. Other people had ceased to matter very much.

She had somehow contrived to reach the summerhouse before him. The door was wide open, the lamp lit, she was half undressed. As usual, she seemed a different person in the dark of the woods, there was no sign of her headache now. He fell into her arms but almost at once tore himself away. A groan broke out of him.

'I'm leaving tomorrow! I'm leaving tomorrow and I can't bear it!'

She put a finger on his lips. 'Hush. Let's not talk about it. Let's be wild and reckless instead. Let's swim!'

She darted away, ran through the trees in her chemise, her hair flying. He chased after her in his shirt and long johns, arrived at the Lake just in time to see her wading out. The water looked dark as oil and fathomless.

Her carefree mood was infectious. Roderick found himself laughing as he threw off the rest of his clothes and dived into the Lake. They cavorted in the water. He showed off for her amusement. The sound of their voices resounded round the pool, echoed in the silent wood. She seemed heedless, as if she didn't care, snapping her fingers at danger.

At long last she grew weary and made her way out of the water. Her sodden chemise was moulded to her, accentuating every line and curve of her body. Roderick made haste to follow. Water cascaded off him as he hauled himself up onto the bank. The air was still and heavy, not a breeze stirred. Tall and naked, he looked down at her as she sat wringing out her long tresses. He remembered the first day, swimming here with H-S, the feeling of being watched. He wanted her to watch him now as she'd done then.

'You were watching!' he said. 'When I swam with H-S, when I got dressed, you were watching in the trees.'

'Watching?' She didn't look up, busy with her hair. 'Don't be silly, darling. What an absurd thing to say!'

Her voice was rather shrill suddenly. He knew she was lying. He was shocked to the core, that she could lie to him. He felt a sense of panic. He remembered now that he was leaving tomorrow.

Anxiously, he reached for her. She responded. Her body was hot to the touch, her hands eager. But as they grappled amongst the tufts of grass, Roderick felt a cool air on his skin. He could hear it whispering amongst the rhododendrons and stirring in the leaves of the trees. And then, in the far distance, came the faint sound of thunder.

* * *

They lay by the pool, his head cradled in her arm. The temperature had fallen noticeably now. The wind was strengthening. Leaves rustled, branches swayed. Every so often, the tops of the trees were silhouetted sharply against the sky as lightning flashed and dazzled. The thunder crawled ever nearer.

Aldora sighed. 'It was not how I thought it would be. I always liked the idea of it, out of doors, by the water. But it's cold, it's dirty, and the stones hurt one's back. It's not nice.'

‘I’m sorry. I’m sorry.’ He put his arms round her, buried his face in her breast. ‘I don’t want to go. I want to stay here with you. I . . . I want us to be like Lord Nelson and Lady Hamilton!’

‘I don’t know what you mean. I’ve never heard of Lady Hamilton.’ She sat up, disentangling herself. ‘You mustn’t be difficult, darling. You can’t change your plans at this late stage. What would Humphrey say? What would your mother think? I shall consider you quite a *boy* if you make trouble over this.’

He sat up too, scowling. ‘I don’t care what Humphrey says! I don’t care about Humphrey at all, or anyone! But you do! You think more of Humphrey than you do of me!’

‘*No*!’ She was vehement. ‘I don’t care about Humphrey at all! I hate him! He is so *old*! He sucks the life out of me. You can’t imagine what it is like for me here, slowly suffocating. Sometimes I think I shall go mad.’

Roderick clutched his knees, miserable. In the summerhouse nothing could touch them but out here he felt exposed. They were caught up in the relentless working of the world, grinding on and on, insensible.

‘I’m *cold*!’ Aldora’s voice rose, petulant, protesting, railing against — against what? The night, the thunder, Humphrey — the whole world, perhaps?

Hugging his knees ever tighter, Roderick watched as she got to her feet and, without a backward glance, began picking her way through the trees. She disappeared into the dark.

Thunder growled in the heavens. The wind gusted. Waves of hopelessness washed over him. *I always liked the idea of it, out of doors, by the water.* How many years had she nursed this fantasy? How long had she waited to fulfil it? Who in all that time had she pictured herself with? Not with him!

Rain began spotting. The trees surged and tossed as the wind rose to a gale. Roderick jumped up, grabbed his shirt and long johns, pulled them on as he ran, hopping and stumbling in the dark. As he reached the lawn, the heavens opened and the deluge began.

* * *

Departure was pure agony. H-S seemed to sense it.

'Never mind, Rodders. You can come again soon. Perhaps Christmas. What do you say, Pater?'

'Boy's welcome any time, any time.'

'You have to hurry now, Rodders, or you'll miss your train.'

'But H-S — your mother — I haven't seen her this morning — I haven't—'

'Oh, she won't be down. She hates goodbyes.'

With a heavy heart, Roderick took a seat in the gig. Jones the burly groom swung his trunk up effortlessly.

When he reached Orsley Halt, there was still a quarter of an hour before the train was due, despite H-S's fussing. The little station was quiet and empty, milk churns lined up on the platform, the name picked out in flowers on a raised bed. The sky was overcast, the air humid.

After pacing up and down for a while, Roderick sat on a bench and searched out a pencil and some paper from his pockets. Chewing the end of the pencil, he set about composing a first letter to his goddess.

He put pencil to paper. *Dear Aldora*, he began.

CHAPTER SIX

Other letters followed the first, letters sent from Clifton and then, as autumn came, from Downfield. He framed each letter carefully. He was eloquent, gallant, earnest, quoting the classics. 'Love conquers all things. Let us too give in to love.' She could not fail to be impressed.

But she did not reply.

'Oh, mater never writes,' said H-S when quizzed circumspectly. 'I've only had two, maybe three, letters from her in all the time since prep school.'

This did not make Roderick feel any better. If he was to be denied even the solace of a letter, it was more than he could bear. A desperate plan began to form in his mind.

'Who . . . what . . . ugh . . .' Roused from sleep in the dim light of dawn, H-S threatened to wake the whole dorm as he floundered in his bed.

Roderick shook him urgently, hissed in his ear. 'Hush, you fool! Listen! If anyone asks, say I'm in the sicker. Do you understand?'

'But Rodders, what time is it? Where . . . ?'

'I can't explain now. I have to go.'

H-S struggled to sit up. 'The beaks are bound to ask questions. There'll be an awful stink if—'

'I don't care. I'm going. Just do your best. I'm relying on you, H-S.'

The journey was a nightmare. Trains were damnably snail-like. One had to change. Connections were never on time. Roderick found himself, of all things, envying Henry Fitzwilliam. If one had a nippy little motor, one could have been at Orsley in no time. It was a novel idea. He'd never seen any real purpose in motors before.

At last he caught the final train. Unable to sit still, he stood in the corridor, looked out through a rain-blotched window as the train wound its way along the Severn valley. The wide brown river rolled sluggishly in its gorge. Barges slid by, labouring against the current, even more snail-like than the train. Tall chimneys came into view, belching clouds of grey smoke that merged with the grey clouds in the sky.

Ugly chimneys. Choking smoke. So much for being the workshop of the world.

Ah, but look, Father would have said, pointing to the famous iron bridge curving gracefully over the swollen river. *Isn't that a thing of beauty, my boy? A monument to the industrial genius of England! That's why Britain is the workshop of the world!*

The iron bridge slid out of sight as the train trundled on. So things came, so things went — Father too.

I was so very sorry to hear about your father . . . what a horrible time for you . . . Almost the first words she'd said to him on his last visit. Empty platitudes, he'd thought. He hadn't realised back then how perceptive she was, how understanding. He'd been blundering around in a fog of ignorance. Only she'd known how he felt and what he needed.

He had to see her again, he *had* to. How much longer would this infernal journey take?

Jackfield, Coalport, Linley came and went before the train stopped at Bridgnorth for an eternity. Roderick grabbed the strap, lowered the window, leaned out, trying to find the reason for the delay. The hissing locomotive was crouched by the end of the platform, poised to spring forward — but dallying, dallying. He closed his eyes, groaned in frustration.

The whistle blew. The locomotive exhaled. Steam billowed. At last they were underway. Puffing and panting, the train gathered speed.

Roderick's frustration evaporated. He was on the last lap, almost there. He stood by the open window as the train wound its way along the valley. Grey clouds scudded across the sky. Smoke from the locomotive poured upwards, shredded, trailed away behind them. Specks of soot swirled in the mist.

Orsley Halt came in sight. The train began to slow. Roderick had the door open a hundred yards before the platform slid alongside. He jumped down while the train was still moving, landing with a jolt. He straightened up. What next? He could hardly march up to the front door and demand to see her. A knight errant would have galloped up on his charger and swept her into the saddle. But he didn't have a charger — or even a motor car, for that matter. What did he have? He felt in his pockets. His ticket. Some loose change. A packet of cigarettes. Matches. Nothing of any consequence.

The platform trembled beneath his feet. The train slowly rolled away. It snaked around a curve in the line. The guard's van trailed out of view. The locomotive's fevered panting faded into the distance. The station lapsed once more into a timeless slumber.

Roderick stirred. The sound of his footsteps was muffled in the clammy air. Surrendering his ticket to the lugubrious stationmaster, he passed through the little booking hall and emerged onto a rutted lane. To his left he caught a glimpse of the river meandering amongst the water meadows down in the valley. His way, however, lay to the right, following the lane uphill between tall hedgerows.

The mist began to lift. The clouds too began to clear, receding into the east, leaving a washed blue sky and rich autumnal sunshine which glowed in the puddles on the road. As he swung up the hill, he met a cart creaking down, the horse in front treading warily, almost fussily, looking askance at the wet and stony track. The wizened driver, hunched over the reins, was chewing a stalk of grass. His eyes were small, beady, regarded Roderick candidly, his face impassive. Roderick stared back, holding his own. As they passed each other, the driver slowly nodded, as if in obeisance. The cart was empty.

Round the next bend, Roderick came to the rusty gates of Orsley, wide open as ever. The weed-infested driveway — worse even than the one at home — led away from the lane and deep into the woods. The house was hidden, lost in the thickets. Roderick checked his watch. It was just the right time. Old Humphrey — Roderick curled his lip, despising old Humphrey — would be having his postprandial nap. Indeed, the whole house would be dormant. Afternoons were long and dull at Orsley. It would be like breaking into Sleeping Beauty's castle.

He began to walk up the drive beneath the overhanging trees, his mind racing ahead. He pictured himself prowling round the walls, peering in at the windows. Humphrey would be in his usual chair, his head tilted back, eyes closed, mouth open, the newspaper spread across his lap. One could climb in through the window as if it was one of the Sixth's studies. And then what? Wake the old fool up and challenge him to a duel? Or creep from room to room in search of Aldora? But though old Humphrey might be asleep, the servants wouldn't be — not all of them — and one was bound to be caught sooner or later. So that was no good, no plan at all.

Roderick slowed then stopped. He stood frowning, looking all round, listening. There was an immense silence. No birds, not even an insect: nothing. The wood stretched away in every direction. Shafts of sunlight penetrated the canopy in places. The leaves glowed in many colours — leaves that were fading, dying.

He needed time to think. It was no good blundering in and trusting to luck. What about the summerhouse? He could take refuge there, prepare himself. It would be so apt, their trysting place: the memories it held would fortify his sense of purpose.

He set off into the wood, thrusting branches and brambles aside, wading through wilting nettles, kicking up last year's dead leaves. Far off, a dove began to coo.

He came to the clearing at last, paused at the very edge. In the broad light of the autumn afternoon, the summerhouse looked ruinous rather than romantic, the warped, mossy roof on the verge of collapse, the wooden walls rotting, the dusty windows hung with countless cobwebs. Was this really where they'd come? It had seemed so different in the summer dark.

He walked slowly towards it. He placed one foot on the bottom step — and then froze. There was a muffled sound inside, a shuffling, scraping noise that might have been anything, rats, mice or crumbling timber. But what if it was *her*? What if, somehow, she'd known he would come and was waiting for him?

He stepped up eagerly and put his face against the miry window. It had seemed much too much to hope but it was true, she was there, she really was!

Only she wasn't alone.

His eyes widened as he peered through the grimy glass. A brawny figure in a grubby shirt and coarse breeches was standing with his back to the door. A scuffle was taking place: that was what it looked like. The brawny fellow was reaching for her, she was trying to ward him off. Her flailing hands knocked his cap to the ground, she seemed to want to scratch his eyes out. The man retaliated, grabbed a fistful of her hair, pulled her head back so that she had to look up at him. And then, to Roderick's utter consternation, the man leaned down and cold-bloodedly kissed her.

It had all happened in the blink of an eye. Now, as he watched them kissing, Roderick heard a voice in his head, a rough, insolent voice with a Welsh lilt to it: *I thought you'd be here sooner, sir . . .*

The Orsley groom, Jones.

Roderick wanted to rip the door open and drag him off her: to rescue Aldora, to kill Jones. He had his hand on the door handle in readiness. But he couldn't move, transfixed with shock. He watched helplessly as Jones shoved Aldora roughly up against the far wall and pressed his body against her. Aldora raised her arm again — but not to fight him off. She caressed him, she cradled the nape of his neck. Her movements were all so familiar that Roderick could almost feel her touch, as if it was him in there and not Jones. Another voice echoed: hers. *Sometimes I think that anything is possible here — anything . . .*

He turned away, fell headlong down the steps, picked himself up, stumbled blindly across the clearing, collided with a tree. He clung to the rough, knobbly bark, seeing stars. There was a buzzing in his ears. A mist had descended in his eyes. But he forced himself to go on. He had to. He couldn't stay here.

Half running, he staggered through the autumn wood, tripping over tree roots, sunshine dazzling him. It seemed no time at all before he was walking through the booking hall at Orsley Halt. He sat down on a bench on the platform — the very bench where he'd sat in August on his way home. It was here, just a few short weeks ago, that he'd set about composing his first letter to her. And now—

He swallowed. His mind was in revolt. It refused to accept what he'd seen. He sat there blankly, hunched over, staring down at the platform.

A distant whistle sounded, echoing along the valley like the mournful shriek of some lost and lonely animal. A train was coming.

It came. He got on.

Then, nothing.

* * *

Sometime later the clickety-clack of wheels going over points penetrated the haze in his head. He looked up, became aware of his surroundings: a compartment with faded seats and blinds half down; blasts of warm air from the heater; a man in a bowler hat reading a newspaper. Roderick sat back, frowning, unsure how he'd got here. He had vague memories of the train stopping and starting several times, people getting on, getting off, shrill whistles blowing. Had he changed somewhere? Now he came to think of it, he was sure he had. At Shrewsbury, perhaps? Or Birmingham? Was he even on the right train?

What was *wrong* with him? He felt weak and dizzy. Flu perhaps? Or shock?

He shook his head. Not flu, or shock. Hunger. That was what it was. He was hungry. He hadn't eaten a thing all day. Idiotic of him.

He got up, slid open the door. The bowler-hatted man carried on reading. Swaying along the corridor, Roderick located the dining car, was shown to a table, sat down, studied the menu. The words swam before his eyes. He half-imagined he could see sentences written there in a scrawling schoolboy hand: *oh, beautiful Aldora . . . my own goddess . . .* He cringed in his chair. The things he had written! The ignominy of it! Did she have them still, all those fulsome letters? The thought sent a chill up his spine.

He blinked, brought the menu closer to his face. Soup to start, then perhaps steak and kidney pudding?

He sat back, waiting for his food. Just the thought of it made him feel better. He rallied. What was he getting in a funk about? She could never use those letters against him.

But what was he saying? Why would she want to use those letters *against* him? She couldn't use them at all without ruining herself.

As he drank his soup, the train gently rocking, the countryside at dusk fleeting past the window, it began to seem incredible that he'd ever been taken in by her. Why had he run away just now? He should have stood his ground. He should have horsewhipped that insolent Welsh lackey and sent him packing. He should have grabbed Aldora by the hair and dragged her round just as the groom Jones had done. She seemed to *like* it. She was monstrous!

But she wasn't, she wasn't, she was beautiful, he loved her—

No, he told himself, spooning soup. He didn't love her, he'd never loved her. Love? Ha! But he shouldn't have wasted his journey. He should have stayed, taken what he wanted, then pushed her into the dead leaves. That was what she deserved because she was nothing but a . . . a . . . His mind groped for the right word. A *whore*! That was it. She was a . . . a *whore*.

He shivered, savouring the word as he'd savoured his soup. A filthy word. A sinful word. Yet somehow . . . exciting . . .

He pushed his soup plate away, watched as it was removed and replaced by the steak and kidney pudding. The smell of the pudding made him salivate. Steam rose from the gravy.

Slicing open the pudding, he began to paint Aldora in his mind as a Jezebel, all dressed in lurid colours. But the more he layered it on — whore, harlot, Jezebel — the less like Aldora she seemed. It was ridiculous to think he could ever have been taken in by a woman like *that*.

He shovelled food into his mouth. He was ravenous. But as the food filled him up, his sense of unease grew. *Never do anything your mother would be ashamed to see you do*. That was what they'd taught him back in prep school. The ideal man was a chaste man. Temptation was the work of the Devil.

Roderick swallowed the last of his food, wiped his mouth with his napkin, surveyed the smear of gravy which was all the remained on his plate. Mother *hadn't* seen him with Aldora, just as in the old days she'd never seen him swimming in the canal or fighting Nibs Carter. His rule had always been that what Mother didn't know wouldn't hurt her.

He stood up, thrust his chair back, threw down his napkin. Rules and precepts and the suffocating hold of tradition: like pie crusts and promises, these things were made to be broken. It was the duty of any thrusting young fellow to break them. But as he made his way back to his compartment, swaying with the motion of the train, he began to wonder about the possible consequences of playing truant today. What if he'd been missed at school? What if he'd been seen in town that morning on his way to the station? And now he had to find a way of sneaking back without being caught.

He wished more than anything that he'd never set out on this hopeless odyssey in the first place.

* * *

There was a short cut one could use on the way from the station. One scaled a wall on Grey Hill Road, crossed a driveway, skirted round a large, square-faced house, and ventured across some open parkland before squeezing through a gap in a hedge to join a footpath which led up to the back of the Ransom's buildings on top of the escarpment. There were dangers. One might run into a gardener or two on the driveway, or the gamekeeper in the parkland; and if one was spotted from the house, the people there complained to the Big Man and there was a fearful stink about it. For this reason the short cut was strictly forbidden. But Roderick felt that at this time of night it was worth the gamble.

The house, indeed, proved to be all in darkness. The only hazard was the danger of losing one's way in the gloaming but as Roderick hastened across the parkland, tripping over molehills, the clouds suddenly parted and the moon was revealed. It was rather a thin moon, yellow and wan like a cheese rind or a pared toe nail, but it gave enough light to see the line of the hedge.

He pushed his way through. The footpath glimmered faintly, climbing the hill. Roderick kept the hedge on his right. To the left, a big field receded into the black night. Somewhere up ahead was the stile where he'd sat after his interview with Raynes back when a place in the house Eleven had been nothing more than a dream. It seemed a long time ago now. As he laboured up the slope, far off in town, carrying clearly in the still air, a dog began barking.

He reached Ransom's courtyard at last. All was quiet. Tiptoeing across the cobbles, he began probing the ground floor windows. There was usually at least one left ajar. He found it. Sliding it up, he swung his leg over the sill, was just climbing in, fighting the curtains, when a sudden and heart-stopping voice spoke out of the darkness within. He was too startled to take in what it said. Losing his balance, he fell head-first into the room with a noise like an avalanche. He landed with a thump on the carpet. Silence fell.

After what seemed an age, the voice spoke again. 'Hell's teeth, Brannan, it's only you. I needn't have put out my candle.'

The voice was familiar, posed no threat. Picking himself up off the floor, shoving his cap in pocket, Roderick said, 'Is that you, Westaway? I can't see a damned thing!'

'One second.' There was a shuffling sound, a rattle, then the scrape of a match against a box. 'And he said, "Let there be light," and there was light.'

A candle flame leapt up. Roderick found himself facing Westaway across a desk. Dancing shadows gave Westaway's face a diabolical look.

'What the devil are you doing in here, Westaway?' asked Roderick, sitting down at the desk, smoothing his hair. 'You made me jump out of my skin, you swine. I ought to report you.'

'A more apposite question is what are *you* doing, Brannan, climbing in through the window at gone midnight?'

'How else would I get in? Everyone uses the windows at this time of night. It was either that, or shin up the drainpipe.'

Westaway took a perch on the edge of the desk. He was holding a book, his finger marking his place. 'I wouldn't trust my weight to that rusty old thing.'

'One has to take a chance once in a while — though it's not really in your line, is it, Westaway. You're more of a skulker.' Roderick relaxed in the chair, his heart rate back to normal but his stomach rumbling. 'Lord, I'm hungry! I had something to eat earlier, but—'

'You're a growing boy, as nanny would say.'

'Your nanny might have said that. Mine was always too busy getting crapulous on cooking sherry to notice if I was growing or not.'

Westaway did not crack a smile. He was a damnably serious chap. Nodding towards the desk, he said, 'Howlett keeps chocolate in his drawer.'

'Of course, this is Howlett's study. I wondered what the smell was.' Roderick pulled open the drawer, rummaged inside. 'Hold that candle still, for Hades' sake. Ah, yes. Eureka. Chocolate.' Roderick peeled back the wrapper, offered some to Westaway.

Westaway shook his head.

Munching, Roderick said, 'What's wrong with your own study? Why use Howlett's?'

'Mine is up a corner, rather. There's no way of escape should the beaks come prowling. Here the corridor goes both ways, and there's the window too, as you have just admirably demonstrated.'

'What *are* you doing here, anyway? You never said.'

Westaway held up the book. 'Reading. I was reading.'

'You risk your neck — or your backside — for the sake of a book?'

'Not just any book. It's Keats.'

Roderick licked his fingers, the chocolate all gone. He regarded Westaway quizzically. 'Poetry? I didn't know you were a poetry fiend.'

'There's a lot you don't know about me.'

Roderick grinned. 'But I know more than you would like, isn't that right? And this is Howlett's study, too. How very droll.'

'Glad you find it amusing, Brannan. I think blackmail is pretty low, myself.'

'Be fair, old chap. You left me no choice. You wouldn't take that shooting test for love nor money — not for the love of your house, that is, nor when you were offered a very generous postal order. I had to find some other way of persuading you.'

Westaway furrowed his brow. 'I still don't know how you found out. About the divorce, I mean.'

'I like to read, too, Westaway. How did that letter go?' Roderick closed one eye, trying to remember it word for word, going back three years to the afternoon he had spent in Mother Moxon's office after the ordeal of the firing squad. It had been quite a discovery, coming across Moxon's files, finding the drawer unlocked. There had been a file for every boy in the house. Westaway's file had contained a letter from his mother. *May I ask at this difficult time if you would be so kind as to keep an eye on Patrick?* Something like that. He couldn't remember the exact words now. He'd only seen the letter once. The drawer with the secret files had been locked ever since.

'A neat turn of phrase, your mother. How is she getting on — her and her new husband?'

Westaway grimaced, his shoulders hunched as if warding off bad memories. 'You really are a weasel, Brannan.'

Roderick laughed, tilting his chair back, putting his feet on the desk. The chocolate was reviving him. He felt, too, a glow of achievement at having made it all the way back to school. He was safe now. He had nothing to fear at school — not these days. So he could afford to be munificent.

'There's no shame in divorce these days, Westaway. It happens all the time.'

'It wasn't just the divorce that gave you a hold over me. I knew you could make my life unpleasant in all sorts of other ways if I didn't do as you asked. You could have made my life even *more* unpleasant than it already was. You've a sadistic streak in you a mile wide, Brannan.'

'That's absolute rot! I wouldn't have said anything, even if you'd refused to cooperate. I wouldn't have told anyone what I knew. What would have been the point?'

'Revenge.'

'Revenge? I say, Westaway, I think you've got the wrong idea about me, the wrong idea entirely.'

But Dorothea last spring after Father's death had said something similar. *That's all you ever think about, revenge, revenge, revenge. You're petty and spiteful, you're a bully . . .*

'It wasn't personal, Westaway. It really wasn't. All I wanted was to get Howlett into the Eleven.'

'That makes it alright, does it? That justifies blackmailing me? Isn't it rather against the whole spirit of the school? What about fair play? What about playing the game? You could have just *asked* me to help.'

'You wouldn't have done it. You said yourself that the house means nothing to you.'

'All I wanted was a little consideration. If you'd come up to me and talked like this instead of dictating terms—'

'I get carried away sometimes, that's all. I apologise, Westaway, if I was heavy-handed. Here's a chance now for *your* revenge. You can turn me in. You can tell them you found me climbing in through the window. You can tell them while you're at it that I haven't been in school all day, that I've been in Shropshire. Tell them that and I'll be gated forever.'

Westaway looked at him curiously. 'Shropshire, eh? I did wonder. It's the wrong term for the Shrove Tuesday Fair. I thought it might be a girl.'

'A girl? Rather not!' Roderick felt his cheeks burning, wondered if it would show up in the candlelight. Not that Aldora was a *girl* as such but Westaway's shrewd guess was disconcerting.

A silence had fallen. Westaway put his book aside, fixed the candle on Howlett's blotter, went and sat in Howlett's battered arm chair. Roderick watched him, waiting for him to speak. Cold air was coming in through the window behind him, autumnal air with a nip in it. The candle flame danced in the draught. Shadows flickered on the walls and the ceiling.

Westaway was unpicking a seam in his dressing gown. At length he said, not looking up, 'It's alright for you, Brannan. You fit here. You belong. For the rest of us — for the outsiders — school is hell.'

'It's hell for everyone to start with. Things get better, I've found.'

'Not for chaps like me. The hell never ends for chaps like me. I thought, once I got my own study . . . but I'm not safe even there. They come in uninvited, they smash up my furniture, they throw my books out of the window, they kick me around the room. Do you know what it's like, Brannan, to be flogged and hairbrushed, kicked and cursed every day of your school life? I'm treated worse than a dog and nobody gives a damn — least of all the masters.'

'You don't think it was the same for me in the beginning?'

'But not now. People respect you now.'

'I've had to work for that, Westaway. It didn't just happen. And if I may say, you *do* rather leave yourself open. You make a point of being different, and the chaps don't like it.'

'What am I meant to do? Pretend to be someone I'm not?'

'You could at least stick up for yourself.'

'All very well for you to say, with half the house ready to fight your battles. It's different for me. I'm one boy alone. They hunt in packs, like wolves.' Westaway laughed bitterly, his long, thin fingers picking insistently at the stitches in his dressing gown. 'Do you know, Brannan, my father told me that school would make a man of me. A man! I'll be lucky if there's anything *left* of me by the time I'm finished here. It's such a damned waste. That's what really rankles. We're sent here to be educated, but education is the last thing that matters at Downfield. Think about it. Science is dismissed as *stinks*. Music, art, literature are treated as a sort of joke. All that counts is games — games and the OTC.'

'But my dear chap, it's the same everywhere. This is how Englishmen are raised. And Englishmen are the finest race on Earth, so the system must have *some* merits.'

'Not *English*men, Brannan. You're talking about *public school* men. Believe it or not, the majority of Englishmen have never been anywhere near a public school. In any case, if the system is so perfect, why are you always fighting against it?'

'I don't! That's rot!'

'Not much, you don't! You do realise that getting me to take Howlett's shooting test was tantamount to cheating? And climbing in at the window after midnight, that's hardly playing by the rules.'

'One can't play by the rules *all* the time. I thought you at least would recognise that, Westaway. It was you, after all, who put me onto Machiavelli. How does it go? "A man who wants to act virtuously in every way necessarily comes to grief among men who are not virtuous."'

'I'm not sure that Machiavelli is a good role model, Brannan. Isn't he rather immoral?'

'Pragmatic, surely. Look, Westaway, things aren't perfect, I know that. But one has to carry on as if they *were*, or the whole house would go to wrack and ruin.'

'Would that be such a bad thing?'

'Of course it would! How can you even ask? The house is everything.' But even as asserted this, Roderick found doubts creeping in. School was the whole world, one's house like an extended family, and to win the Cricket Cup the only worthwhile aim in life. He'd been certain of this ever since coming to Downfield. But just lately, with Father dying and Orsley intruding, he'd begun to feel as if he was standing on shifting sands, nothing fixed or certain. The wide world, the world beyond Downfield, was tapping quietly but insistently on the window.

'The Cricket Cup—' he began, seizing hold of this one fixed point in all the state of flux.

Westaway interrupted. 'Cricket! Good Lord, Brannan, don't talk to me about cricket! You can't *begin* to guess how much I despise cricket!'

Roderick raised an eyebrow. 'You do realise, I suppose, that this proves you can't possibly be *normal*?'

'Do you really think blind worship of the golden calf of games is *normal*? You're the one, Brannan, who's out of step with the world, not me.'

'Out of step, am I? So now we're getting to it. No, come on, Westaway, let's have it. What do you *really* think of me?'

Westaway looked at him circumspectly. 'Rather rash of you to ask, surely? I might be honest.'

Roderick spread his arms. 'Be honest, then — if you dare.'

An almost malicious expression crossed Westaway's face. He spoke with relish. 'What can I say? You're . . . you're arrogant, asinine, something of a tyrant when your blood's up. You pick people up, you use them for your own ends, you drop them: Scotson, for instance—'

'Yes?' Roderick gave Westaway a menacing stare. 'What about Scotson?'

'You were rather jealous of Scotson, I think. Jealous of his success, his popularity. That was what you wanted to destroy him, to turn him into a pariah.'

'You do talk the most utter bilge, Westaway. Anyone would think I was a *monster*. I liked Scotson. He was my friend. But there was no helping him.'

'He was a tortured soul, that's true.' Westaway cocked an eye, challenging. 'He was in love with you, of course.'

'Don't be so foul! What a foul thing to say! It's not even true.'

'You don't *want* it to be true: there's a difference. "There are more things in heaven and earth, Horatio, than are dreamt of in your philosophy."'

'What do you know about it, anyway? What do you know about *love*?' Roderick spoke the word with contempt.

'Well, nothing, of course. Absolutely nothing. It's something else we never get taught. We spend most of our lives locked up here, boys amongst boys, never meeting a woman from one term to the next. We have no idea about women.'

'I do! I know about women! They are all . . . *Jezebels*!' He'd been going to say *whores*, but he was afraid of the word, afraid of saying it out loud.

Westaway looked at him astutely. 'So that's it, is it? This girl of yours. An inconstant heart. Or has she given you the heave-ho?'

'What girl? What are you talking about?'

'The girl you have obviously been to see today. You haven't bothered to deny it.'

Roderick said hotly, 'Why would I want to visit some Jezebel? They're all Jezebels!'

'All? Even your mother? Alright, Brannan, there's no need to look at me like that. I'm not suggesting that your mother actually *is* a Jezebel. I'm just making a point. You can't tar everyone with the same brush. Not all men like cricket and not all women are Jezebels. That's the way of things.' He smiled grimly. 'My mother, of course, is the Jezebel of all Jezebels — or so my father would tell you. Hence the divorce. But she is still my mother.' He sighed, a sigh that seemed to contain a whole world of misery and heart ache, that encompassed the whole sorry story of the divorce — whatever that story might be: his mother's letter in Moxon's file had not quite made it clear. It was like getting a glimpse into Westaway's soul.

Why was it, Roderick asked himself, that he suddenly felt as if he *understood* Westaway? Why was it suddenly possible to *talk* to him? Was it simply the lateness of the hour, the feeling of being cast away, as if he and Westaway had been washed up on some desert island? He watched runnels of wax slowly solidifying on the side of the candle. Westaway was right. Not all women were the same. He could at a pinch paint Aldora Harrington-Shaw as a Jezebel but any suggestion that Mother or Dorothea resembled Aldora in any way was not just nonsense, it was obscene. But this only made things even more confusing. Why did Westaway have to constantly muddy the waters?

Or maybe it wasn't Westaway. Maybe Westaway simply saw the world for what it was.

In the lengthening silence came very faintly the sound of the church clock striking one.

'I wish—' Roderick began, then stopped.

Westaway looked at him quizzically.

'I wish I *didn't* know about women!' Roderick burst out. 'I wish I could *forget*!'

'There's no going back once one has bitten the apple,' said Westaway quietly. 'I think you'll find that one can't very well live without them.'

'But Westaway — Patrick — how does one . . . how do you . . . ?'

'One sublimates. One reads Keats.'

Their eyes met. Westaway gave a sheepish grin. Roderick found himself grinning too. 'So. Keats is the cure, eh?' He picked Westaway's book up off the desk, turned it over in his hands. 'Poets are all worthless. That was Wellington's opinion.'

'Good grief, Brannan! Who nowadays takes a blind bit of notice of the Duke of Wellington? What heroes you have — Wellington, Machiavelli!'

'But what's the *use* of poetry, Patrick? What's the *use* of it?'

'What's the use of anything?' Westaway got to his feet, crossed to the desk, took the book out of Roderick's hands. '"Truth is beauty, beauty truth." Poetry is . . . is something different. Outside of school. Outside *myself*.' Westaway's eyes glinted in the candlelight.

Roderick shivered. There was cold air on the back of his neck. He got up, closed the window. It was an act of finality. The midnight parley was at an end.

'Well, Patrick,' said Roderick as he crossed to the door, 'if there's ever anything I can do for you — stop them smashing up your furniture and so on—'

'Why would you do that?'

'To prove I'm not a monster — because I'm not, whatever you might think.'

'Well, there is one thing. If you could find a way to spare me the torture of games, let me waste my time as I see fit, reading poetry or painting—'

'Painting too? Is there no end to your talents, Patrick?' They were face-to-face by the door now. 'I shall certainly do my best for you. I give you my word. If, that is, you can trust the word of a — what was it, now? *Arrogant, asinine*—'

'Well, you did ask.' Westaway looked him in the eye. 'Do you know Brannan — Roderick: I've always felt I ought to loathe you, but somehow—'

'Now, now. None of that. Keats is the cure, remember?' Roderick opened the door. 'Good night, then, Patrick.'

'Goodnight, Roderick.'

* * *

'Why are you in such a temper?' asked Dorothea in the nursery.

'I am not in a temper. Alright, I am. But I have every reason — as you'd know if you'd been listening to a word I've said.'

Why, he asked himself as he prowled round the day room, did he even bother coming up to see her? Let her come to him if she wanted to talk (did she?). He needn't lower himself by running up to the nursery first thing — the very first morning of the Christmas holidays. It wasn't as if she was even *trying* to pretend that she was glad he was home. No one was glad he was home. Except Hecate. And Mother, of course. But at least with Hecate one didn't get the feeling of being silently *judged* the whole time.

He set the rocking horse going and sighed. Dorothea looked up from whatever it was she was doing with her needle and thread.

'I can't keep up with you. I thought cricket was the be-all and end-all? Why are you now fretting about rugby football?'

'It *is* possible, you know, for a chap to have a taste for both.' Especially when that chap was guaranteed a place in the house Fifteen next term. His first stint in the Fifteen last winter had been less than memorable. He was determined to do better this time, for the sake of the house and for his own peace of mind. And God, it seemed, was on Ransom's side. Why else would He have sent them Cunningham?

Roderick had explained all this, he'd told Dorothea how Cunningham was only a fourth year but was something of a phenomenon; how Cunningham had quickly become known as 'the Prodigy' because of his unprecedented prowess at games. He'd explained to her how Mother Moxon was going out of his way to ruin Ransom's chances by vetoing any suggestion of Cunningham playing in the Fifteen — all because the boy had to cram for . . . for something (Roderick forgot what).

'Honestly, Roddy! Is that all you've got to complain about? It's not the end of the world!'

'But it is, it really is! The house Fifteen stands no chance without Cunningham. And what about the Cricket Cup? Cunningham could make all the difference. But Moxon's got him lined up for one of the school prizes instead.'

'Lucky Cunningham, to be spared the Cricket Cup.'

He looked daggers at her but she didn't see, poring over her needle and thread.

Flinging himself into what was still known as Nanny's chair, he said, 'Oh, you're hopeless! A fellow simply can't talk to you!'

'Perhaps I might like to talk about something *other* than cricket once in a while. But I don't suppose you *can* talk about anything else other than games.'

'That's not fair! I am interested in all sorts of things, not just games!'

'Such as?'

'Well, I . . . I . . . I read poetry!'

'Poetry?' She looked at him dubiously.

'Alright, I have *friends* who read poetry, it amounts to the same thing.'

'H-S?' she said, even more doubtful.

'I do have other friends apart from H-S.'

Roderick sighed. What a homecoming this was. Nothing to look forward to. Christmas would be unutterably dull. Mother could not give out invitations, she was still in mourning — though she had made one exception.

'What was Mother thinking, inviting that old fool to dinner tomorrow?'

'Colonel Harding is not so bad once you get to know him.'

He looked at her in disgust. 'Are you feeling quite well? Because you can't be in your right mind if you really believe that! There are no redeeming features at all, even you can't persuade me that there are. Father couldn't stand the bumptious idiot, and Father was right.'

'The Colonel has been a great comfort to Aunt Eloise. As a widower, he can sympathise.'

'Colonel Harding has never been a comfort to anyone. I expect his wife died of boredom while waiting to get a word in edgeways. I expect *both* his wives died that way. You've heard, I suppose, that his second wife had been his housemaid?'

Dorothea looked at him. 'You're making that up.'

'It's true, it's perfectly true.' As a matter of fact, Roderick did not believe that old chestnut either but there was no harm in repeating it — especially when it appeared to be a story which Dorothea had not heard before. 'My God, Doro, have I actually found a snippet of local history which you *haven't* got off pat?'

If looks could kill . . . He grinned at her from Nanny's chair as she sat at the table with her needle and thread. But she pursed her lips and turned her back and resolutely refused to see the funny side.

* * *

Roderick did his best to stave off the impending horror of the Colonel's visit by going hunting, a mad dash across the winter fields and over leafless hedges, coming back spattered with mud and blood, exhausted. He'd scratched his hand quite badly on some brambles but it was not deemed a serious enough injury (a mere graze, Mother said) to warrant missing dinner. The Colonel awaited.

The Colonel's conversation — or monologue — ran on the usual lines: the iniquity of the government, the diabolical evil of the motor car, the scandalous neglect of the Army. And Mother found comfort in *this*?

But then, unexpectedly, the Colonel changed tack. He'd added a new theme to his repertoire. Suffragettes, a national disgrace — those Pankhursts and so on — smashing windows, planting bombs, setting fire to pillar boxes. Where were their fathers? Where were their husbands?

This talk put Roderick in mind of the group of women he'd seen outside the Oval two and a half years ago. They'd worn sashes with *VOTES FOR WOMEN* in bold letters and they'd been handing out leaflets. Father had said . . . but what *had* Father said? It was strange to think that this time last year . . . that this would be the first Christmas without—

But enough of that. Enough. This roast pheasant, it was delicious. There was something missing, though. More gravy, perhaps?

As he poured brown gravy, his thoughts went back to suffragettes. Aldora Harrington-Shaw wasn't a suffragette but her husband had no control over her either. But what in heaven's name had Aldora Harrington-Shaw got to do with anything? He didn't give two hoots for Aldora Harrington-Shaw? (Was it still possible in this day and age to get hold of a chastity belt?)

'Roderick! You are not paying attention!' Mother's voice was crisp, admonishing. It had the effect of a dose of salts, clearing one's head.

'Sorry, Mother, sorry. What was it you said?'

'Not me, Roderick. The Colonel. The Colonel is talking to you.'

The Colonel was asking about school. He'd heard good reports about Downfield recently (*Condescending old fool.*), though he'd opted to send Charles to Harrow, Julian too for that matter. (*And look what it's done for them, one a blithering idiot and the other — well, isn't Julian Harding the housemaid's son, if the scandalmongers are to be believed?*) 'Downfield, I always think, is much the best of our second-line schools.' (*Very generous of you to say so, you bumptious idiot.*) 'Mind you, Teddy was always a sharp operator. When we were out in India—' (*Oh lord, please, not India, not again!*)

Roderick stifled a yawn, smoothed his hair using his injured hand conspicuously, accusingly (*Must I be submitted to all this in my delicate state of health?*), waited impatiently for the apple charlotte as the plates were cleared. Was that *another* new footman or did he just *look* new? Timms had been a hopeless clod, of course, but one had got *used* to him.

The Colonel droned on, Teddy this and Teddy that. Only slowly did it sink in that Teddy, obviously some antediluvian acquaintance form regimental days, was none other than the Big Man, headmaster of Downfield. Roderick perked up. This was interesting. Very interesting. But just as he opened his mouth to make further enquiries, the apple charlotte finally arrived. Teddy and India were forgotten. The apple charlotte had to be examined and discussed. Colonel Harding — naturally — was the world's expert on apple charlottes.

With pudding finished there was a hiatus as the ladies (Mother, Dorothea) left the room. Taking his seat again, Roderick jumped in quickly, turned the conversation back to punctilious Teddy.

'Oh, yes, young man, I know him well, know him very well: known him for years. We served together in India, don't you know. There was one time when—'

'Do you still see much of him, sir?'

'Well, ah, yes, now and again, now and again, at the club and so on. But I'm not in town as often as I used to be.' The Colonel puffed on his cigar, inflating puce cheeks. 'Capital fellow, Teddy. We're both old Downfieldians, don't you know. We were in the same house as you, from what your mother was telling me.'

'More brandy, sir?' Roderick picked up the decanter. It was rather unsettling to find that one had *any* sort of connection with Colonel Harding. The same school — the very same house! But there had to be a way, he felt, that this could be turned to his advantage. The situation with Cunningham loomed large in his head. 'You must come and visit the old place, sir. See how things have changed. I'd be very glad to show you round.'

'Jolly good idea, young man. Capital notion. See Teddy in his element, as it were. Now, as I was saying, when we were in India—'

'I don't suppose you'd recognise the place, sir. There have been a lot of changes. Ransom's had a new extension built a few years back and there's talk now of improving the latrines. Then there's the Big Man's plan for every boy to have a study of his own, and not just the Sixth.'

'Quite right, quite right. What did I tell you? Teddy always was on the ball! Tell me, young man, who's your housemaster these days? When Teddy and I were at—'

'Funny you should ask, sir . . .' Roderick layered it on thick, Mother Moxon's obsession with school prizes, his neglect of games. As for the general tone of the house . . . The sentence was left hanging. The Colonel could draw his own conclusions.

In actual fact, the general tone of Ransom's was no worse than in any of the other houses. One heard stories, of course. One heard rumours. As a rule, one gave them as much credence as that old chestnut about Colonel Harding and the housemaid. It *could* be true. The bounds of possibility suggested it wasn't.

The Colonel's face grew ever redder. He puffed and spluttered. 'Disgrace! Absolute disgrace! What can Teddy be thinking?'

'I'm not so sure, sir, that the Big Man is entirely aware . . .' Roderick planted further seeds as he poured more brandy.

'*My* old school, *my* old house! It's scandalous! Teddy ought to be told. Someone ought to tell him. Someone *must* tell him!'

'I couldn't agree more, sir.'

Roderick sat back to enjoy his cigar.

When, after a time, they joined the ladies in the drawing room, Colonel Harding made a point of saying to Mother,

'Splendid boy you've got there . . . splendid young chap . . .quite officer material.' Mother gave every appearance of being highly gratified by these remarks but Dorothea glanced at Roderick as if she wasn't convinced.

Later, the Colonel gone, the evening over, Dorothea said as she climbed the stairs with Roderick,' What are you *up* to, Roddy, currying favour with the Colonel?'

'Me? Currying favour?' He was all innocence. But this only served to fuel her suspicions.

'There's always been a devious side to you, Roderick Brannan. I've known that ever since I first met you.'

'Well, I like that! Calling your own cousin *devious*! Why are people always so quick to see the worst in me?'

'Perhaps because you give them good cause,' she said over her shoulder, leaving him standing on the first-floor landing as she carried on up to the nursery.

Heading slowly to his room, Roderick wondered if he should explain to her about Machiavelli, how it was necessary for a fellow to be both a lion and a fox. But possibly — probably — she'd take the same view of Machiavelli as Westaway. What she didn't realise was that a chap had to make his own way if he wanted to get on. It was all very well for Dorothea to be all superior, living her cosseted life at Clifton Park, but he was Roderick Brannan, scion of the Massinghams, heir to the estate, leading light of Ransom's, denizen of the house Eleven. He had his position to think of. He had his reputation to uphold.

There was also the Cricket Cup to consider, he told himself as he began to get undressed. Whatever anyone might say, the Cricket Cup remained the pinnacle of achievement at Downfield. No effort should be spared in the pursuit of that dream.

Using his bandaged hand to unbutton his shirt, he found that even though this was only the first week of the holidays, he was already looking forward to going back to school.

* * *

Even without Cunningham, Ransom's Fifteen that Lent term was stronger than anyone could remember. They strolled their way to the semi-finals — and then were played off the field by imperious Harcourt's. Of course, it had to be *that* match which the Big Man chose to come and watch, though by the end — plastered in mud, bruised, battered, exhausted, taken apart by the Harcourt's backs — Roderick was past caring who might be watching.

As he trudged off the field, however, he passed close to where the headmaster was still standing, muffled against the inclement March weather. The Big Man did not strike one as being a *Teddy*, nor was he a bumptious fool: one actually had a lot of respect for him. Which only went to show that it couldn't be India or the Army which turned a man into a crashing bore. It had to be congenital.

The Big Man was talking to one of the beaks. As Roderick trailed past he overheard a snippet of their conversation.

'A pity that Ransom's did not play that boy Cunningham. I've heard he's rather good.'

Heading for the baths, Roderick tried to console himself with the thought that — as Dorothea and Westaway would have it — Downfield was *not* the whole world. What did the Rugger Cup matter in the scheme of things? But this was no real comfort. If Downfield really didn't matter, then not to triumph even here was more of a poor show than ever.

* * *

It was the most eagerly awaited footer final in years. Some touchline experts were even predicting a Conway's win. It was true that Conway's Fifteen were uncommonly large and fierce. They had left a trail of destruction in reaching the final. Could Harcourt's hold on the Cups finally be weakening?

It certainly looked that way in the first half. Conway's racked up a comfortable lead which would have left most opponents completely demoralised: that was the way it had worked for them all term. Harcourt's, however, were not just any side. As they started the second period, there was not a shadow of doubt in any of their faces. It was as if they actually *believed* the myth of their own invincibility.

Harcourt's finally drew level with less than ten minutes to go but by then, any idea of a Conway's victory had long gone. Conway's had nothing left. They looked like beaten men.

And so Harcourt's were champions again. All those who had doubted now laughed and claimed to have seen it coming all along. As if they'd ever *really* given Conway's a prayer — of course they hadn't!

Harcourt's reign continued. Would it ever end?

CHAPTER SEVEN

Waiting by the stile, leaning on the fence, Roderick looked out at Row Meadow but saw in his mind's eye the churned and muddy Upper on that day a few weeks ago when Ransom's dreams of the Rugger Cup had been demolished by unstoppable Harcourt's with the Big Man looking on. *A pity Ransom's did not play that boy Cunningham.* But how could they, with Moxon's deadly hand stifling the life out of the house?

Roderick shook his head impatiently. The vision of the muddy Upper was shattered. He saw instead Row Meadow green and bright in the sunshine, yellow dandelions scattered in the long grass. A breeze was blowing in fits and starts. Rabbits were nibbling over by the far hedge. It was here he'd played cricket with the village boys. It was here he'd hunted rabbits with Turner. It all seemed a long time ago now.

He took aim with his hand, pointing at the rabbits. 'If only I had a gun.'

'What was that about a gun?'

He turned to find Dorothea coming up the path between the churchyard and the high wall of the vicarage garden. She looked beatific in her white frock with its frills and flounces, the ribbons of her wide-brimmed hat blowing in the breeze.

She was purer than ever, no doubt, after a cleansing Easter service.

'Here you are at last,' he grumbled. 'I was beginning to wish I'd gone back with Mother in the motor. It's cold, standing round waiting.'

'What do you expect? It's not even April. You should have worn an overcoat.' She held out a hand for him to help her over the stile. 'What was that about a gun?' she repeated.

'Nothing,' he muttered, remembering that Father had rather disapproved of taking pot-shots at wild animals. Dorothea probably felt the same. He vaulted the fence, said, 'Who was that fat old woman you were talking to?'

'She is neither fat nor is she old. She is almost the same age as Aunt Eloise. And you know very well that it was Mrs Turner.'

'Never heard of her. All those villagers look the same to me.'

Dorothea laughed. 'You *are* ridiculous. But it's nice to have you home, all the same.'

As they walked slowly across the field waiting for Eliza to catch them up, Dorothea threaded her arm through his. It was a trick she had learned from Mother, who had sometimes walked like this with Father in the gardens. It had given the impression that Father was a tower of strength — which in his own way he had been — while making Mother seem weak and wispy in comparison (there was in reality nothing remotely weak or wispy about Mother). Roderick had to admit that walking this way did make him feel . . . well, the word *valiant* might come into it, not to mention *chivalrous*. Dorothea would laugh at his pretensions, but that was exactly how it felt, having a woman on one's arm.

Did Dorothea at eighteen qualify as a woman?

She was bursting with what she fondly called *news*, some of it gleaned from Mrs Turner (he knew exactly who Mrs Turner was, mother of the ferret-owning stable boy), but most acquired in some mysterious manner which he had never been able to fathom. She seemed to know everything about everybody — everybody within a two- or three-mile radius, that was to say. Beyond that her knowledge failed. And yet she had the cheek to call *him* parochial, claiming he was not interested in anything except school!

Oh, but he was glad to be home! He couldn't explain it. He'd been glad before when the holidays began but this was different, ran deeper. He was content to live in the present. Next term, for now, could wait.

He listened indulgently as Dorothea burbled on. Someone called Milly Carter had married someone called Nolly Keech ('Oh, Roddy, of course you know who Milly Carter is, she was the kitchen maid for eight years! And Nolly is the carpenter's son, you used to play with his brother Harry.'). The Carters were orphans. Milly's marriage had left Roderick's old enemy Nibs Carter to bring up his youngest siblings on his own, without female help. *Serve him right, too*, Roderick said. But he was wise enough not to say it out loud.

Village affairs dealt with, Dorothea turned to the doings of the more important local families. 'I almost forgot. You won't have heard, Roddy. Giles Milton has become engaged to Julia Somersby.'

'Giles Milton from Darvell Hall? Is the man mad? Why does he want to marry that horse-faced fright?'

'Don't be wicked. Miss Somersby has a nice face.'

'If you say so. But I thought Miss Horse-Face was earmarked for Fitzwilliam?'

'That was all forgotten about years ago. Everyone has known for ages that Mr Giles and Miss Somersby would get married *eventually*.'

'In which case, their getting engaged is not *news*.'

'But it's romantic. They are in love.'

'Love! Love exists only in the minds of idle girls.'

'Cynic.'

'Realist. Problem with girls is, they have a very flimsy grasp on reality.'

'Oh really? Then try this for reality!'

Disengaging her arm, Dorothea swung a most unlady-like punch, as if they were ten years old again and squabbling over the spy-hole in the dining room door.

'Ouch! That hurt, Doro!'

'Good. It was meant to.'

She was all prim and proper again in an instant, smiling at him as if butter wouldn't melt. As he rubbed his arm — crippled for life, probably — he turned and looked back.

'Where's that infernal child?'

The infernal child was over by the first stile, hobnobbing with a gaggle of village brats. No doubt Dorothea knew the name and parentage of every single child. Then again, he reasoned, there had been a time when he could identify a dozen species of butterfly without stopping to think — the difference being that he had netted the butterflies and pinned them to a board. Might it be worthwhile considering this procedure for surplus village progeny?

He laughed. Dorothea looked at him suspiciously. But at that moment Eliza came running at last, her skirts flying, her sash undone, holding on to her hat with one hand. 'Yoo-hoo! Roddy! Doro! There's going to be a flying machine! Isn't it thrilling!'

'There's going to be a what?' said Dorothea, catching the girl efficiently and setting about making her presentable once more.

'A flying machine!' Eliza panted. 'Johnnie Cheeseman told me all about it. We have to go to Barrow Hill tomorrow. It's the best place to see it. May we go? Oh we *must* go!'

'Who is Johnnie Cheeseman?' asked Roderick charily.

'His grandfather is landlord of the Barley Mow,' said Dorothea.

'The Barley Mow! That disreputable drinking den! I'm not sure you should be fraternising with people of that sort, Eliza.'

His sister ignored him. 'It's a French flying machine. At least, a Frenchman is driving it. He is going all the way to Manchesting.'

'Manchest*er*,' Roderick corrected, frowning as he watched his sister skipping ahead, making the rabbits scatter, white tails bobbing as they ran for their burrows. Surely a girl of her age ought to be better informed about the geography of her own country, ought to know that Manchester was Manchester and not Manchesting. But how old was she, exactly? Nine, ten? It was time she had a governess. A governess would knock some sense into her. But Dorothea insisted there was no need: she was quite capable of looking after Eliza, she liked to make herself useful.

'May we go to Lawham tomorrow?' cried Eliza as she scrambled up onto the next stile. 'May we see the flying machine? I've never seen a flying machine in my whole life!'

'They're nothing special,' said Roderick, 'just a passing mania. Bits of wood and paper. I wouldn't be seen dead in one.'

'When I grow up,' said Eliza loftily, looking down on him from the top of the stile, 'I shall fly in a flying machine. I shall drive it myself.'

'Lord help us,' said Roderick.

* * *

Eliza gazed out from the wide, flat summit of Barrow Hill, scanning the azure sky. 'Where is it? Oh, where *is* it?'

'There's a wonderful view,' said Dorothea. 'I've never been up here before. It's as if one can see half England!'

'This sceptered isle,' said Roderick, 'this blessed plot, this precious stone set in a silver sea.' He looked sidelong at his sister. 'This empty sky, devoid of monstrous mechanical birds.'

Eliza glared at him and he grinned as he too turned to look at the view. The spire of Lawham church was small and sharp as a needle. Smudges of smoke drifted in the sky where a train was waiting at the station. Far distant hills made an uneven line on the hazy horizon.

Henry Fitzwilliam had brought them here in his motor. It had all been arranged yesterday over luncheon at Clifton.

Lady Fitzwilliam and her son had been guests. The subject of the flying machine had cropped up. Fitzwilliam had been enthusiastic. He would be, Roderick had thought.

He turned to watch Fitzwilliam spreading rugs on the grass. They had brought a picnic as no one seemed entirely sure when the flying machine was due. But the flying machine was neither here nor there. Roderick had decided to take an interest in motors and who better to ask about them than Fitzwilliam? Fitzwilliam's motor was a BFS Mark III, the four-seater version. Roderick felt he had a claim on it, coming as it did from Father's factory. But how exactly did one operate (pilot, drive, whatever one did) a motor car?

'It's quite easy once you get the hang of it,' Fitzwilliam had said. 'Why not try? Why not take the wheel?'

But Roderick had declined for now. He preferred to practise when there wasn't an audience of mocking females (his cousin, his sister).

They had left the motor parked on Market Place in Lawham — Lawham, the most boring town on earth, a place where nothing ever happened, where time had stood still since its glory days as a stop on the old coaching routes. Roderick and Fitzwilliam had carried the picnic hamper between them. There'd been other people on the footpath, there was quite a crowd here on top of the hill.

'Where *is* it?' Eliza repeated, hopping up and down with impatience. 'Why doesn't he come?'

'I expect he's fallen in the sea and drowned,' said Roderick.

Dorothea gave him a look. 'Must you, Roddy?'

'Must I what? I just hope all this fuss is worth it. I've given up the point-to-point to come here.'

'Well, you needn't have. We could have managed quite well without you.'

'But you had to have a chaperone. I couldn't have left you in Fitzwilliam's clutches.'

They ate the picnic. Time ticked by. Still there was no sign of the flying machine. People started to pack up and leave. The 'passing mania' was passing even more quickly than expected. Lolling in the long grass, Roderick listened to Dorothea and Fitzwilliam talking. They seemed to have an inexhaustible supply of subjects. But what a milksop Fitzwilliam was with his chubby cheeks and that ridiculous little moustache.

Dorothea looked up. 'I can't see Eliza anywhere.'

Fitzwilliam jumped to his feet. 'I'll go—' he began, but Roderick forestalled him. 'She is *my* sister. *I* shall go.' Any excuse to get away from that pudding-head for a while. What on earth did Dorothea see in him?

Roderick found Eliza sitting on the slope of a grass-grown dyke: the remains, perhaps, of some ancient fortifications. There was said to be an Iron Age hill fort on Barrow Hill. Eliza grabbed his hand and pulled him down beside her. Did he realise, she said, that she was in possession of a *royal* name? There had once been a queen of England called Elizabeth, imagine that! There had also been eight kings called Henry (Fitzwilliam's name) but no kings called Roderick and no queens called Dorothea.

'But don't worry, Roddy. You don't have to keep your own name if it doesn't fit. You can choose a new name, like the King did. His name is really Albert, not Edward. What name would you have if you were king?'

'Nebuchadnezzar.'

She looked at him, indignant. 'That's silly. A silly name. You made it up.'

'I most certainly didn't. But what's in a name? It's deeds that matter. I would be a good king. I wouldn't spend all my time dallying in France while the country goes to wrack and ruin. I'd shake things up, make people squeal. It's high time everyone was put back in their place.'

'Like who?' asked Eliza curiously.

'Never your mind.' Roderick got up, held out his hand. 'Come on, Pain. Time to go.'

She allowed herself to be pulled to her feet. A wistful look crossed her face. 'I *did* so want to see the flying machine! Do you really think he fell in the sea and drowned?'

'Of course not. I was just talking off the top of my head. You must learn to take things with a pinch of salt.'

'A pinch of *salt*? Why *salt*?'

'Ask Doro. She's eager to teach you all she knows. But never mind all this talk. If we don't hurry, we shan't be back in time for tea.'

It was only when they were all packed up and heading down the hill that Roderick noticed anything amiss. Dorothea went charging down the path as if she hadn't a minute to live. Or was it, Roderick wondered watching her with a keen eye, that she wanted to get away from Fitzwilliam? Fitzwilliam was unusually quiet, too, looked rather flushed. Something had obviously happened. A little disagreement, perhaps? Words exchanged? One could hardly credit it, Miss Goody-Goody and the milksop! Perhaps she had seen through him at last.

Dorothea and Fitzwilliam did not speak, did not so much as look at each other, all the way back to Clifton.

* * *

Roderick was in his room getting changed, had unbuttoned his shirt, was unfastening the cuffs, when there was an urgent knock on the door and, without waiting for a reply, Dorothea came crashing in.

'Do you mind, Doro! I might have been naked or—'

As he hurriedly buttoned his shirt back up, he realised that she was not listening, was in fact close to tears. She had not taken her coat off, was still wearing her boots and even her hat.

'Doro, what's the matter? What on earth is wrong?'

'Oh Roddy! I don't know what to do! Henry has asked me to marry him!'

'He's asked you *what*?'

Roderick was rocked on his heels. This explained a lot: the silence, the awkwardness, Fitzwilliam not staying to tea. But marriage! She wouldn't . . . would she . . . ?

'Doro, hush, listen, listen to me. What did you say to him? How did you reply?'

'Well, I said no, of course. But — oh Roddy — it was such a shock. And . . . oh . . . oh . . .'

Her look of distress was enough to wring the most austere of hearts. He could think of nothing else but to put his arms around her. As she clung to him, tears streaming, he had a feeling of déjà vu. It was less than a year ago since he'd held her in his arms in the nursery when she'd been upset about the semolina pudding.

It seemed a long time before her sobs subsided. Even then she did not let him go. He patted her back awkwardly. His shirt was wet against his skin where her tears had soaked in.

When she finally spoke, her voice was muffled against his chest. 'He was so upset. He . . . oh, Roddy, I think I've hurt him dreadfully!'

'*He* was upset! My God, Doro, what does that matter!' But of course it would matter to her. She was always putting other people first — worrying about other people instead of herself. He tightened his grip, almost angry with her. 'You really shouldn't bother so much about other people. Think of yourself for a change!'

She did not reply but after a moment made a little movement and he realised he was squeezing her rather hard — suffocating her. He let go, lead her to the bed. She sat on the edge, he sat next to her. He passed her his handkerchief just as he'd done all those months ago in the nursery after Father died.

Dabbing at her tears, she said, 'He's always been so kind to me.'

'It's no more than you deserve.'

'He said it was fate. Right from when we first met there was a connection between us.'

'That's absolute rot!'

'And when I ran away and he found me on the Welby Road—'

'When did you run away? Why have I never heard about this?' He put his arm round her as if she might run away again at any moment. 'Why was I never *told*?'

'Oh, of course, you must have been at school, you wouldn't know—' She hiccupped, took a deep breath. 'It was soon after I first came to Clifton. I decided to leave, to go back to London.' Her voice grew calmer, a little firmer, as she focused on the story. 'I ran away with no money and a hat that was too big for me and kept falling over my eyes. I didn't really know what I was doing. On the Welby Road I met Henry in Bernadette. Do you remember Bernadette, his Daimler? Poor Henry! He had a black eye! Someone had thrown a stone at him. They often did in those days. People objected to motors. Henry gave me his dust coat to wear and he brought me back here, back home — except I didn't think of it as home in those days, it was more like a . . . a gaol!'

'I don't understand. Why did you want to go to London?'

'It wasn't London really, it was my papa. I wanted my papa. I thought that was where he'd be: in London, in Stepnall Street. I thought of Stepnall Street as home in those days, not Clifton. But Stepnall Street wasn't home, not really. We lived in one room — there were four of us—'

She broke off, looked stricken. Was she still upset about Fitzwilliam, or had she made herself miserable thinking of her old life and her missing father? One tended to forget that she'd ever been poor. The poor were separate. One had nothing to do with them. One merely had a vague idea of their being drunkards, illiterate, vicious. There were poor people in the village, of course, but one didn't really notice them. It was different in big towns and cities where there were vast swarms of poor people, like plagues of locusts.

He looked sidelong at Dorothea. One might have expected poverty to leave its mark, like smallpox. But there was no sign. She looked ordinary and familiar with her plain round face and her dark curls. Her coat was buttoned to the throat, curved over her breasts—

He swallowed. She'd grown breasts. When had that happened?

'I thought he was my *friend*.' Her voice was getting shaky again. Tears began to roll down her cheeks one-by-one. 'I thought he *liked* me. But *love*! Now he's spoiled *everything*!'

'You needn't think, Doro, that you're not good enough for him. That's absolute rot. *He's* not good enough for *you* — he could never be!'

'But he's so kind, so gentle, he's . . . What *is* love, Roddy? What is it *like*? How does one *know*?'

'Lord, Doro, it's . . . it's no good asking me. I'm not the sort of fellow who thinks much about love.'

He felt his cheeks burning. He wanted to ride roughshod over love, to stamp it out, destroy it. He wanted to wipe her tears — to catch them on his fingers. But he wasn't fit to touch her. The things that went on his head, his thoughts about women, his filthy mind. And he'd been looking at her breasts just now! He ought to be ashamed. He *was* ashamed, sitting next to her. He'd laughed at her over the years, poked fun, called her Miss Goody-Goody. But that was exactly what she was: good. The nicest, truest, most gentle-hearted person he'd ever met. How dare Fitzwilliam put her through all this! How dare he think he had the right to even *ask* such a question! He was old enough to be her father!

She was still talking. Roderick forced himself to concentrate, to pick up the threads.

'. . . and I *do* like him, I like him very much, and . . . well . . . if that's all it takes . . . I could still say yes, couldn't I? It's not too late, is it? I wouldn't want him to be unhappy for the world!'

'He'll get over it soon enough. We're sturdy fellows, us men. Don't think you owe him anything, because you don't. It's *you* that matters, what *you* want.'

He helped her to her feet, wiped the tears off her cheeks with his thumbs — because he wanted to, because he could, because he was a sturdy fellow who would never let her down.

'Go on now, Doro. Go and lie down. Don't worry about Fitzwilliam or anything else. I shall take care of it. I shall take care of *you*.'

'You . . . you won't tell Eliza, will you? Or—' Her eyes widened in alarm. '—or Aunt Eloise! You mustn't tell Aunt Eloise! Please, Roddy!'

'Hush. I won't say a word to anyone, I promise. And you needn't come down to dinner if you don't feel up to it. I shall tell Mother you had too much sun.'

She looked somewhat relieved, allowed him to lead her to the door. Here she paused. Her eyes searched his face. She smiled.

'Thank you, Roddy.'

She kissed him gently on the cheek and then was gone.

He closed the door, began unbuttoning his shirt again, planning as he did so how he would protect her: protect her from Mother, from everybody — from himself, too. But from Henry Fitzwilliam most of all.

* * *

It did not prove as easy as he'd expected to keep the news of Fitzwilliam's proposal under wraps. He was in the breakfast room next morning, finishing his coffee and toast after getting up late, scanning the newspaper. Mount Etna had erupted. An explosion on an American warship had killed eight. Two hundred and ninety had died in a disastrous fire in Hungary. Tuppeny-ha'penny stuff. All very dull.

The King and Queen of Bulgaria, he read impassively, *left Constantinople at 6 o'clock—*

The sound of a motor outside made him look up. Tyres scrunched on the gravel.

He got to his feet, crossed to the window just in time to see Lady Fitzwilliam, Henry's mother, being handed down by her chauffeur. A moment later, the doorbell jangled.

Mother was in the next room, the parlour, her place of business. She wouldn't normally be in to callers at this time of the morning but she'd probably receive Lady Fitzwilliam, who counted as an intimate friend if anyone did. Abandoning his coffee, Roderick ducked through the connecting door into the empty drawing room, waited. He heard Basford come into the breakfast room, cross to the parlour door, knock. A murmur of voices. Basford retraced his steps to return a moment later with the visitor.

'Lady Fitzwilliam, ma'am.'

When he heard the parlour door close, Roderick went back into the breakfast room, startling the footman who was clearing the table.

'That'll be all, Basford.'

'Sir?' Basford glanced at the breakfast things with a conscientious eye.

'I don't need you, Basford. Shoo, shoo.'

Reluctantly abandoning his task, the tall footman retreated. As soon as he'd gone, Roderick took up a position by the parlour door. Mother was speaking.

'I had no idea, Alice. Nothing has been said.'

'I can't understand why she would turn him down. It's incomprehensible. Henry is quite shaken by the whole affair. If I could just have a word with her . . . ?'

'You can be sure I will be having words with her myself,' said Mother firmly. 'I will make sure she sees sense.'

Mother was not having any outsider interfering in Clifton business. Bully for her! But things did not look too bright for Dorothea. No one liked being made to 'see sense' by Mother — not even him. The least he could do was warn his cousin before the summons came.

He hurried up to the nursery, packed Eliza off with the maid to 'walk in the garden or something'. He'd only just finished explaining when one of the housemaids appeared with a request that Dorothea go down to the parlour.

'Roddy!' Dorothea grabbed hold of his hand, panic in her eyes. 'Will you come with me? Please!'

'Of course I will.' He squeezed her hand, braced himself. 'Come on, then. Let's get it over with.'

She continued to hold his hand all the way downstairs, only let go as they reached the parlour door. She patted her hair into place. Roderick recognised the gesture as an unconscious imitation of Mother. It would have amused him at any other time.

Mother was seated on a stool at her bureau, turned to face them as they came in. Her eyes narrowed a little at the sight of her son.

'Thank you, Roderick, you may go. This doesn't concern you.'

'Doro wants me here, Mother,' he said stoutly.

Mother sighed — not a good sign: one could never be sure where Mother's sighs might lead.

'Very well. Sit down, both of you.'

Mother got straight to the point as one might have expected. She outlined at length all the advantages of what she called 'a match' with Henry Fitzwilliam. Roderick grew impatient, tapping his knee. He glanced round the room, looked out of the window. There was a grey March sky. Starlings were chirping in the lime trees. The sight of the rampant rhododendrons made him uneasy for reasons he could not put his finger on. He blinked and looked away.

Did Mother really believe all this soft soap? It was never easy to gauge what she was thinking. She was certainly rather less forceful than usual — or was that merely the effect of her widow's weeds?

Mother's speech came to an end. What objections, she concluded, could Dorothea possibly have to marrying Henry Fitzwilliam?

'I . . . I don't love him, Aunt.'

'Love?' Mother was dismissive of love. 'Love rarely has anything to do with it. Love comes later, if it comes at all. But if you are determined to die an old maid—'

'Really, Mother! Dorothea is eighteen, not twenty-eight!'

'But you can't count on many better proposals,' Mother continued, ignoring her son, looking keenly at Dorothea. 'You can't rely on that. You do realise, I presume?'

'Yes, Aunt. But . . . but . . .'

This was cruel, thought Roderick. He must intervene, cut Mother off. If Mother didn't like it, so much the worse for her.

He opened his mouth to speak but Mother got in first.

'Very well, Dorothea. If that is your final word, we will draw a line under the whole business. It shan't be mentioned again.' She turned back to her bureau and the household accounts.

Dorothea was only too glad to get away but Roderick paused in the doorway. Mother looked round with vague impatience as he spoke.

'What about Lady Fitzwilliam, Mother? What will you tell her?'

Mother sighed, laying down her pen. 'I'm afraid Alice has brought this on herself. She has always encouraged Henry to seek out the most inappropriate matches.'

Such as Miss horse-face Somersby, thought Roderick; but even Fitzwilliam had not been fool enough to fall for that one.

'I shall have to tell her, I suppose.' Mother spoke softly, as if to herself. 'Pay a visit to the Grange. Henry is inconsolable, Alice says.'

'He would be, the duffer.'

Mother looked at him sharply. Roderick expected a swift rebuke. But all she said was, 'I must get on, Roderick.' She picked up her pen once more and turned away.

Roderick closed the door softly. Henry Fitzwilliam was an idiot. Was it possible that Mother believed this too? She would never say so, of course, but there were no flies on Mother.

Slowly climbing the stairs, Roderick wondered if he ought to have been more on his guard all these years. He'd felt that Fitzwilliam's proposal was a bolt from the blue but that was not strictly true. Last year at Father's funeral, for instance, the way Fitzwilliam had been gazing at Dorothea with doggy devotion. And there'd been other signs over time. Once, on Dorothea's birthday years ago, Fitzwilliam had danced with her to music from his gramophone. Roderick remembered the fierce anger he had felt; he remembered how he'd felt compelled to butt in and dance with her himself, even though he despised dancing. But he hadn't realised what it meant. He hadn't realised what Fitzwilliam was up to.

But it was all over now. Dorothea was safe.

He expected her to be all smiles when he entered the nursery, was perplexed to find her in tears instead.

'What if Aunt Eloise is right? What if I've missed my chance? What if I die an old maid?'

'Surely you don't think it's worth marrying Fitzwilliam just because of that? Why should you get married at all? Why shouldn't we keep you to ourselves? I shan't get married. I really think I shan't. General Gordon never married and he got on alright.'

'Oh, Roddy, you and your generals — Wellington and Nelson and the rest. And all those tin soldiers you used to play with. Do you remember?'

She was off again. It was hopeless. One couldn't say anything without bringing on fresh floods of tears. It wouldn't have mattered so much if she'd been the kind of girl who cried all the time. But this was totally out of character, not like Dorothea at all. He wanted the proper Dorothea back. What could he do to put things right?

He seized on the first idea that came into his head.

'I say, Doro. Why don't we go on a trip this summer? It would be something to look forward to.'

'A trip?' She showed interest. The tears were checked. 'But where could we go? And you know that Aunt Eloise hates to travel.'

'Mother shan't come. It will be a trip just for us.'

'And Eliza.'

'If you must.'

'We couldn't leave Eliza. Oh, Roddy, we couldn't—'

'Yes, yes, alright. We'll take Eliza. We'll take anyone you like. We shall go to the continent—'

'Oh!' Her eyes widened.

'We could visit that French governess of yours—'

'Could we? Could we really?'

'—and see the Alps and so on.'

'Roddy! How wonderful!'

He patted himself on the back. He'd turned things round at last, changed tears into smiles.

It was only afterwards, when he'd left the nursery and gone to find Hecate to take her for a walk, that he began to wonder what he'd let himself in for. Someone would need to persuade Mother, for a start — and that someone would have to be him. And what on earth had possessed him to mention the Frog governess?

But summer was months away. There was a whole term to get through first. And the Easter hols weren't half over yet.

Hecate was nowhere to be found, which was not unusual. She was an independent-minded creature. Searching for her all through the house and out into the stable yard, Roderick — in one of the disused loose boxes — chanced upon his long-neglected bicycle in a forgotten corner: last in a series of bicycles, each one a step up from the last, largesse from Father's factory.

How long since he'd used it? The Clifton craze for cycling had rather fallen into abeyance in recent times. Dragging it out into the yard, brushing off some of the dust and cobwebs, Roderick decided that it still looked the part, blue and red and sleek, with the letters *B.B.C.* prominent on it: the Brannan Bicycle Company. It would perhaps need some oil, the nuts and bolts might need tightening, one of the tyres was flat. It was no good asking Turner. He was an expert with horses (and ferrets) but when it came to machines he hadn't any idea. Turner had never in real life looked askance, crossed himself and said, *They be the work of the devil, they be*, but it was easy to imagine him doing so.

Roderick decided to fix the bike himself. Why not? Father had never shied away from getting his hands dirty. He'd always kept the Clifton bicycles in tip-top condition. If it was good enough for Father . . .

Besides, how difficult could it be?

* * *

Freewheeling down the Lawham Road, Roderick basked in a sense of achievement. It had taken several days longer than expected and more than one outburst of invective, but he had persisted and now his bicycle was as good as new. He had taken to the open road, fresh air rushing past, Clifton and all its tangled affairs left far behind.

Traversing the humpbacked bridge over the canal, he took to the pedals. He passed on his left the turning to that old track known as Hunter's Lane; on his right was Ingleby Wood, its budding trees just coming into leaf. He would go as far as Lawham, he decided; maybe even Broadstone. There was nothing to stop him. He was strong as an ox, cycling was child's play.

He was out of his saddle, treading down on the pedals, making his way up the rise, when a motor car suddenly swept past him, making light work of the climb. The motor slowed and stopped. As Roderick drew level with it, a voice hailed him.

It was Henry Fitzwilliam.

'Hello there! Out on your bicycle, I see! How are you? How is everyone at Clifton? How is . . . is . . . ?' Fitzwilliam's voice faltered.

'How is Dorothea?' Roderick gave a malicious smile. 'She is fighting fit, never better. Why do you ask?'

There was a certain satisfaction in seeing Fitzwilliam colour up at the mention of Dorothea's name. He looked particularly ridiculous just now with that silly little moustache and rings round his eyes where his goggles had been. But, balanced on his bicycle, Roderick felt rather at a disadvantage. His machine seemed something of a kid's toy next to Fitzwilliam's monster motor, that throbbing engine, all that easy power. It looked even more imposing than usual, somehow sturdier yet sleeker.

'That motor, Fitzwilliam, is it new?'

'The motor? Oh, the motor! Yes. Yes, it's new.'

It was the BFS Mark IV, apparently, in the process of being road-tested. There were all sorts of marvellous improvements over the old BFS models which Roderick could not make head or tail of — except for the detachable wheels which even he could see would make punctures easier to deal with. Production of the Mark IV was due to begin shortly at Allibone Road, to be ready in time for the Motor Show later in the year.

Roderick decided then and there that he would get his hands on a Mark IV at the earliest opportunity. It wouldn't take much to talk Mother round. The biggest headache would be learning to pilot the damned thing. Would it be too much of a cheek to ask Fitzwilliam to help?

But never mind piloting a motor! Oughtn't he to be learning how to pilot Father's businesses? It had never occurred to him before. It wasn't a bad aim to have in life, to fill Father's shoes. Allibone Road: that was where the largest of Father's factories was situated up in Coventry. What was it like? Dorothea, he seemed to recall, had once visited one of the earlier, smaller works but even she had never been to Allibone Road. Roderick experienced an unwonted desire to see the place, the fruit of Father's labours.

Fitzwilliam did not look exactly thrilled at the prospect, grew decidedly worried when Roderick dropped hints about taking up the reins as Father's heir.

Roderick smirked. For reasons he couldn't fathom, he felt unusually magnanimous towards Fitzwilliam today. 'Of course, I've not finished school yet, and then there's Oxford: everyone's frightfully keen on my going to Oxford.' Let Fitzwilliam play at being the captain of the ship for a while longer. One might need his help, after all, in the matter of learning to drive. 'Nice to see you, anyway, old chap, but I must dash. Places to be and all that.'

'Yes, of course. Do give my regards to . . . to everyone.'

As he pedalled away, working hard to get up the slope, Roderick felt that life after Downfield was beginning to take shape, as if he could see ahead for the first time. Not just vague dreams, the world his oyster: the future was becoming as real as this road, with any number of turnings and by-ways, Oxford and Coventry and Clifton.

But first there was school. He had unfinished business at school. And time was running out for him to achieve there all that he wanted to achieve.

* * *

It was a term like no other. The wind of change was blowing through Ransom's. Mother Moxon had taken his leave of the place.

It came as a complete surprise. There'd been no hint of it in the Lent term. Had he gone of his own accord? Or was it possible that the Big Man had been hobnobbing in his London club with his old friend from India, hearing disquieting rumours? But the world did not operate like that, Roderick told himself. It was never a simple case of cause and effect like the workings of a bicycle. The chances of fortune, the vagaries of fate meant that no one could be congratulated, no one blamed, the changes must simply be accepted as a *fait accompli*.

The headmaster himself took temporary charge of Ransom's. He was full of enthusiasm for the prospects of the house Eleven. There would be no repetition of that business over Cunningham last term. At last the whole house was united.

The wind of change continued to blow, not just in Ransom's, not just at Downfield, but across the whole country. The King was dead. The Edwardian era was over. Might other eras be drawing to a close, too? The outlook for the inter-house matches began to look a little brighter.

* * *

Ransom's Eleven progressed majestically to the semi-finals. They were to face Rimmer's, a repeat of the contest that Roderick had missed last year because of Father's untimely demise. In the other semi-final, Harcourt's were drawn against Conway's.

The neutrals found little to get excited about in either match. Harcourt's comfortably outplayed Conway's. Ransom's confounded predictions of a close-run contest by producing a virtuoso display against Rimmer's, the most one-sided match of the term.

The final of the Cricket Cup began to loom large. People were asking by how much Harcourt's would win this year. Because there was no doubting they'd win. They always did.

* * *

It was cool, overcast, the air thick and gloomy, not summer weather at all. Heavy grey clouds pressed down on the Upper for a second day in succession, the second day of the final. The spectators were oddly subdued as if they weren't really there, as if they were ghosts of themselves. The two teams eyed each other circumspectly like boxers sparring. There was nothing to choose between them. Their first innings had been all but identical. It was a match awaiting a knock-out blow. Would it come from a moment of genius — or from some unthinkable mistake?

And all the time, at the back of one's mind, the old refrain: *Harcourt's are unbeatable.*

* * *

Harcourt's captain was the best batsman in the school. He'd had a nervy time of it yesterday but was coming into his own in Harcourt's second innings. He had opened his shoulders, was getting into his stride. The runs were mounting up.

The sound of the church bell chiming the hour came faintly through the gloom, like an intimation from another world.

'Never send to know for whom the bell tolls,' muttered Roderick, fielding at fine leg. 'It tolls for thee.'

Poetry. It was infectious. Westaway had a lot to answer for. Did he perhaps know any decent poems of consolation after a bitter defeat?

* * *

Harcourt's captain was on strike again. A grandiose sweep of the ball and he was off. Another run. Another nail in Ransom's coffin.

Out of the corner of his eye, Roderick saw young Cunningham throwing himself across the grass. What was he doing, the bloody idiot, all out of position?

At once the action seemed to slow down. Roderick felt that he was seeing it as a series of vignettes: Cunningham's arms stretched out across the turf; Cunningham's fingertips brushing against the ball as it passed; the ball slowing, stopping, spinning on the spot; Harcourt's captain suddenly out on a limb, dithering between one crease and the other. Cunningham was on his feet. His back arched as he hurled the ball with all his might. The ball hung in the murky air. It seemed to hang for all eternity. Harcourt's captain in a flat-out sprint was reaching with his bat for the shelter of his wicket.

Several things happened in the blink of an eye. The ball was in the wicketkeeper's hands. The bails were down. Harcourt's captain was in a heap by the stumps. But in which order had these things happened?

The cry went up. 'Owzat?'

Roderick held his breath. Silence, silence, silence. His lungs were fit to burst.

Then — a raised finger. 'Out!'

As Roderick gulped for air, Howlett's face appeared before him, eyes shining, mouth agape.

'Rodders! Rodders! We—'

Roderick put his finger to his lips. No words were necessary. Howlett understood.

‘Right-oh, Rodders. Right-oh, captain. You can depend on me.’

Howlett went back to his place, steady as a rock. Young Cunningham too was brought back to earth by a look. The next Harcourt’s batsman was already walking out.

Roderick adjusted his cap. Once more unto the breach.

* * *

The long morning trailed to an end. Lunch came and went. The afternoon slowly wore away. The weather took a turn for the better. The sun, as elusive as victory for most of the last two days, could now be seen glowing behind banks of white cloud massed in the sky. The heavy air lifted. As it did so, a weight descended on Roderick’s shoulders. He was more than the captain now. He was a puppeteer. Only his strength of will was keeping his team going as Harcourt’s formidable bowlers ground away at the Ransom’s batting order.

The last of the tattered clouds ebbed into the east as the sun sank in splendour towards the horizon. The stand of oaks cast long shadows across the boundary. Ransom’s were still chasing Harcourt’s total. They were down to their last two batsmen now. Roderick was at the crease. He had been batting for some time. He could not have said exactly how long. He was dizzy with fatigue, his stomach in knots, the blisters on his hands throbbing. It had never been like this in those old adventure books.

Still the ball kept coming.

He steeled himself for the next effort. There was a deathly silence all round the field. Taking a pace forward, he met the delivery head-on. *Crack*! A half-volley. The follow-through took him down onto one knee. He held this position, squinting into the sun, watching the ball run away into the shadow of the oaks. A four.

He heard cheering. It grew louder, louder, become a deafening roar. The beaten fielders were starting to leave the pitch, their heads bowed. Slowly Roderick got to his feet. His tired brain struggled to take it in.

The crowning moment. Everything he had dreamed of. The Cricket Cup.

Could it really be true?

* * *

Roderick smoothed his hair as he hurried along Market Street, replaced his cap, put on a burst of speed: he didn't want to be late. But why was he going at all?

'The mater is coming to take me to tea,' H-S had said. 'She has been visiting Aunt Prudence, is on her way home. You must come too, Rodders.'

'Did she ask for me?'

'Well, no, she didn't as it happens. But of course she'll want to see you!'

Tea at the White Hart. That was all it was. No need to be nervous.

He wrinkled his nose. He *wasn't* nervous. Just late.

As he took his place, he found himself blushing. He felt shy of her. It was the last thing he'd expected. She was looking all around, a distracted expression on her face, as if she felt that much more interesting conversations were taking place somewhere just out of earshot.

H-S made a valiant attempt to gain her attention, even going so far as to ignore the cakes on his plate. 'You can't imagine, Mater, how jolly it is to be a Ransom's man just now! We are the toasts of the school for winning the Cricket Cup, for beating Harcourt's. We were up half the night celebrating. You've never seen such celebrations.'

'How lovely . . . how nice . . .' She played with the string of her Dorothy bag. She crumbled cake with her long, pale fingers.

'Rodders is *such* a celebrity now. You should have seen him, the way he played in the final: he was batting for hours, he was simply magnificent. He's bound to be captain of the First Eleven next year, he'll probably be head of house too. Imagine me being chums with such a fellow!' H-S jumped to his feet. There was just time, if they were quick — before her train — to make the pilgrimage to the Upper. She couldn't possibly go without seeing the scene of their triumph.

'Whatever you say, Alfie darling.'

They walked along Market Street, cut through the alley past New Hall and came out in North Street. Aldora began to look round with interest.

'So many boys,' she murmured.

'It's a school, Mater. There are bound to be boys about. Come on, this way.'

'No,' said Roderick, pointing. 'We'll go *that* way.'

'Are . . . are you sure, Rodders?'

'Quite sure.'

Leading the way along the Jitty, smiling scornfully at the Conway's boys hanging out of the upper windows (let them see how far they got with their measly court martial now), Roderick was aware of a growing feeling of discontent. H-S, of course, was pop-eyed at the audacity of it, making free with Conway's Jitty, but to Aldora it meant nothing, just as the Cricket Cup meant nothing — and *he* meant nothing. But it was not just Aldora. There must be vast swathes of the world that had never heard of Downfield or the Cricket Cup. It made him angry to think of it.

They stepped onto the Upper. The sun shone fitfully. The grass in places was as threadbare as a worn carpet. There was no one about except for three or four fellows clowning around by the pavilion. Their laughing voices faded in and out as the wind gusted.

Half way across the field, Aldora stopped and put her hand to her mouth, theatrical as ever. 'My bag! Oh Alfie, my bag! I must have left it behind! How silly of me!'

'I'll go, Mater! I'll fetch it! Don't you worry!' H-S was overjoyed to be of service, went lolloping off towards Little Lane.

Roderick watched him. *Poor Harrington-Shaw*, Dorothea had called him. *You ignore him, you don't listen to a word he says.* But nobody ever listened to H-S, not even his own mother.

Roderick turned to look at her, H-S's mother. She had walked on, was taking tiny steps because of her hobble skirts, placing one foot precisely in front of the other, her heels sinking into the turf. The ostrich feathers in her hat quivered in the breeze.

He ran to catch her up. His discontent grew. His anger surged.

Under the spreading boughs of the oaks, she turned to face him. They were in almost the exact spot where the last ball of the cricket final had ended up.

'You never wrote!' His voice sounded harsh in his ears. He didn't care. 'I sent you so many letters. You never replied.'

She was looking at him now properly for the first time that afternoon. Her gaze lingered. 'Darling, those letters, I meant to tell you. You mustn't send any more. Humphrey might read them and then where would we be?'

You mustn't send any more . . . But hadn't she realised that the letters had stopped coming months and months back, as long ago as last autumn? Hadn't she even noticed that he'd *snubbed* her?

Sunlight danced and dazzled as the wind tossed the branches of the trees and seethed amongst the leaves.

He took a step towards her, then another, as if drawn against his will. She watched him from under the wide brim of her hat.

'How I enjoyed your visit last summer,' she murmured. 'We had such fun.'

She reached out and touched his cheek. Her fingers lingered, stroked his skin, brushed across his lips. He could hear the boys by the pavilion laughing, one moment loud, the next fading to nothing.

'Don't!' he growled. 'Someone might see.' People were always watching him now. He was, as H-S had pointed out, a celebrity.

She didn't take her hand away. He reached up to push it aside. Somehow his fingers got entangled with hers. They were holding hands, standing close. The fingers of her free hand caressed the back of his neck, drawing him still closer.

Suddenly he didn't care if anyone was watching or not. His knees shook, his heart was thumping. She had cast her spell on him again. She had cast her spell even here on the sacred ground of the Upper. Or was it that she had drawn something out of him, something from deep inside; something that was a part of him, that wanted her, that wanted more, more, more—

'Ahoy, Mater!'

H-S's voice carried faintly across the Upper as if from half a world away. Roderick tried to step back. She wouldn't let him. Frantic, he twisted away from her. Still she held his hand in hers, gripping it, a smile playing on her lips.

She let him go only at the very last second. He snatched his hand away as H-S came puffing up.

'Your bag, Mater!'

'Alfie, you found it, how clever of you.'

H-S beamed from ear to ear as she took his arm, drew him away, began to walk with him across the playing field leaving Roderick forgotten, standing beneath the swaying branches of the trees. He watched the pair of them turn into Little Lane, dwindle, disappear.

Stuffing his hands in his pockets, whistling a tune — the first thing that came into his head — he rambled across the Upper, reassembling himself: the casual hero of the Cricket Cup, one of the foremost celebrities of the school; a man with a future.

CHAPTER EIGHT

'England's never been invaded,' said Roderick grandly as he watched the white cliffs recede. He was uncomfortably aware of the deck swaying beneath his feet. Dry land already seemed a distant memory. The sky above was a deep blue flecked with streaks of white cloud. There was a brisk wind blowing. The sea surged and swelled. Waves dashed themselves against the side of the boat in explosions of spray.

'That's not entirely true,' said Dorothea. 'What about 1066?'

Roderick sighed. 'Must you do that?'

'Do what?'

'Spoil the effect. Introduce superfluous details. What I said was substantially correct.'

'But not entirely true.'

'Nor was 1066 entirely an invasion. It was just a boatload of old Normans.'

'Normans?' Eliza, holding Dorothea's hand, looked at Roderick in some doubt.

His sister was being literal again, Roderick realised. She was probably imagining a cross-channel steamer packed with bowler-hatted bank clerks: who else but a bank clerk would have a name like Norman? This was the problem with girls.

They took things far too much at face value. They were also obsessed with petty-fogging detail.

'Normans are people from Normandy,' explained Dorothea, expunging the image of the bank clerks. 'It's a part of France.'

'Does the Mam'zelle live in Normandy?' asked Eliza.

'No. We shan't be going to Normandy, not on this trip.' Dorothea turned her back on England. 'Let's walk along the deck. But you must hold on to your hat, Eliza, or else it will blow away.'

Roderick reluctantly let go of the rail, moved to follow his cousin and his sister. It was impossible to walk in a straight line the way the deck was swaying. The horizon rose and fell alarmingly. There was also a nauseating smell of smoke. Smoke was belching from the white funnels, being snatched away in billowing clouds by the breeze, leaving tendrils to twist and twirl towards the deck. Roderick tried to whistle to keep his spirits up. But that didn't help. He found he was whistling the same old song, the tune he'd begun to whistle on the Upper a month ago, the tune couldn't get out of his head: *Boiled Beef and Carrots*, completely ludicrous.

'Look!' Eliza was pointing. 'A motor car! How extraordinary, to have a motor car riding on top of a ship!'

There was indeed a motor on the foredeck. 'One of ours,' said Roderick.

'Ours?' said Eliza.

'A BFS Mark III coupe. Rather old hat now. It doesn't even have detachable wheels.'

Dorothea shot him a glance. 'You are something of an expert all of a sudden.'

'I am taking an interest in the family business.'

'The businesses do very well as they are. There is no need for you to interfere.'

'What do you mean *interfere*? You make it sound as if—' He stopped, swallowed uneasily.

Eliza was staring up at him. 'You *have* gone a funny colour, Roddy!'

'I feel a bit . . . a bit queasy, actually. The sooner we get off this what's-its-name, the better.'

'The *Prince of Wales* is its name.'

'*Purgatory* would be more apt.'

'You are just a little sea-sick, that's all,' said Dorothea, know-it-all.

'Sea-sick!' Eliza was scornful. '*I* don't feel sick in the least!'

'Well hurrah for you. I'll have you know that Nelson himself . . . that Nelson . . .' He couldn't finish. Much as he'd have liked to stay and squash his annoying little sister, he felt a more pressing need at that moment to find somewhere to be quietly indisposed.

On his knees in the heads, throwing up his lunch followed by his breakfast, Roderick wondered if there was a moral to be drawn from this, the hero of the Cricket Cup brought low by seasickness. It there *was* a moral, Dorothea would be sure to point it out. She was helpful like that.

Don't live like vegetarians

On food they give to parrots . . .

Oh Lord, that song, that ludicrous song. Now was not the time. Why couldn't he just wipe it from his mind? And why did he feel so ill? Hubris, Dorothea would say. But that was completely unfair. He'd been a perfect gentleman ever since the triumph of the Cricket Cup. He'd not boasted inordinately. He'd been nice as pie to everyone. He'd gone through the end of term, the OTC summer camp, and preparations for this trip, being so magnanimous he barely recognised himself.

Boiled beef and carrots, boiled beef and carrots . . .

He sat back on his haunches as the song went round and round in his head. Was it safe to get to his feet, or was he stuck down here in the bowels for the duration?

Perhaps give it just a bit longer.

He'd made up his mind about one thing, however: he would never depart from England's shores again.

* * *

The station was in the middle of nowhere, nestled amongst rolling hills and green woodland. Blinking in the bright sunshine outside the station building, they could see no sign of the village — Jeancourt-en-Argonne — that was their final destination. There was, however, a rickety-looking cart driven by a taciturn man who had a bushy moustache and no English. He slung up their cases and trunks, then indicated with a Gallic shrug of his shoulders that *les Anglais* should climb up amongst them.

The plodding horse clip-clopped down a long straight road striped by the shadows of trees. The creaking cart swayed and jolted. It was hardly a dignified way to travel. Positively medieval. There was also a certain smell, suspiciously like dung. But what else could one expect in a country like France where the food was inedible (no boiled beef), the currency ridiculous, the railways abominable, and the people — well, where did one begin? They were completely perfidious. They even professed not to understand their own language — at least, they did when he spoke it to them. Dorothea, on the other hand, hobnobbed with the locals at every opportunity, and the greasy, sneaky so-and-sos buttered her up by pretending they understood every word of her execrable nursery French.

There was only one person who looked to be enjoying the ride even less than him and that was the maid, Turner. Mother had insisted on a maid for the girls, rightly suspicious of Continental ways. But Turner looked as if she was wishing that anyone had been chosen rather than her — and no wonder, what with the heat and the stink and the flies.

Turner, thought Roderick, watching her from under the peak of his hat. *Our Daisy*, as the stable boy had called her: Billy Turner's younger sister. She liked her own space, he'd said. But she lived in some tiny little hovel in the village (*a cottage*, Dorothea called it). What were they like, hovel-girls?

She was English, which was something. But she wasn't exactly pretty — not in this mood with a face like sour milk. She was different from that other maid, Hobson, the one he'd caught dallying with Nibs Carter. Funny how that had stuck in his mind, the way Hobson had giggled and fluttered her eyelashes, the way Carter had put his impertinent arm round her as if—

Roderick with an effort tore his gaze from the miserable maid, sat up, looked round. They were coming to a village at last — or what passed for a village in these parts: a few ramshackle buildings that looked like they'd been thrown up around the time of the Hundred Years War, and a stumpy church of that foreign religion they all practised over here.

The former governess, it transpired, lived at this near end of the village. Gates in a high brick wall opened onto a yard. There was a rickety barn to the left, another high wall to the right, and straight ahead a house. It wasn't too peasant-like if hardly luxurious. Chickens were roaming in the yard, pecking in the dirt right up to the steps of the porch. Here the crusty cart man deposited them, luggage and all, before turning his horse round and clopping off. The wooden gates banged shut. They had arrived.

Mlle Lacroix appeared on the porch to greet them. She looked at first sight the same as ever: tall, slim, her hair up. On closer inspection, however, one could see flecks of grey in that hair and there were one or two more lines on her face than before. Four years had passed, after all, since she left Clifton.

Mlle Lacroix embraced Dorothea, insisted on embracing Roderick too. One didn't exactly appreciate it. She kissed Eliza, kissed the maid, Turner. 'You are so very like your dear sister!' Turner did not look best pleased about *that*.

After being shown to their rooms (passable), having a wash (there was clean water: hot no less) and getting changed, they gathered on the cool shady veranda at the back of the house. It overlooked a garden wilderness. Roderick glimpsed a swing between the trees but there was no sign of a summerhouse.

'Tea is ready!' Mlle Lacroix emerged carrying a tray. 'See how I keep up my English habits!'

'Civilisation comes to Jeancourt,' muttered Roderick. Dorothea gave him a look.

'And so, *mes amies,* how do you like *la belle France*? You have been to Paris, I think? So exciting! It is so long since I was there!'

'It was only a brief visit,' said Dorothea, 'but we saw Notre Dame and the Eiffel Tower.'

'A load of scrap metal bolted together,' scoffed Roderick.

Mlle Lacroix laughed. 'I remember your sense of humour, *Monsieur*!'

He attempted a smile, rather thought he'd failed, but the governess didn't seem to notice, too busy talking in that sing-song voice that had once been so familiar. She'd always given herself airs, Roderick was reminded: she'd always been insufferably self-contained and had not seemed to realise that she was one of the servants.

Balancing his cup and saucer on his knee, Roderick found he was listening despite himself. Mlle Lacroix lived in this backwater with her *maman* and her brother Gabriel, a law student. Maman had been poorly of late, bedridden. The brother had been called away to stay with acquaintances who might later prove useful in his career.

If the brother was still a student, thought Roderick, then he must be a good deal younger than his sister. But how old *was* Mlle Lacroix? Younger than Mother. Of a similar age to Aldora Harrington-Shaw, perhaps? And yet so very different! An old-maidish sort of woman though not entirely faded. It was odd. One had, in the old days, always thought of her as a governess, never as a woman. One had become rather curious recently about women — about how old they were and . . . well . . . everything.

She caught his eye just then, as if she was aware of his thoughts. He was furious to feel his cheeks start glowing.

She clapped her hands together. '*Alors*! Here we are, all together again! What fun we shall have these next weeks!'

Weeks, thought Roderick. Two whole weeks in the back of beyond. He would surely die of boredom — if Mlle Lacroix did not talk him to death first.

* * *

The time passed tolerably quickly as it turned out. There was the village to explore and the surrounding hills and woods. Picnics were taken into the meadows, there were expeditions in the dung cart and further afield by train. A helpful neighbour kept an eye on Maman. Mlle Lacroix had more facts and figures at her fingertips than a Baedeker. In Varenne, they saw the grocer's shop where the King and Queen of France had been arrested in 1791 as they tried to flee the revolution. At Verdun, they saw Vauban's great fortress and heard the story of the commander in the revolutionary wars who had committed suicide rather than surrender to the enemy. Roderick would have preferred to hear less about the Queen of France's jewels and more about the guillotine which chopped off her head, and as for the suicidal commander, his death seemed pointlessly quixotic.

Mlle Lacroix also kept abreast of events in England: the election in January, the death of the King, the furore over the People's Budget.

'Monsieur Asquith, Monsieur Lloyd George, I think they try to help the poor with their pension for old people, yes?'

'We shall all be poor if that pair of rogues have their way.'

'Oh, *Monsieur*, you are so *drôle*! But tell me, all of you, about Clifton Park! Ah, how I miss it, the village too! How are Dr Camborne and Lady Fitzwilliam and Henri with his motor cars?'

Roderick glanced at Dorothea at this point, but she showed no signs of being perturbed at the mention of Fitzwilliam's name.

'Madame Bourne, how is she? And Monsieur Ordish, so very *effacé*! Tell me of Monsieur Becket and his vegetables, and those great friends Nanny and Cook: do they still sip the cooking sherry in the kitchen and sample wine from the cellar?' Mlle Lacroix laughed at their expressions. 'Oh la la! You did not know?'

Roderick called it sly — sly and sneaky — sitting back and seeing everything yet saying nothing: nothing to the point, that was, for Mlle Lacroix never seemed to tire of the sound of her own voice. Every piece of furniture in the house — every picture, ornament and trinket — seemed to have some tale attached, from the mysterious gold locket with the stranger's likeness to the escritoire which Gabriel had won in a bet. There were photographs to look at too: the elusive Gabriel (so handsome, said Dorothea; rather po-faced, thought Roderick); a younger, healthy Maman; a whiskered gentleman standing next to what looked like a giant picnic basket.

'*Mon père*,' said Mlle Lacroix. 'He died when I was sixteen.'

'And this?' Eliza pointed to the basket.

'It is a balloon, *ma petite*! *Mon père* as a young man lived in Paris. When the war came, Paris was besieged by the Prussians. People grew hungry. They ate rats. There was only one way of escape. Can you guess?'

'In a balloon!'

'That is correct, Eliza. But it was dangerous! The wind might take the balloon out to sea or straight into the arms of the Prussians! *Mom père*, he was lucky. He came to Belgium and he was safe.'

After the war, *mon père* had married Maman and decided that he wanted to live off the land. He had purchased this house together with a smallholding. Now only the house remained, the land being rented to a local farmer. And so the tales went on and on, interminably.

Eliza was much taken with the anecdote about the balloon: a rather far-fetched story in Roderick's opinion. But he had no objections to helping Eliza make model balloons. He was particularly proud of one with a real fire in the gondola — until, that was, the whole thing caught fire and went floating out over the roof tops, nearly setting half the village alight. Dorothea put a stop to balloon making after that.

* * *

Roderick stood at the window of his room, yawning and scratching his head. Their two weeks at Jeancourt were nearly up. The weather had continued hot the whole time. Now, the last night but one, it was too sultry to sleep. The garden was all in darkness. There was a smell of dry earth and chickens. Next to the window was a drainpipe. He'd always wanted to shinny down a drainpipe, the way heroes did in books. Here was his chance. Anything was better than lying awake with his head full of French history and faded photographs and incendiary balloons.

He pulled on his trousers, dropped his boots out of the window, climbed down the drainpipe. It was very old and very rusty. The rust got all over his hands. The heroes in books never had this problem, he thought ruefully as he pulled on his boots.

The garden felt like a neglected hothouse tonight, as if one was encased in glass walls, the dark French countryside securely shut out. He soon discovered that he was not the only one up at this hour. He saw a glimmer of light, heard a murmur of voices, Dorothea and the Frenchwoman. Making his way silently, stealthily, he peered out from the bushes. Mlle Lacroix in a long, shapeless robe was sitting on the swing, Dorothea in her dressing gown leaning against one of the uprights. A lantern hung from the cross bar.

Roderick's eyes lingered for a moment on the Frenchwoman. She looked different with her hair down, less prim and proper, yet somehow still aloof. Not cold or stand-offish: it was as if she wasn't quite human, as if she was a supernatural spirit of the woods, a dryad, ageless, virginal. But there was also a brittleness about her which one never noticed in the daylight, which seemed to show up in the feeble glow of the lamp. So many different facets to a woman who at first sight seemed so dull! How odd women were, so very unalike each other, and so far-removed from men that they might have been a different species.

He became aware that they were talking about Henry Fitzwilliam. Roderick's ears pricked up.

'He was, I think, always a little in love with you, Dorossea. The seed was planted when you were a little girl. It sprouted, grew and blossomed.'

'But what *is* love, Mam'zelle?'

'If you do not know, then you have not yet felt it, *ma petite*. It is as it is.'

'And . . . and you, Mam'zelle? Have you ever . . . ?'

'Once, long ago. He was . . . he said . . . Ah, but it doesn't matter now. I had Maman, and Gabriel was but a child, and *mon père* had passed away. It was impossible.'

'Oh, Mam'zelle, how sad, I'm so sorry!'

'*Alors*. It is in the past. Forgotten. Poor Henri too will forget by and by. He will be unhappy for a time but it will pass.'

'And will I . . . will I ever . . . ?'

'You are, I think, a girl assured of love, Dorossea. But no one can say when love will come. When it is least expected. Sooner, perhaps, than you think.'

What rot they talked, thought Roderick listening in the shadows. All this rubbish about love, about it growing and blossoming as if it was some delicate flower. It wasn't. It was more like a weed. It grew where it wasn't wanted, it flourished despite one's efforts, its roots went deep. Or was that lust, not love?

If you do not know, then you have not yet felt it . . .

Dorothea was saying goodnight now, kissing the mam'zelle's cheek, taking her leave. The governess remained. Roderick watched her swaying gently on the swing, resenting her, jealous. But he couldn't take her place, he couldn't talk to Dorothea about love: that was the devil of it. One had to share Dorothea with so many different people. It was intolerable!

He took a last look at the mam'zelle on her swing, feet dangling, pale hands gripping the chains, dreaming perhaps of the man who once had wanted to marry her (what had she looked like in those days?). But as he turned to go, her sing-song voice rang out, making him jump.

'Oh, *Monsieur*! Will you not stay and talk to me for a while?'

He felt as if he'd been wrong-footed. He stepped from the bushes at a disadvantage dressed only in his flimsy night shirt with the collar open and his trousers with the braces dangling. His hand went up automatically to smooth his hair.

'How long have you known I was there?' he challenged her.

She laughed, did not answer his question. 'I saw you lurking, *Monsieur*, like *un loup* in the woods. What is the word, *un loup*?'

'A wolf.'

'Ah yes, a wolf. See, Monsieur, how quickly I forget my English!'

'I don't suppose you have much call for it in this backwater.' He scowled. 'What do you mean, anyway, by calling me a wolf?'

She sidestepped the question once more. 'You thought perhaps we were talking about you, *Monsieur*? You wanted to hear what we say?'

'But it wasn't about me! It was all *poor Henri*!'

'Ah yes. Poor Henri. All this time his mother think him immune to the charms of women. He would not look at Miss Somersby.'

'Old horse-features.'

'Oh, *Monsieur*! So cruel! A cruel and heartless wolf!'

'Fitzwilliam had a cheek, asking Doro to marry him!'

'He was not immune after all, you see. I think all along he was waiting for Dorossea. Perhaps he did not even realise in the beginning. It is easy, I think, to fall in love with Dorossea.'

'What do you mean by that? You needn't talk to me as if I was a kid! I'm not a kid! I'm eighteen! You are more of a child than I am!'

He was not sure what made him say this last bit but it seemed as if he might have struck a nerve. Her smile faded. There was something like a look of doubt in her eyes.

He pressed home what he took to be his advantage. 'You know nothing about me, Mam'zelle. You were never *my* governess. I'm not a fool. I'm not naive. I'm not *innocent*.'

He'd meant to boast, he'd meant to show her that he was a man of the world, but somehow his words sounded like a confession. What if she took more from his words than he'd intended?

'You are right, of course, *Monsieur*. You were away so often at school; so much of your life was lived elsewhere. We knew nothing about it, Dorossea and I — Madame too, and Monsieur. Poor Monsieur! It is a sad loss! You are very like Monsieur, I think, to look at. In spirit you are more like Madame. How tall you have grown! How strong and fierce you have become! Such a dangerous wolf! And so pleasing to look at. You will be much admired, I think. Women will notice you. But take care, *Monsieur*! Remember that your body is a temple which belongs to God.'

'Oh yes, your precious *Dieu*!' Her estimation of him was rather disconcerting. He covered his feeling of unease by going on the attack. 'What has *Dieu* ever done for you, Mam'zelle? After all these years, you are back here, back where you started!'

'This is true. And it is so often the way. Women get left behind. Women must do the work that men do not care to do. Who else would look after *Maman* but me?' She shot him a keen glance. 'You are, I think, a little afraid of women, *Monsieur*, no?'

'Afraid? What rot! I'm not afraid of *anything*!'

This sounded rather too much like a boyish boast. There was more he could have said on the matter, much more, but at that moment a tremulous voice came floating faintly from the direction of the house.

'Francine? Où et tu, Francine?'

Mlle Lacroix sighed. 'Maman.' As she stepped off the swing, a look of intense weariness briefly crossed her face. 'Maman requires attention at night as well as in the day.'

He saw her for a second as a slave, shackled to her home, at Maman's beck and call, doing the work that men did not want to do. He'd been angry with her, he'd resented her, but now — well, he felt differently, somehow, seeing yet another facet to her.

'Your name is Francine. I . . . I never knew that.'

'Did you not? *Incroyable!*' Laughter returned as she unhooked the lantern. 'But that is how it is, *Monsieur*. There is always something new to learn even about those people we think we know. Well, *bon nuit*, my brave, my fearless wolf!'

Her laughter and the light of the lantern slowly faded as she walked away through the trees. Shadows closed in around him.

He sat down on the swing with a profound sense of dissatisfaction. What was it about her? It was as if she held up a mirror and one saw a reflection of oneself. She held up a mirror, said nothing, smiled. It made one's blood run cold.

Was she really a slave? Did she *feel* like a slave? What about Dorothea? Did she feel that way, too? Dorothea never travelled much — to Lawham now and again, to London once in a blue moon — whereas for him there was school, there were visits to friends, there was Oxford to come.

He kicked off his boots, swaying on the swing, dragging his toes through the grass. He felt anxious about Oxford. He felt sudden nostalgia for school. He had three terms left but already it seemed as if the place was slipping away from him. The grey buildings, the leaky roofs, the windows which wouldn't shut, the desks that were falling to pieces, the draughty rooms, the cold baths, the stink of the earth-and-bucket latrines, the interminable divine services: all these things seemed indescribably precious.

He sighed, dug his heels into the dry earth, stopped the swing. Jumping down, picking up his boots, he made his way slowly back to the house.

* * *

The weather broke as they journeyed into Switzerland. The hot, dry spell came to an abrupt end. Clouds swirled in a sullen grey sky, rain came down in sheets. Against this backdrop, the mountains looked even more dramatic, rearing up into craggy mist-shrouded ridges and bitter, stony peaks, snow capping the tallest. The lower slopes were pine clad.

Lower still there were narrow green valleys, meandering rivers, picturesque villages, the clang of church bells.

Mrs Somersby had known just the place they could stay: a *Gasthaus*, she called it. Mother had felt it necessary to consult Mrs Somersby, the local expert on all things exotic (a Continental holiday in Mother's eyes was wildly exotic). The *Gasthaus*, Mrs Somersby had explained, was a place her son Mark used whenever he went climbing. Being near the Rhône valley, it was convenient both for Geneva and for the Matterhorn. Mark had climbed the Matterhorn on several occasions. Perhaps Roderick might consider it too?

Roderick had asked himself if Mark Somersby's climbing had been fitted in before or after winning the South African War single-handed. But all he had said out loud was that he'd heard the Matterhorn was old hat these days and that everyone was now climbing Monte Rosa instead.

The famous *Gasthaus* or pension, 'so perfect and convenient', was just outside the village of Anderdorf on the western slopes of a tributary valley. There was a cart to take them and their luggage up from the station. It was a good, sturdy cart, scrubbed clean. It did not smell of manure. Roderick was dubious about the *Gasthaus*, however. Wood was all very well for a garden shed, but he didn't think it entirely suitable for human habitation. The place was crawling with people, too.

'Oh, Roddy, there's hardly anyone here!' said Dorothea. 'Apart from the four of us' — she counted the maid Turner as one of 'us', naturally — 'there's only the Frenchman and his wife, the two German gentlemen and—'

'Are they Prussians?' asked Eliza. 'Are the German gentlemen Prussians like the ones that besieged Paris and made the people eat rats?'

'They'll be arrogant,' said Roderick. 'All Teutons are arrogant.'

But the elder Herr Kaufmann — he was in his early thirties, perhaps — showed no immediate signs of arrogance. Indeed, he soon proved a most useful acquaintance. Roderick was determined to do some climbing if only to rub Mrs

Somersby's nose in it later, and Herr Kaufmann knew about the clothes and equipment one needed, how to hire guides, and which climbs to attempt. He was in need of a companion, too, as his cousin — the younger Herr Kaufmann — was convalescent and forbidden any strenuous activity.

Roderick was eager to tackle the Matterhorn.

'Perhaps we will start with something a little easier, yes?' said Herr Kaufmann.

'If you say so, old chap.' But the Matterhorn remained his goal. Anything Mark Somersby could do, Roderick Brannan could do just as well, if not better.

* * *

As soon as the weather improved, Roderick and Heinrich — they soon got on to first name terms if only to avoid confusion between the two Herr Kaufmanns — set about their climbing itinerary. It wasn't long before Roderick forgot all about trying to outdo Mark Somersby. He was enjoying himself too much to bother about that. The wild terrain was like nothing he had known. There were fragrant woods, slopes of scree, sombre cliffs of weathered rock, sudden alarming crevices, and mountain peaks thrust up into the blue sky like gnarled knees or pointed horns. Unexpected waterfalls plunged wildly over worn lips of rock. Snow lingered in remote and shady cols. Green valleys glimmered impossibly far below. The tinkling bells of goats grazing on high pastures barely scratched the deep silence. Tanned goatherds grinned from under shapeless felt hats like boys who'd stepped from an older, more rustic, more honest world. Roderick had acquired sturdy boots, a knapsack, and a walking stick called an *alpenstock*. He was happy to follow Heinrich and the tireless guides for hours at a time with no idea where he was going. Once or twice they stayed overnight in chalets and mountain huts of wood or slabs of grey stone. Tired, aching, hungry, Roderick stretched by the fire eating stew and goats' cheese and strange-tasting bread, listening to Heinrich and the guides gabbing away in German. Most of the conversations went over his head despite Heinrich's halting translations. Sometimes it felt like school: the spartan existence, the absence of perturbing females. But it was better than school, for they were competing against the elements, not each other. Heinrich, though more experienced, did not pull rank or put on airs; and Roderick did not feel the need to show him up or put him in his place.

Most of the time there was too much going on, too much to take in, to bother with thinking. But whenever he did snatch a moment for quiet reflection he felt that this — *this* — was how life really should be lived.

* * *

Returning to the *Gasthaus* late one afternoon after the longest expedition yet (two days away), Roderick — washed and changed and pleasurably weary — went down to the balcony where he found Dorothea sitting alone, reading. She smiled at him and returned to her book. He leant on the balustrade. It felt right, this silence between them: not empty but full of promise. Why rush to fill it? They had all the time in the world.

He gazed at the view. The cottages — chalets — in the village below looked like dolls' houses from this distance. The deep valley was sunk in shadow, but sunlight lingered on the upper slopes opposite, the rock faces stained red and gold. The air was cool and completely still. He could hear, remote but clear, the sound of water trickling, the bleating of goats, a distant bell clanging.

'A magical place.'

He looked round at the sound of her voice. Dorothea had joined him. They were the only people on the balcony.

He smiled at her eagerly. 'Magical is just the word! So you feel it too! Doro, you should come with us, come climbing, up to those places over there where the sun is still shining. It's even more magical up there.'

'I'm quite happy here, nice and safe.'

'You'd be safe with me.'

'Until you decided to haul yourself up some cliff by your fingertips, or went running like a goat along an inch-wide path.'

'Are you calling me a goat?'

'I've called you worse.'

'Perhaps I deserved it.' He looked round. 'Where is the child?'

'In bed.'

'Not ill, is she?'

'Asleep.'

'At this hour?'

'It's the mountain air. It tires her out. That, and long walks in the sunshine. We're not exactly idle down here either, you know.'

He turned, leaning back against the balustrade. Dorothea's book lay abandoned on her chair.

'What are you reading?'

'Voltaire.'

'Voltaire!' He looked at her in astonishment. 'What on earth do you want with Voltaire? Or is that the mountain air too?' He went across and picked up the book. Flicking through it, he saw that it was in French. What swagger, reading Voltaire in the original French! 'One of the mam'zelle's books, I presume?'

'No.' She looked a little sheepish, he felt. 'Actually, Johann leant it to me.'

For a moment he was at a loss. Then he remembered. 'Oh, you mean the younger Herr Kaufmann, the pale convalescent. But this is in French, not German.'

'Johann speaks French and English, as well as German.'

'I'm surprised to learn that he speaks at all. Never deigns to, usually.'

'He's just a little shy, that's all.'

'Teutonic arrogance.'

'Johann is *not* arrogant!' She snatched the book out of his hand. 'Johann only speaks when he's got something worth saying — unlike some people I could mention!'

He watched perplexed as she swept off in a huff. What had he said this time?

Johann, he said to himself. Not *Herr Kaufmann*.

His suspicions were aroused. Perhaps it was time he started taking an interest in young Herr Kaufmann.

* * *

Roderick at dinner studied Johann Kaufmann whom he had not taken much notice of previously. The younger of the two German cousins was perhaps twenty-one or -two, looked rather pale and thin after his recent illness, a weedy specimen. What was it about him that Dorothea found so fascinating? One could at a pinch — using the language of Westaway's poets — describe his hair as the colour of ripe corn and his eyes as blue as the Alpine sky, but did that add up to his being handsome? What *was* it that made a chap handsome? What did girls look for? Roderick remembered that the French mam'zelle had said he would be *much admired*. But when it came to Dorothea he didn't want to be *admired*; he simply didn't want to be ignored.

After dinner Heinrich excused himself, went off to write a letter to his wife back in Hamburg. Roderick joined Dorothea and Johann by the fire in the sitting room. There were no other guests around. It was all very cosy, thought Roderick. Must have been cosier still when he'd been absent, sleeping in a hut half way up a mountain. What had Dorothea and Johann been doing on all those evenings alone? Speaking French? Discussing Voltaire?

Roderick couldn't shake the uneasy feeling that he'd been neglecting his duties. His sister and his cousin were in his care. He was their chaperone. It was time he started acting like one.

He watched the German distrustfully, casting round for a suitable opening. What was it the French mam'zelle had said about Alsace and Lorraine? These provinces had been taken from France by force of arms. The French people would not forget.

Johann Kaufmann did not seem in the least put out when the subject was raised. 'These are lands where Germans are living. The names of the towns are German: Metz, Strassburg, Mulhausen. It is only right that such places are part of the *Reich*. But we have only taken the German parts: all of Elsass, but only half of Lothringen.'

'The French tell a different story, old fellow. No doubt there'll be another war over it sooner or later.'

'I do not think so, Herr Brannan. In ten, twenty years it will all be forgotten. For instance, Germany is now the ally of Österreich, but Königgrätz was only four years before Sedan.'

Why did the fellow have to be so damned serious about it? Who or what were Königgrätz and Sedan? Roderick considered bringing Turkey into it. Everyone knew that the Germans wanted to get their hands on Turkey. But then he caught Dorothea glaring at him and thought better of it.

Johann did not sit with them for long. He was tired, he said: still recovering from his recent illness. No sooner had he gone than Dorothea burst out, 'How dare you, Roddy! How dare you be so rude!'

'What? I don't see what I've done. I wasn't making it up. You were there when your precious mam'zelle told us all about Alsace and Lorraine and the Prussian War and her father eating rats. In any case, it's obvious to anyone the Germans are out for everything they can get. Look at the Baghdad railway!'

'You don't know the first thing about the Baghdad railway! As for Alsace and Lorraine — well, it's not as straightforward as it seems. Johann says—'

'*Johann says, Johann says.*'

His tone was rather more sneering than he'd expected. He couldn't understand why they were both getting so hot under the collar over someone as puny and insignificant as Johann Kaufmann.

Dorothea's eyes were blazing. 'Why must you be so rude, so horrible—'

'There's no need to bite my head off. I don't see that it makes any difference to you if I'm rude to some filthy sausage-eater.'

'He's not well. I . . . I feel sorry for him. I know what it's like to be ill. I had diphtheria once, if you remember.'

'Your little friend is so delicate a sneeze would finish him off, never mind diphtheria.'

'How can you say something like that? How can you be so cruel, after what happened to Richard?'

'Richard?' His cousin Richard, Uncle Fred's ailing son. 'Good Lord, what's Richard got to do with anything? I haven't thought about Richard in ages.' Not since Lench's Latin class three years ago.

But this was the wrong thing to say, obviously. She gave him such a look of contempt he was nearly knocked out of his chair. By the time he'd recovered his composure, she'd gone. He was alone.

Twice in one evening, he said to himself. She'd stormed off first on the balcony, now here in the sitting room. He stared at the glowing fire and the pile of sawn logs next to it. What was it about that German boy that made her so touchy? This would need careful watching. Mother would never forgive him if anything untoward happened. There could be no more gallivanting up mountains. A pity, but there it was: some things were too important to be ignored.

* * *

When next morning Heinrich Kaufmann suggested a new expedition, Roderick cried off, citing a sprained ankle — a spur-of-the-moment excuse which he soon came to regret: he had to hobble whenever Heinrich was around and it was a devil of a job trying to remember which ankle was supposed to be the injured one. But this was neither here nor there. He was free now to keep a close eye on Dorothea. And with Heinrich at a loose end too, the German cousins spent more time together leaving Johann less opportunity for getting Dorothea alone.

Everything was working out well. The day of departure grew steadily nearer. And then Eliza decided to do a disappearing act.

The first Roderick knew about it was when the maid, Turner, came to him on the balcony in tears with some story about Eliza going off to pick flowers.

'I told her no, sir, I told her it was too far — she wanted to go to the high meadow, see, and it's *miles* — but she must have gone anyway because I've looked all over and I can't find her nowhere and it's been *hours* now, sir, hours and hours, and I'm sure she's done it just to spite me!'

Roderick rolled his eyes. Girls! They were impossible, more trouble than they were worth, he'd been right about that all along. It was enough to drive a fellow out of his mind, Dorothea consorting with foreigners, Eliza running wild, and now Turner weeping and wailing and showing him up in front of several of the other guests.

'Stop snivelling!' he hissed. 'That won't help! You've only yourself to blame if Eliza falls off a cliff or drops down a crevice!'

'Oh, sir . . . oh, Master Roderick . . . oh, oh, oh!' Tears were streaming down her face, her nose was running, she looked quite repulsive. But something stirred within him. She was a girl in his care, a proper English girl — Billy Turner's sister at that. A fellow mustn't shirk his duty.

He was reaching for his handkerchief, he was trying to summon some words of comfort, when Dorothea appeared on the balcony.

'Whatever's going on? What have you said to Daisy?' She put her arm round the maid, faced up to him. 'How dare you shout at Daisy! You're nothing but a bully! You should be ashamed of yourself!'

He tried to explain but she was in no mood for listening and all the while Turner was sobbing and whimpering in the background. The Frenchman and his wife, and one or two others, had been watching all this with great interest. Now other guests began to appear, the two Germans amongst them.

Heinrich took charge with typical Teutonic high-handedness (it was funny how one could go off a chap). An air of excitement swept through the normally placid *Gasthaus*. Turner was mollified and sent to lie down. Search parties were despatched to look for Eliza. Roderick with his 'injured' ankle was not expected to join them. In any case, he was not really worried. Eliza, though rather soft in the head, was not stupid — not stupid enough to fall down a crevice, anyway. But as he watched the search parties dwindling into the distance, he realised that he'd lost track of Dorothea. She had not gone with the search parties, so where was she?

He went first to Turner's attic bedroom but the maid was alone and fast asleep. Not as upset as all that, then. Going back down, he headed for Dorothea's room. The door was ajar. He could hear voices. Peeking inside, he saw Dorothea sitting on the edge of her bed, Johann Kaufmann sitting next to her. The arrogant young Teuton was even holding her hand! Roderick's blood boiled, but he stepped back. It was no good barging in like a bull in a china shop.

He kept out of sight behind the doorpost, listening. He heard the name *Richard*. So that was it. She was telling that snub-nosed sausage-eater all about Richard. Why? Richard was dead. He'd been dead nearly six years.

'I think of death in this way, Fraulein Ryan: it is like someone leaving the room. That is how I think of *Mutti*, that she is in some other room, some other place.'

'Oh Johann — your mother — I didn't know! When did she—?'

'Since many years, Fraulein Ryan. She was killed by cholera. That was when I decided to become a doctor. When I am qualified, I will be able to save others, even though I could not save Mutti.'

It was enough to make one sick, Mutti this and Mutti that, whispering in Dorothea's ear like a pious priest. And what was he saying now? Some trumped-up tale about his mother's name being Dorota: a likely story! Worming his way in, that was what *he* was doing.

Roderick could not stay to hear more. Someone was calling for him. He made his way downstairs. The search parties had returned. Eliza had been found. She was standing on the front steps looking very pleased with herself, enjoying all the fuss. Roderick waded in. Showing him up in front of all these foreigners: he'd make her pay!

But this was Eliza, not Turner. Eliza did not burst into tears. She turned red with fury instead.

'I am *not* disobedient or naughty or any of those other things you said! I did *not* run away, I only went to pick some flowers! I don't see why I shouldn't pick flowers if I want to. I don't care if you forbid it or not. I don't care about you at all. I hate you.'

And with that she ran off, leaving him in the centre of a staring crowd. He laughed. Little sisters: what could one do with them! But wasn't it getting a bit chilly out here? They should all go indoors, get in front of the fire.

As he climbed the steps side-by-side with Heinrich, the German said, 'Your ankle is better now, I think, Herr Brannan?'

'So it is. Clever of you to notice. Can't have been as bad as I thought.'

* * *

In the corridor on his way down to dinner, Roderick bumped into Dorothea. He grabbed her wrist before she could get away.

'You shouldn't talk so freely to that sausage-eater.'

'I shall talk to whomever I like. Let go of me, Roddy!'

'He's a foreigner and a fraud. He'll probably die of consumption in any case.'

'You're hurting me!' With an almighty effort, she wrenched her arm away from his grip. 'I never realised you could be so *despicable*. I *hate* you.'

She went running back the way she had come, slamming the door of her room.

Roderick stared after her. 'So you hate me, too. Aren't I the lucky one.'

But when he took his place at dinner he found that, for the first time since arriving in Switzerland, he had lost his appetite.

* * *

Eliza knelt on her seat in the train, waving goodbye to the mountains. The Matterhorn had gone unconquered, Monte Rosa too, but Roderick had no regrets about leaving them behind if it meant leaving the Herr Kaufmanns as well.

Eliza sighed as the mountains slipped out of view. She sat down next to Dorothea. 'I wish we could have stayed longer. I wish there were mountains in Northamptonshire. I wish—'

'You only get three wishes,' said Roderick. 'It's the same in every fairy story. You had best use your third wish wisely.'

'I wish . . . I wish . . . I wish needn't have left Herr Kaufmann and Herr Kaufmann behind! It feels like we've lost them and I liked them so much!'

Dorothea stirred. 'Johann has promised to write and I have his address.'

'Then we haven't lost them after all!' cried Eliza. 'How super, how lovely!'

Roderick looked at Dorothea through narrowed eyes. She wouldn't meet his gaze. She'd been avoiding him for days. They'd barely spoken since Eliza's disappearing act. She must think she'd been very clever, she must feel so very smug, outsmarting him and getting hold of that sausage-eater's address. What a pity Johann Kaufmann had not been strong enough for climbing. It would have been the work of a moment to push him off a precipice.

Roderick turned to the window, watched the rain falling, watched green fields passing in a blur. The gentle hills were half hidden by lowering clouds. The mountains seemed like a dream already. Dorothea would forgive him. She always did. And the holiday had not been *all* bad. He'd enjoyed the climbing. He'd enjoyed too a certain *Mädchen* from the village who'd spoken no word of English but who'd been very obliging in all sorts of ways and so sorry to see him go. But now, thinking about her as the train rattled along the rain-sodden valley of the Rhône towards Lake Geneva, he found that for the life of him he couldn't remember the girl's name.

* * *

Rain pursued them still as they set out on the last lap from Welby station. The motor purred up the drive. Clifton swung into view. It looked breathtaking, lit by an eerie light as dark clouds massed overhead while sunshine still glowed on the fields sloping down to the canal. Spots of rain were falling as they got out of the car. Mother was waiting on the doorstep, so eager was she to see them. Her smile was every bit as electrifying as the gathering storm.

Despite an early start that day and a tiring journey, Roderick when he went up to bed found he was unable to sleep. He got up, donned his leather slippers and his dressing gown, went downstairs. The house was in darkness, silent. But when he turned on the electric light in the drawing room, he found Dorothea sitting on the couch, lost in thought and still fully dressed.

He hesitated in the doorway. Here they were, alone together at midnight. She couldn't ignore him now. But would she have anything to say to him? And what was she thinking about, so solemn and pensive? But they were home now. Things would soon get back to normal.

As he poured himself a brandy, doubts assailed him. Would they really get back to normal? Would she forgive him this time? He'd never seen her as angry as that evening in the *Gasthaus*. She'd said that she hated him. She'd never said that before — at least, she'd never said it as if she *meant* it.

He cradled his glass. 'Doro, I . . .'

She looked up.

'I . . .' He swallowed. 'Do you want a drink?'

She nodded, surprising him. He poured brandy, held the glass out to her. She took hold of it. For a moment, he didn't let go.

'Write to him, if you want. Write to your German.'

'Thank you,' she said coldly. 'I shall. But I don't need your permission.' She wrenched the glass out of his hand, put it down at once beside her on the couch.

He retreated, sat down on the piano stool, miserable. Why did he get so angry around her? Why did he resent that German boy, and Richard too: why did he still resent Richard after all this time? It was silly, senseless, to wish things were different. She made friends, she made an effort. And people liked her, went out of their way for her: the servants, the villagers, everybody — even acquaintances met on the road. Dorothea wouldn't have been Dorothea if it had been any other way. And he wouldn't change her for the world. She knew that. Surely she knew that?

He sat hunched on the stool, staring down at his leather slippers. He'd never felt tongue-tied with her before. Things were not back to normal.

After a while she got up and left the room. Her brandy was left untouched.

He sighed. He wished he was back in the mountains. He wished he was sitting by the fire on some high Alpine meadow eating stew and strange bread, listening to Heinrich and the guides talking in low voices, their guttural German words indecipherable. He wished he could breathe clean, cold air and lie back on the dark grass and see the mountain peaks silhouetted against the night where stars were strewn in infinite number. He wished he could go to sleep listening to that deep mountain silence, a silence which had remained unbroken since the beginning of the world.

CHAPTER NINE

The Big Man's garden was teeming. Such a clamorous din could surely never have been heard before in this peaceful plot on the edge of the escarpment overlooking the distant, hazy valley. Roderick had found a breathing space in the greenhouse, was smoking a furtive cigarette as he looked out between a profusion of tomato plants at the wide lawn crammed with wooden chairs and with tables draped with white cloths. It was a day of excess, from the brilliant sunshine beating down out of a cloudless sky, to the endless cups and saucers, the great plates of sandwiches, the vast array of cakes. Musicians from the school orchestra were playing genteelly in one corner. A hundred conversations were going on at once. Snatches of talk hung on the hot, still air.

'. . . and his housemaster tells me he is doing very well . . .'

'. . . one simply couldn't move in town — the coronation, you know . . .'

'. . . my dear, this weather, positively tropical, and no end in sight . . .'

Tropical didn't do it justice by half, thought Roderick, wrinkling his nose. One was sweating profusely in all one's finery. But nothing could spoil today, this day of days, the very last day of all.

The devil of it was, time speeded up when the end came in sight, time went ever quicker the more you wanted to slow it down. Terms had once seemed interminable. Now they passed in the blink of an eye. No sooner had he returned to Downfield to start his final year than the final year was over. There'd been nothing he could do to halt the headlong march of time.

As he smoked, the Big Man's valedictory speech in the New Hall echoed in Roderick's head.

. . . and was it not Disraeli who said, 'Almost everything that is great has been done by youth'? Today, as we say farewell to so many of our boys, as we send them out at last into the world, we look forward with anticipation to all that they will achieve, the youth of Downfield . . .

Roderick had not slept a wink last night, waiting for the last day to come. He'd got up early in the clammy dawn. By the time he met Mother and Dorothea for breakfast at the White Hart, he'd been awake for hours.

. . . what great good fortune, then, to be born an Englishman, to have the honour of carrying out God's work across the greatest empire Man has ever known . . .

After breakfast, Roderick had paraded with the Corps on the Upper. They had been inspected and eulogised by the Big Man, their proud parents looking on. But the main event of the day had come after lunch: the concert and prize-giving in the New Hall which concluded with one of the Big Man's celebrated speeches.

. . . 'beware,' as it says in the Good Book, 'lest any man spoil you though philosophy and vain deceit.' Therefore be on your guard. Remember all that you have learned here. It will serve you well, I think. It will serve you well as you venture into the world . . .

The Big Man's voice had boomed out as he reached his peroration. It had filled the Hall, echoed from the vaulted ceiling. Row upon row of rapt faces had hung on his every word.

. . . and my final advice to you all — the best advice, I think, that anyone can ever give — is simply this: fear God, honour the King, and always do your best. God bless you all!

The applause had been thunderous. Then had come the opening bars of the School Song. The orchestra, the choir, the whole congregation had joined as one. A crescendo had been reached with the final thrilling verse:

For England and Almighty God
We march tall in the van;
Proudly let us each proclaim,
I am a Downfield man!

The last notes had faded. Utter silence had fallen. It was the end. Roderick had felt pain in his chest. He had fought to keep his composure.

Now, as he stubbed out his cigarette amongst the roots of the tomato plants, he felt that he'd already left the school behind. He was a Downfield man but no longer a part of Downfield. The cord had been cut.

He stepped out from the greenhouse into the blazing sunshine and sauntered across the lawn, weaving between the tables and chairs and the swarms of people. Boys clustered round him as if he was magnetic. This was what it meant to be popular.

'I say, Brannan,' said Benson, a rather nondescript inhabitant of the Upper Sixth, 'isn't that your sister over there? She's rather a stunner!'

'That's not my sister, Benson, you ass. It's my cousin, Miss Ryan.'

'She's on her own. Had we better not go over?'

'I shall go over, but not you, Benson, or you others.' One couldn't take just anyone to meet Dorothea. Roderick looked around. He espied a familiar face, solitary as ever. 'Westaway! Over here! Come and meet my cousin!' Patrick Westaway, he felt, was just the sort of chap Dorothea would approve of.

Westaway bowed and kissed her hand. He could get away with it, being an individual: it didn't seem like ostentation when it was Westaway. How was it that an oddball like Westaway could impress girls so easily? And yet he did — easily and effortlessly. Girls liked him. They warmed to him.

Dorothea was no different. 'I'm so pleased to meet you, Mr Westaway. You're the one who paints, is that right? And you read poetry.'

'I do, Miss Ryan. It's considered awfully antisocial. I'm ostracised and persecuted on account of it.'

'But didn't you win four prizes earlier?'

'That counts for nothing, I assure you.'

'Patrick is talking his usual rot, Doro. The whole house is very proud of his achievements. Well, I certainly am, anyway.'

'Tell me, Mr Westaway: is Roddy one of the boys who persecutes you?'

'He was something of a tyrant at one time, Miss Ryan, but he has improved with age. That will be your influence, I expect.'

'Oh, no. Roddy *never* takes any notice of *me*! He ended up a prefect, I believe. We at home expected him to be head of house, from all that he said.'

'That is something of a sore point, Miss Ryan. Perhaps we should talk instead about his triumph in the Cricket Cup. Ransom's Eleven won the Cricket Cup for the second year in a row. Your cousin was captain, leading from the front again.'

'Cricket bores me to tears, Mr Westaway.'

'And me, Miss Ryan.'

Roderick spoke up. 'I say, you two, I am still here, I am listening to every word!' They were poking fun, laughing at him. Yet oddly enough he didn't really mind, not today, not when it was Dorothea, not when it was Westaway.

He minded, though, about not being head of house. He minded even now, all these months later. It had more or less been promised him, he'd felt. Everyone had expected it. But he'd been passed over for an absolute plodder called Marchant.

Men are wretched creatures who would not keep their word to you.

Quoting Machiavelli, Westaway had said, was hardly good form. Such details added up, he'd argued. There was a feeling in certain circles that Roderick was *not quite one of us* (as Westaway had phrased it). Marchant, on the other hand, could be relied on not to rock the boat. Marchant was pure-blooded, too, his father something in government and his mother the daughter of a duke.

Roderick wondered if perhaps he'd never quite learned the rules of the game — that elusive game that Raynes had spoken of all those years ago in the head of house's study. Had he sailed at times too close to the wind while looking the other way? How much, for instance, had Raynes really known about that business with Martineau and the Petty Pilferer? And what exactly had Colonel Harding said to his old friend Teddy in their London club? Whatever the case, the upshot was clear. He, Roderick Brannan, stood here in the busy garden on the last day of all as the hero of the Cricket Cup, the captain of the house teams, a doyen of the First Eleven, but he was not head boy and he was *not quite one of us*.

Nor was he entirely back in Dorothea's good books, he admitted ruefully.

She was still talking to Patrick . . . 'Roddy's mother over there with your headmaster, Mr Westaway. What do you suppose he is telling her?'

'He is extolling your cousin to the hilt, you may be sure.'

'Aunt Eloise will enjoy that. She needs no convincing that Roddy is a hero.'

'And you, Miss Ryan? What do *you* think of him?'

But Dorothea did not say, merely smiled a mysterious smile.

Westaway took his leave. 'There's my father. I must go and speak to him again. I have been trying to persuade him that four school prizes go some way to making up for the fact that I never made the house teams. He is not yet convinced. It was a pleasure to meet you, Miss Ryan.'

Westaway bowed once more then walked away, threading through the crowd.

'You have the nicest friends,' Dorothea said.

'It just goes to show, I can't be all bad.'

‘No,’ she said, ‘not all bad.’ She smiled. This was a different sort of smile, a nice smile, a candid smile, a smile that one remembered. ‘We shall be glad to have you home. Eliza can’t wait.’

‘I have the OTC summer camp first. Then there’s that . . . that chap in Lincolnshire. I promised I’d pay a visit.’

‘Lincolnshire? I thought you said Bedford just now?’

‘Er, no, definitely Lincolnshire.’ He took her arm. She didn’t object. ‘Shall we join Mother?’

‘Yes, let’s. We can find out exactly what it is your headmaster’s been saying about you!’

* * *

Kicking his heels, Roderick looked out from the shade of the porch of the National Gallery, watching the traffic surging round Trafalgar Square, crowds seething on the pavements. People were baking and bad-tempered. The heat was never-ending. Far above the noise and hurly-burly, Nelson stood poised on his lofty column. A pigeon wheeled round his hat before gliding slowly down to take a perch on one of the window ledges of Morley’s Hotel.

As he mopped his brow, smoothed his hair, replaced his homburg, Roderick half-wished he was as remote and unreachable as Nelson. He half-wished he was at home where Mother would still be glowing from the Big Man’s report of him. Nobody knew he was here in London — nobody except *her*, Aldora Harrington-Shaw.

She had brushed against him as if by accident in the Big Man’s garden on the day of the farewell tea. She had not even looked at him as, under cover of the noise of the crowd and the sound of the music, she had murmured that she would be in town for a time and wouldn’t it be extraordinary if they happened to bump into each other by accident — outside the National Gallery, say, at two p.m., two weeks next Tuesday.

Why had he come? And why did he relish all this subterfuge? He couldn’t explain it. All he knew was that he had the audacity to be here.

But when he picked her out in the crowd on the pavement below, walking towards him, he experienced a moment of doubt, felt an almost overwhelming urge to duck behind one of the pillars and wait for her to pass.

He was furious with himself. This was no way for the hero of Downfield to behave, skulking like new boy — and with Nelson watching too! It would all have been for nothing, a wasted trip, if he funked it now.

He ran down the steps. She saw him and waved, smiling under her wide-brimmed hat. Heads turned to look at her. She was dazzling in the sunshine. He hastened towards her.

She took his arm, led him across the expanse of Trafalgar Square.

'Where are we going?'

'To the Hôtel Métropôle, darling. I have booked us rooms as mother and son. Clever of me, don't you think?'

'I shall have to call you "mater".'

'And I shall call you "darling", darling.' As they waited at the kerb for a gap in the traffic, she stroked very gently with a gloved finger the underside of his chin. 'I knew you would come. I knew you would come to me.'

* * *

Noise from Northumberland Avenue drifted in through the open window as Roderick sat up in bed and lit a cigarette. Beside him, Aldora stretched out luxuriously. He watched her out of the corner of his eye as he blew out smoke. She caressed his arm. Her well-manicured fingers rasped against his skin.

'You were very masterful, darling. You used to be so gentle.' She did not sound unduly disappointed — just the opposite, if anything. 'When you are at Oxford, we will be able to meet all the time.'

He scowled. This airless room, the heat of the afternoon, the dishevelled sheets (*the rank sweat of an unseamèd bed . . .*): it all seemed stifling, suffocating, somehow disheartening.

And now this talk of Oxford: why did that make him want to run, run, run?

'What is it, darling? What's wrong? You look so fierce.' She reached up to touch his face, running her fingers across his lips and up the line of his nose. 'When you frown, darling, your eyebrows meet in the middle just *here*.'

He shook her off, leaned across to flick ash into the ash tray on the bedside table. 'What would Humphrey say? What would Humphrey say if he could see us now? What would he do?'

She looked up at him, her hair spread across the pillow, her eyelashes dark against her pale skin. 'He would shoot you, I imagine,' she said mildly. Then, without warning, she shuddered and looked away. 'Let's not talk about Humphrey. He disgusts me, so old and wrinkled, falling asleep in front of the fire!'

'What, then, *shall* we talk about?'

'We must decide what we are going to do, how we shall spend these few days together.'

'I thought we would stay in bed. That *is* the point of all this, isn't it?'

'We can't stay in bed *all* of the time, darling. It's bad for one's complexion. Besides, I want to be out and about with you. I want people to notice us. It's quite safe to be noticed here, where nobody knows us. We could go to Hampton Court or Box Hill. There are coaches that leave from the hotel.'

Despite her words, she showed no sign of moving just yet. After a while, Roderick stubbed out his cigarette and swung his legs out of bed. As he reached for his long johns, he glanced down at her lying tangled with the sheets. One large breast was partly exposed. There was a sliver of areola like the sun in eclipse. But she looked plain and rather threadbare without her finery. She was so very different to the tender girl in Anderdorf.

'You won't be able to do this much longer, Aldora.'

'Do what, darling?'

He reached for his shirt. 'Play the regal harlot.'

'I am not sure I care to be called a *harlot.* It's not nice.'

'But that's how you see yourself, like Cleopatra with her eager young lovers.'

'There's just you, darling. Only you.'

'And the groom at Orsley.'

He paused in buttoning up his shirt to watch the words sink in. If she was surprised, she covered it well.

'How do you know about that?'

Stooping to pick up his tie, he did not answer.

'He was nothing, nobody, a mistake. He was not nice.' A touch of petulance came into her voice. 'He tried to blackmail me. He threatened to tell Humphrey. As if Humphrey would have believed the word of a man like that! I made Humphrey dismiss him.'

'How many others?' Roderick asked harshly, knotting his tie in the mirror.

'Others?' she murmured, stroking her own neck. 'Yes, there have been others. Why not? Why shouldn't I? Why must I live a cloistered life when so many men desire me? So many.' It was as if she was reciting the words of a well-worn story.

Roderick frowned into the mirror. (His eyebrows did *not* meet, that was a gross exaggeration). All those shopping trips. All those visits to Aunt Prudence. How long was it since H-S had discovered that Aunt Prudence had been dead for years? That had given even him pause for thought. But, being H-S, the thought had soon passed him by.

Roderick shrugged into his jacket, pocketed his loose change. 'You might as well cancel my room. I shan't be needing it.'

She struggled to sit up. 'But where are you going, darling? We've only just arrived!'

'I'm eighteen, Aldora. Eighteen. I should be with girls my own age.'

'Why would you want girls of that sort? You don't need anyone but me. I don't look my age. I don't look more than thirty. I can pass for twenty-five in the right light. Do stay, darling.'

'I'd really rather not, if it's all the same.'

As he opened the door, she called out, 'You'll come back, darling, I know you will.' She added as if to herself, 'They all come back in the end. They all come back to me.'

'I shan't,' Roderick muttered, closing the door behind him. 'I *shan't*.'

But out in the corridor he felt adrift. He was supposed to be in Lincolnshire. He wasn't expected home until the end of the week. He was alone in London with nowhere to go, nothing to do.

This was where his audacity had led him.

* * *

He was barely inside the front door when Eliza came flying down the stairs, scattering ribbons from her hair.

'You're back! You're back! Oh, Roddy, I'm so glad! You'll believe me, won't you? I know you'll believe me!'

She danced around him, enough to make him dizzy.

'Steady! Slow down!' He grabbed hold of her to keep her still. 'Now, tell me slowly and calmly: what's all this about?'

'About the ghost, of course.'

'What ghost?'

'The ghost I saw on the stairs. A white lady.'

'Are you sure it wasn't just a dream? What did she say, this ghost?'

'She wasn't a dream, she was real! But she didn't speak. She turned round — like *this* — and looked at me — like *that*.' Eliza shivered. 'I thought it was Mama at first, or Mrs Bourne, but then I realised . . .' Her eyes grew wide. 'No one else was awake. There was just me and *her* in the dark!'

'And just what were you doing, wandering around the house in the middle of the night?'

'It wasn't the middle of the night. It was almost dawn. I had to get up early so I could meet Johnnie Cheeseman and pick mushrooms. You have to pick them at first light, before the snakes eat them.'

Ghosts, mushrooms, snakes . . . Roderick shook his head, bemused.

In the nursery, Dorothea was sitting sewing.

'What-ho, Doro.' He did his best to act as if there'd never been any awkwardness between them. 'Do you believe in this ghost, then?'

'Eliza believes in it.' Dorothea didn't pause in her work. 'You are standing in my light.'

'Sorry.' He moved aside, shoved his hands in his pockets. 'What are you *doing*, anyway?'

'Mending Eliza's clothes.'

'There are servants for that sort of thing.'

'Eliza's clothes need so many repairs it seems unfair to leave it all to Daisy.'

'Where is Turner, anyway?'

Dorothea didn't answer his question, as if it was none of his business, as if he didn't belong, as if he was surplus to requirements.

'Why are you back so soon?' she asked. 'We expected you to stay in Lincolnshire until the end of the week at least.'

'Oh, well . . .' He shrugged.

She cocked an eye at him. 'I don't believe you went to Lincolnshire at all.'

'What rot!' He turned away, pretended to look out of the window, shoving his hands even deeper into his pockets. 'You do talk rot!' He could feel the colour flaring in his cheeks. He was an absolute fiend, bringing Aldora into the hallowed precincts of the nursery — even if she was only inside his head (she was still inside his head). He had a ridiculous urge to get down on his knees and beg Dorothea's forgiveness. Forgiveness for what? For Aldora, for Switzerland — for everything he'd ever done? But why should he apologise? He could do what he liked, he didn't need Dorothea's permission. He was glad he'd gone to London, he was glad he'd come away again, he was glad that nobody knew about it but him. He was glad, too, that he'd got Nibs Carter the sack, glad about Martineau and Moxon, glad of all those other things people blamed him for. He wasn't sorry in the least. He was fiercely unrepentant.

Staring between the bars on the window, he said challengingly, 'Alright, then. If I didn't go to Lincolnshire, where did I go?'

'Young Stan told me that you caught the train for London.'

'Smith the chauffeur, you mean? Well, you might tell Smith to mind his own business in future. And if you must know, one has to go to London in order to get a train to Lincolnshire. Welby to Euston, Euston to King's Cross, King's Cross to Lincoln.' He was not sure if this was entirely accurate — what about cross-country services? — but at least it *sounded* plausible.

Thankfully, before Dorothea could interrogate him further, Eliza interrupted them.

'Roddy, will you stay up all night and watch for the ghost?'

'Certainly not.'

'But *someone* must, and Mama says I mightn't.'

'Aunt Eloise disapproves of ghost hunting,' said Dorothea.

'What about mushroom picking?' asked Roderick.

'That too. But Aunt Eloise's disapproval did not deter Eliza. She put a hairbrush on her pillow so that she would keep waking up and not miss the time. As it happened, the ghost intervened before any mushrooms could be picked.'

'You're incorrigible, Eliza.' Roderick yawned, stretched. He felt it safe now to leave his station by the window. Dorothea's suspicions — if that was what they were — had been allayed, and he had nothing to feel repentant for: he was decided on that. A truce had been called. That was what if felt like. 'I suppose one ought to think about getting ready for dinner.'

'We have Lady Fitzwilliam and Colonel Harding this evening.'

'*Both* of them? Couldn't I be spared on my first evening back?' But oddly enough, the tedium of a Clifton dinner with guests was almost welcome by dint of its very normality.

He made his way to his room where he surprised a maid in the act of turning down the bedcovers and closing the curtains.

'Oh sir! You did give me a start!'

'What are you doing in here?' asked Roderick, removing his jacket and tie and staring at her.

She blushed. 'I'm sorry, sir. I'd be finished usually, but Sally's poorly and I've had to do all her work today as well as my own.'

She was edging towards the door, but he moved to block her way, memory stirring. 'Hobson, isn't it?'

'That's right, sir. But if you'll just let me pass, I've the other rooms to do.'

No time for dallying with Nibs Carter today. Was it true that the poor had loose morals?

She had a strand of hair hanging down. With one finger, he looped it up and tucked it inside her cap, then he stepped aside.

'Off you go.'

'Thank you sir,' she mumbled, and fled.

* * *

'Eliza has been telling me about her ghost,' said Roderick at dinner.

Mother sighed. 'Is she still persisting with that nonsense?'

'Ghosts?' boomed Colonel Harding. 'Don't believe in 'em! Load of old rubbish!'

'Quite right, sir.' Roderick added cunningly, 'I hear you've bought yourself a motor car, sir.'

'What's that? A motor? Who told you that? I've had Julian pestering me, Eileen too, but no child of mine will persuade me that motors are anything other than the work of the Devil. The Devil!' He banged his fork on the table.

'All the same,' said Lady Fitzwilliam mildly, 'one can't deny they are catching on. Even I use one since the floor of the carriage fell out. Of course, motoring is not as cheap as it was, with the new petrol tax and so on.'

'This government!' cried Colonel Harding. 'Taxing us out of hearth and home! Where will it all end, I want to know! People's Budget my eye! Lloyd George ought to be shot!'

Roderick began, 'Actually, I rather admire—', but Lady Fitzwilliam deftly interrupted, spoiling his fun.

'This is excellent pork, Eloise my dear.'

'I've been so lucky, Alice, in the matter of a new cook. Good cooks are usually so hard to find.' Mother cast a forbidding glance at Roderick before turning back to her guests. 'I had to let the previous cook go. A weakness for drink, I'm afraid. Rather remiss of Mrs Bourne never to have noticed.'

* * *

Eliza sat on the library floor surrounded by books. Roderick, on a stool, was searching through other books along a high shelf. They were looking for clues about the ghost — the White Lady, as Eliza had christened her.

'I don't think she was a *wicked* ghost,' Eliza said. 'She didn't mean to frighten me. There was no terrible warning. She just looked at me and *shimmered*, then she dissolved. Do you really think she might have lived here once upon a time?'

'Why else would she be haunting Clifton?' Roderick was dubious about the existence of the White Lady but encouraging Eliza's obsession irritated Mother and disrupted the routine of the nursery. It was one way of making his presence felt. He was, after all, the man of the house.

'Here. Try this.' He threw down a book from the self he was searching, a rather weighty volume, many of the pages still uncut. 'Yet another tome by the indefatigable Sir George. There may be some family history in it.'

'Who *was* Sir George, and why did he write so many books?'

'He was a Massingham, one of our ancestors.'

'But we are called Brannan.'

'That was Father's name. The Brannans never lived here. They have no family history.'

'Mama's name was Rycroft before she got married, not Massingham.'

'Mama's mother was a Massingham. The Massinghams lived here for hundreds of years right back to Tudor times, long before this house was built. Has Mother never told you any of this? I know it by heart.'

'Mama never tells me *anything*.' Flicking through the book that Roderick had thrown down, Eliza said, 'There are such a lot of Massinghams. They all have the same names. I get confused.'

'The writer of the books was the second Sir George, the fifth baronet and a Member of Parliament. He lived around the turn of the last century.' Roderick had once read in an encyclopaedia that Sir George's works had *met with overwhelming indifference and soon vanished into well-deserved obscurity*. It was a sobering thought. What would be written in encyclopaedias a hundred years hence about Roderick Henry Brannan?

'Roddy, do you think there will be lots of Brannans one day just as there were lots of Massinghams?'

'Of course. If you could see into the future, they'd all be lined up like Banquo's descendants.' Children: they were one way of achieving immortality. But to have heirs one would need to marry. The idea of marriage was too near the knuckle so soon after escaping Aldora's clutches. (But it hadn't been an *escape*, it had been a *denouement*: he must remember that.)

'In a hundred years' time,' said Eliza, 'there will be a hundred Brannans—' She was off on one of her flights of fancy. 'Everyone in the whole village will be a Brannan. There will be no room for anyone else. In a hundred years . . . Roddy? What's a hundred years *like*?'

'Let's see.' He looked down at her. 'How old are you now, kiddo?'

'Eleven years and nine months.'

'Well, then. Imagine you'd lived your whole life nine times over. That's a hundred years.'

She wrinkled her nose. 'I don't like to think about time. It makes my head ache.'

'Then don't think about it. Any luck?'

Eliza shook her head. 'This book is all about the Combination Acts. What are Combination Acts?'

'It was a Law that said everyone had to wear clean underclothes at least once a week.' Roderick jumped down from the stool, rubbed his hands together briskly. 'Enough of this idling. I'm off to Lawham to see my tailor. I need lots of new clothes for Oxford.'

Eliza scrambled to her feet. 'May I come?'

'If you can be ready in the blink of an eye.'

'I'll be quicker than that! Can Doro come too?'

'If she must.'

Eliza paused in the doorway. 'Oughtn't we to tidy up? Doro says one should always tidy up after oneself.'

'The servants can do it.'

'But what if Mama—'

'Mother never comes in here.'

'That's right. She doesn't. Why?'

Roderick shrugged. 'Don't ask me.' He took hold of Eliza's hand. 'Come on, kiddo. Let's go.'

* * *

Having completed his business with the tailor, Roderick sauntered along Lawham High Street in search of Dorothea and Eliza. The cattle market was in full swing on the main square. Calves watched with lugubrious eyes as he passed. Flies buzzed. The stink was revolting.

He found the girls on the grassy space behind the old school on the far side of Market Place. There were some crumbling ruins, all that was left of a medieval priory. He paused by the wooden gate, watching unseen. Eliza was galloping around in her usual breathless manner but Dorothea was sitting calm and composed on the stump of a long-fallen arch in the shade of an oak. There was a letter in her hand, a smile on her lips.

The Druids had worshipped oaks, he told himself. Perhaps they'd worshipped the very tree under which Dorothea was sitting. It must have been a sapling when the priory was built. It was still here now that the priory had gone. Some things endured far longer than Sir George's boring books.

Roderick shook his head. This was Eliza's fault, all her talk about time. Her mad ideas had a way of insinuating themselves. But the past was the past and the future could take care of itself. All he had to do for now was enjoy himself.

He opened the gate. Dorothea looked up, saw him, smiled. As he approached, he saw her tuck away the letter she had been reading. He experienced a burning curiosity to know who it was from. Surely not that sausage-eater from last year?

'Have you been measured up?' she said.

He nodded. 'I shall cut quite a dash at Oxford, you may be sure.' He leaned against the divine tree. 'I was thinking . . .' But what had he been thinking? Tailcoats and dress shirts, calves' eyes and Druids, oak trees and crumbling walls, the future and the past. 'I was thinking . . .' He plucked an idea from the air. 'We should go on a picnic. The three of us. You, me and Eliza.'

'A picnic?'

'Yes, a picnic. People *do* have picnics, it's not unknown. The weather is set fair, it's my last hols before Oxford, why not enjoy ourselves?'

She warmed to the idea. 'We could go in the motor. We could take lunch *and* tea. We'd need rugs, a hamper—'

'Anything you like. Tomorrow. We could go tomorrow.'

'No, not tomorrow. There's the funeral tomorrow.'

'What funeral? I don't know anything about any funeral.'

She explained. He might have known it would have something to do with the village. The shopkeeper had died, Mr Cardwell.

'So that was his name. I often wondered.'

'You knew his name, Roddy. Everybody knew his name. He was very popular. Poor Daisy is so upset. That's why she hasn't been around these last few days.'

He looked at her blankly.

As if explaining to an ignoramus, she said slowly, 'Mr Cardwell was her uncle.'

'I expect half the men in the village are her uncles. They're all related one way or another.' But he found himself thinking not of Daisy Turner but of her brother Billy. Mr Cardwell had been *his* uncle too. Roderick remembered ferrets and beer two years back. He remembered cricket and rabbiting in Row Meadow. He remembered the ambush in the Spinney long ago. 'I suppose I ought to show my face at this funeral.'

'You?'

'Yes, me. There's no need to look quite so astonished. Why shouldn't I go?' He felt himself colouring up, added hurriedly, 'We can still go on the picnic next day, or the day after.'

'Well, yes, we could . . .' A smile crept over her face. 'That would be nice, Roddy. Something to look forward to.'

'I do have my uses,' he muttered, scowling. But for once, it seemed, he had done something right.

* * *

He had wondered if the funeral would be anything like Father's. It turned out to be a much smaller, more rustic sort of affair. He felt out of place. The peasants — he was careful not to refer to the villagers as *peasants* in front of Dorothea — looked at him askance as if he was a visitor from another world, whereas they greeted Dorothea like one of their own. Billy Turner glanced at Roderick in passing, said nothing, but gave a little nod of his head before moving on. One couldn't help but notice that Turner's suit (Sunday best?) was far too small for him.

Sitting in a pew towards the back of the cold church, Roderick felt Dorothea's hand reaching for his.

'Oh, Roddy . . .'

He hadn't the faintest idea what to say — was she *really* this upset about some old shopkeeper? — so he just squeezed her hand instead. This, it seemed, was just what she needed. She turned to him for a moment with shining eyes, whispered, 'Sometimes you can be so *lovely*, Roddy!'

Was he to understand by this that Switzerland had been forgiven and that they were back to the way things had always been? Was it too much to hope?

Walking back across the fields with her hand still in his, she said, 'It was a lovely, lovely service.' Everything was *lovely* today. But to Roderick's mind the service had been rather brief and perfunctory, the elderly vicar — 'A lovely old man, so lovely!' — rather going through the motions.

Anyway, it was all over now. He'd done his duty. And with the weather still hot, the sunshine blazing, everything was set fair for the picnic tomorrow.

* * *

The curtains flapped listlessly in the faintest of breezes. Outside the afternoon was hot and dazzlingly bright; here in the bedroom it was dim, sultry, soporific. Roderick put a restraining arm round Susie Hobson's shoulder as she tried to slip from under the bedclothes.

'No you don't!'

'Oh, sir! You must let go of me!'

'I shan't.'

'I've work to do, sir! Bossy Bourne will have my guts for garters. She isn't best pleased with me as it is.'

'I am the master of the house. You've to please me first, not the Dreadnought.'

'You please yourself, sir. I've had quite enough of you for one day.'

'Very pert, Susie Hobson.' Roderick exerted himself, pulled her back onto the bed, wrapping his arms round her. 'Of course, if you really must go, there's always Kirkham.'

Susie pouted. 'Kirkham? What would you want with Sally Kirkham?'

'She's a pretty girl, Kirkham. Very pretty. I'm sure *she* wouldn't run off and leave me.'

'But I'm much prettier than Sally! You can ask anyone and they'll say the same!' Susie Hobson sighed, yielding into his embrace. 'Very well then, sir. I suppose you'd better kiss me again.'

* * *

Roderick in his room lay back in his bath, hot water lapping at his chest. He was very pleased with himself. Who would have guessed that Susie Hobson would prove so biddable? But evidently she had a soft spot for him.

'You're a handsome one, aren't you, sir!' she'd cooed as she stroked and patted him. 'You will be good to me, sir, won't you?'

Handsome. It was what *she* had said: Aldora. *I've never seen such a handsome boy*. But he did seem to have this effect on girls, on women. Aldora, Hobson, the *Mädchen* in Anderdorf; even old Lady Fitzwilliam the other night had been dribbling on to Mother about how tall he was, how well-proportioned, and so pleasant-looking!

Dangling his arms over the side of the zinc bath, Roderick's grin faded. To take such a risk with Hobson when the Dreadnought was on the prowl and Mother somewhere about was rather foolhardy to say the least. And he very much doubted whether Dorothea would regard what he'd done with Hobson as being 'good' to her.

Slugs and snails and puppy dogs' tails: that was the long and short of it. Sometimes he had the Devil in him and he couldn't help it. He'd always been the same. And it was impossible — simply *impossible* — not to feel smug at getting one over on Nibs Carter, for Carter and Hobson were still courting, Dorothea had told him not long ago.

With Hobson, one didn't feel such a novice as one had with Aldora. The boot was firmly on the other foot. Was it *his* fault if Hobson was so smitten? She had a devil of her own, *that* was obvious enough.

But what if it had been Daisy Turner batting her eyes at him and not Susie Hobson? How would he have felt next time he met Daisy's brother?

Ducking his head under the water, Roderick rinsed himself clean, deciding as he surfaced that he would turn over a new leaf.

Unless, of course, Hobson—

He ducked his head again then sprang out of the tub to stand dripping on the oilcloth. He reached for the towel laid ready. Tomorrow the picnic. He'd be on his best behaviour. He'd even make an effort with Eliza. He would, in fact, and from now on, be a model cousin, brother and son, the new Roderick Brannan. He wouldn't lose his temper, he wouldn't even grumble. This he solemnly promised. Starting tomorrow.

* * *

'Useless idiot!' muttered Roderick, glaring at the gangling chauffeur who was forging ahead across the meadow lugging the picnic basket, Eliza skipping at his side. 'This wouldn't have happened if I'd been allowed to drive.'

They hadn't even got as far as Broadstone before the motor broke down. Smith didn't have the spare part he needed. Roderick had wanted to make him walk back and fetch it but Dorothea had said no, they could just as well have the picnic here as anywhere else. They had left the motor by the roadside and begun tramping across endless fields in the torrid heat, trying to find a spot which met with Eliza's approval.

'Young Stan is not an idiot.' Dorothea beneath her parasol looked effortlessly cool. 'It's not Stan's fault that the motor broke down. And I had enough of your driving the other day when we went to Lawham. You go far too fast and you don't keep your eyes on the road.'

'That's slander, that is! I'm an expert driver!' *Impetuous* was the word that Fitzwilliam had used while giving Roderick some coaching recently. Fitzwilliam fussed like a maiden aunt, but no one knew more about motors. But perhaps it was best not to mention Fitzwilliam in front of Dorothea.

The chauffeur had stopped to catch his breath and Eliza was sitting on the picnic basket as Roderick and Dorothea joined them.

'Why not stop here?' suggested Roderick. 'There's nothing wrong with this place. I want to eat.'

Eliza wrinkled her nose, looking round. 'What are all these humps and bumps?'

'I've heard as it's a dead village, miss,' said Smith. (How did he know, a Coventry boy, a stranger in these parts?)

'A dead *village*?' Eliza looked at Stan in wonder. 'But how can a village *die*?'

'A village dies when there's no one left living in it,' said Roderick. 'I expect this place was finished off by the Black Death.'

'What's the Black Death? Will the Black Death come to Hayton? Will Hayton die too?'

'Of course not, you goose. The Black Death only happened in medieval times. Don't you know *anything*? You ought to, at your age.'

'When was medieval times?'

'From the fourth of September 476 to the twenty-ninth of May 1453. Now let's spread the rugs and have our picnic.'

But Eliza was adamant: they couldn't possibly have a picnic on top of a dead village.

Roderick sighed. 'Very well. If we must traipse to the ends of the earth, then let's get on with it. There's one saving grace. We shall all bake to death in this heat long before we starve.'

They weaved between the mounds and hummocks, came to a cart track. The rutted earth was dry and cracked. They followed the track, Smith sweating and stumbling under the weight of the hamper, Eliza running ahead. The midday sun beat down on them. The verdant landscape rippled in the heat. There was an airless quiet.

Passing under a brick railway bridge, they came to a place where there was a grassy bank shaded by an elder. The cart track went on, passed through a gate, faded into the fields beyond. But Roderick threw down his boater and refused to walk a step further. Eliza for a moment looked likely to argue but then thought better of it. They got out the rugs and spread them on the grass, and Dorothea set about unpacking the picnic.

Lounging in the shade of the elder, Roderick eyed the chauffeur narrowly. 'Off you go, then, Smith.'

'Sir?' Smith's eyes swivelled from Roderick to the picnic then back again.

'Off you go and fetch the part for the motor.'

'Don't listen to him, Stan,' said Dorothea. 'Eat your lunch first.' She passed him a piled plate along with a glass of champagne.

'That's *my* champagne,' hissed Roderick. 'I fetched it myself out of the cellar.'

'It's Aunt Eloise's champagne,' Dorothea corrected. 'I don't suppose you asked permission, either. I don't like champagne, in any case. The bubbles go up one's nose.'

'Only if you *sniff* them.' Roderick snatched the bottle and propped it by his elbow.

Dorothea looked at him rather pityingly. He tried to come up with some crushing remark but it was too hot to concentrate, too hot to pick a fight with Dorothea, too hot to bully the chauffeur. Besides, what about his new leaf?

But the new leaf could wait until the weather was cooler. It could wait until tomorrow, or next week — or never.

Roderick yawned and lay back, the food all eaten, the champagne all gone. Smith with his coat off and his sleeves rolled up was now flat on his back with his cap over his face. Dorothea and Eliza sat nearby, chattering, laughing, drinking lemonade. Whatever did girls find to talk about? His fuddled brain couldn't follow their tortuous conversation.

Roderick closed his eyes. The heat, the food, all that champagne: he suddenly felt very sleepy. He breathed in the scent of grass, of the elder blossom, of the leather of Smith's jacket, of discarded orange peel. He listened to the murmur of the girls' voices, the gentle snoring of the chauffeur, the faint buzzing of bees. The sounds grew distant, indistinct. Sated and somnolent, cradled by the grassy bank, swaddled by the heat, in no time at all he was fast asleep.

* * *

It was pitch dark. He couldn't breathe, he couldn't move. He'd been buried alive. He'd been buried along with the dead village. Someone had made a dreadful mistake, thinking him dead from the Black Death when he'd only been asleep. He opened his mouth to call for help but his mouth was full of cold, wet earth. He was choking, suffocating, dying—

He woke with a start. He found himself squinting into a dazzling light. He pressed his hands to the ground expecting to feel damp earth, but all he felt was dry grass. He breathed a sigh of relief, remembering the grassy bank and the picnic and the elder tree. The shade had moved as he slept and now the sun was in his face.

Slowly he sat up, looked around. Everything was almost the same but not quite. The sun was in a different place, the afternoon had deepened; the fields, trees, hedgerows, embankment baked in heat and silence. Eliza and Smith were nowhere to be seen, Smith's coat lying abandoned. Dorothea was sitting under her sunshade surrounded by pens, pencils, paper, envelopes, newspaper cuttings.

Roderick stretched sleepily, the terror of his dream fading. 'Writing letters?'

'Trying to.' Dorothea sighed. 'The heat makes the ink run. There are blots all over the page. I shall have to start again.'

'Writing to your serious little sausage-eater?'

She didn't deign to reply, crumpling a piece of paper in a way that made Roderick think it was how she would like to crumple *him*.

He envied the sausage-eater but found it impossible to hate him on this drowsy afternoon, in these perfect surroundings. Emotions flowed through him as incontinent as Dorothea's ink. He couldn't decide if he was happy, sad, angry or what. His emotions seemed something entirely new, as if they had as yet no name.

He reached for Dorothea's newspaper cuttings to anchor himself in the printed words. Asquith, the Parliament Bill, hedgers and ditchers; suffragettes in the Albert Hall, striking railwaymen shot dead in Wales: none of it seemed real on this endless afternoon.

He picked up another cutting, blew off an ant, began to read: *If a situation were to be forced upon us in which peace could only be preserved by the surrender of the great and beneficent position Britain has won by centuries of heroism and achievement, by allowing Britain to be treated where her interests were vitally affected as if she were of no account in the Cabinet of nations, then I say emphatically that peace at any price would be a humiliation intolerable for a great country like ours to endure . . .*

It was Lloyd George. Good old Lloyd George. He had to be doing something right to get up Colonel Harding's nose — Humphrey Harrington-Shaw too. Old men with old ideas. *Centuries of heroism and achievement . . . a great country like ours . . .* He had a way with words, Lloyd George, the sly old dog, there was no doubt about that.

The piece of paper slipped through Roderick's fingers. He stared up at the sky, shading his eyes with his arm. Wellington and Nelson, Trafalgar and Waterloo; Crécy, too, and Agincourt and the Spanish Armada and the Battle of Blenheim. All the centuries of heroism and achievement, all in the past. What in the modern world was left to be done? The entire globe had been mapped and explored. Even now Captain Scott was about to conquer the last untrodden land on earth. England's enemies had been eternally vanquished, the Royal Navy ruled the seas, the Pax Britannica would endure forever. It was just his luck, thought Roderick, to have been born into this mellow autumn of the world when the great cycles of history had all been played out. What was left for him? Oxford, and Father's factories, and Clifton; marriage, perhaps, and children (Banquo's heirs) — if a girl existed he could really love, if love really existed.

Was he even a man *capable* of love? Did he *want* to be?

He picked up the piece of paper he'd dropped. 'Do you send all these clippings to your Teuton? Is he interested in such things?'

'His name is Johann, and yes, he's interested. He's interested in England.' She reached across, took the paper from his hand, looked at it. Her face clouded over. 'This, though . . . I decided not to send this. It made me feel . . . I don't know. Roddy, do you think there really will be a war? Some people say so.'

'A war over Morocco? It's all rot, Doro. Just sabre-rattling. What's Morocco to us? The Germans like to kick up a fuss now and then, it's in their nature. Look how they meddled with the Boers! But they'll roll over in the end, they always do. There won't be a war, not in this day and age.'

'Germans are patriotic too, you know. They have history and culture. Johann tells me all about it in his letters: Schiller, Goethe, Kant—'

'Pah! None of that lot are a patch on Shakespeare and Newton and . . .'

'And?'

'There name is legion.'

'Roddy?'

'What is it?'

'I can't *not* write to him, not after all this time.'

'You must do what you want, Doro. Whatever makes you glad. I only want you to be glad.' Was this the new leaf turned? 'It's a jolly thing, I suppose, to write letters to a chap. You used to write to me.'

She smiled at him. 'I shall write to you when you are at Oxford. Are you very nervous about Oxford?'

'Of course not! I'm not some sort of sap! It's only the same as going to school.'

'But it isn't. It's different. I'd be nervous, if it was me. I think you are nervous too. I think you're frightened like a little boy. In fact, I *know* you are.'

'If you know, why ask? What is it about girls that makes them want to cut a chap down all the time?'

'What is it about boys that makes them want to build themselves up?'

'I don't need to build myself up, Doro. I'm perfect as I am.'

'And so very modest too. If you're not too high-and-mighty, perhaps you could look for Eliza. I haven't seen her for ages.'

'I pity your sausage-eater,' Roderick said as he got to his feet. 'No doubt you've got *him* wrapped round your finger, too.'

'You are ridiculous,' she said laughing; and he laughed too as he made his way up the grassy bank past the elder. There was a thicket of bushes at the top. Red Admirals and Meadow Browns were flitting in and out of the dappled shade. He pushed his way through the tangled branches. His feet crunched on gravel and he found himself walking on the permanent way of a railway. It must be the Great Central, he decided, shielding his eyes to follow the line of it running along embankments and over bridges across the low-lying fields. The rails curved into the distance, glinting in the slanting sunlight.

A restlessness awoke in him. He thought of everything that lay over the horizon. He thought of the trains that could take him there. But the tracks stretched empty in the golden afternoon, the timeless peace unbroken.

He kicked at the rails with his hands in his pockets, thinking about Oxford, wondering if it really would be so different to school. Would Oxford help with the new leaf, make him a changed man, civilised, enlightened, easy-going

— a man who, like Dorothea, gave people the benefit of the doubt?

His thoughts were interrupted by the faint sound of laughter. He turned towards it, stepping from sleeper to sleeper until he came to a bridge. He looked over the parapet. There was another railway below, a single track running at right angles to the one above, the LNWR branch line from Lawham to Leamington. His sister was down there bedecked in buttercups and harebells and purple vetch, which were slung in chains round her neck and tucked into her sash and fastened in her flowing hair. She was wielding a sprig of nettles, looked down imperiously at the chauffeur kneeling between the rails at her feet.

'Please, your majesty!' he begged. 'Have mercy!'

'I am the Queen of All the Flowers! You have been naughty! You must be punished!'

Eliza raised the nettles. At the very last moment, Smith jumped up and dodged aside. Eliza chased after him. They ran laughing and calling up and down the permanent way. Roderick watched from his lofty position with a smile on his lips.

The smile hardened. 'Smith! Have you fixed that motor yet?'

The chasing stopped. Smith looked up, straightening his cap: from above it looked almost as if he was saluting. 'No, sir, I haven't sir. I'll see to it right away.' The chauffeur hastened to obey.

Eliza looked up at Roderick on the bridge, her head tilted back. 'Why did you send Stan away?'

'His name is Smith and he has work to do.'

'You have spoiled my game. I am the Queen of All the Flowers.'

'Never mind that. Just get off the line before a train comes along and squashes you.'

'Silly! You can hear a train long before it comes! The rails begin to sing.' She held out her hand. 'Look! There's a ladybird on my finger!'

But it was too small for him to see from up on the bridge.

As he stood there looking down, he had the strangest illusion that she was holding out her hand to him in supplication, as if he had the power of life and death, as if he was immensely tall, omnipotent, invincible. But then she began to chant in her sing-song, childish voice and at once the illusion was shattered: it broke into pieces and vanished in the blazing sunshine.

Ladybird, ladybird, fly away home
Your house is on fire, your children are gone
All but one who lies under a stone
Fly away, ladybird, fly away home!

It made him smile to hear her but the smile died on his lips for suddenly the simple words seemed to him more poignant than any of Westaway's poets. Another illusion, he told himself. But if it was only an illusion, why was his heart swelling within him, why could he feel such an inexpressible longing, an inexpressible longing for — for what?

For what?

* * *

They would walk home, Dorothea announced. It was not far, across the fields. Smith could come back for the motor in the morning. They stowed in it the rugs and the hamper, and then took to the canal towpath as far as the tunnel.

The sun behind them was falling towards the horizon, staining the thin clouds red and gold and brilliant purple, as they climbed the slopes of Hambury Hill, tramping alongside the hedgerows. They came upon signs of the harvest: corn piled in stooks; a cutting machine chugging; men, women and children busy in a big field, sparing barely a glance for the passing picknickers. Apart from the machine, thought Roderick as he trailed behind the others, this might have been any harvest in any year, going back, back, back into the mists of time. Crécy and Waterloo, Clifton Park and the venerable Massinghams: they were as nothing, mere ripples on the water, swept away by the great tides of life.

They left the harvest behind as the sun dipped below the horizon. At long last they climbed the stile into the Old Close. Clifton stood tall, framed against the fading sky, its edges softened by the twilight, its windows bright with many lights. Dorothea and Smith led the way. Eliza held Roderick's hand, stumbling wearily through the long grass. They came to a gate which opened onto a well-worn track. Opposite, as they filed through the gate, a single lamp glowed in the downstairs window of Becket's cottage. Rookery Hill with its crown of trees loomed darkly in the near distance. To the left the track quickly dwindled to a grassy bridleway and was lost in the gathering dusk, seeking Brockmorton far away across the fields. But they turned right, towards the house. As they passed the archway that opened into the stable yard, Smith peeled away, heading for his chauffeur's loft. Roderick now led the way, crunching across the gravel. Deep shadows were piled beneath the spreading boughs of the cedar tree but the front door was open wide and light spilled out onto the steps.

They passed from the timeless twilight into the brightness of the hall. They were home at last.

* * *

Before going down to dinner, Roderick looked in on the nursery. There was no one in the day room, no sign of Dorothea. Eliza was in her room next door, already tucked up.

'I kept falling asleep. Doro said I should go to bed.' She took hold of his hand. 'Wasn't it super? Wasn't the picnic wonderful? The most wonderfullest thing that has ever happened.'

He smiled down at her. 'You're easily pleased.'

'I wish—' She yawned.

'More wishes?'

'Only one wish this time. I wish we could stay like this always. I wish we could be together forever: me, you, Doro, Young Stan.'

'Silly goose.' He ruffled her fair hair. Yet her wish seemed to chime with something inside him, one of those nameless emotions from earlier.

She was studying his hand, first one side, then the other, tracing the lines on his palm, stroking the tiny hairs on his fingers. Finally she drew it to her mouth and kissed it.

'What was that for?' he asked, bemused.

'I don't know. I wanted to do it. Sometimes I get an idea to do something and I just do it.'

'That will get you into all sorts of trouble if you're not careful. Well, night-night, kiddo.'

'Good night, Roddy.'

He paused on his way downstairs, examined his hand, the one she'd kissed. He could still feel the tingling touch of her lips. It had been like receiving a benediction, as if he'd been kneeling as Smith had knelt earlier before the Queen of All the Flowers. He was a knight soon to set forth on crusade. He was a knight suffused with piety, devotion, lionhearted courage.

He grinned, flexing his fingers, shaking his head. He was not a knight. Knights were medieval, they were old hat, they were all as dead as the dead village by Broadstone. He was setting out not on crusade but to follow the footsteps of Uncle Fred to Oxford.

His stomach rumbled. Even the knights of old must have needed their dinner.

Leaving the half-landing, he ran down the rest of the stairs to join Mother and Dorothea.

CHAPTER TEN

Waiting for his connection at Bletchley, Roderick paced along the platform, smoking a cigarette, impatient. He wanted to get it over with, to get there: Oxford. He could, of course, have travelled by motor, but that would have made it even more difficult to dissuade Mother from accompanying him. One might have been setting off for the Antarctic with Captain Scott, the way Mother had been carrying on.

Well, perhaps 'carrying on' was rather strong, but he'd never known her give him advice before. He must not spend beyond his means. He should avoid gambling at all costs. 'Your Uncle Frederick,' she had begun, but then stopped and said no more.

'One would think I'd never been away from home before,' he had complained to Dorothea. 'I've been going to school three terms a year for ten years! And what's Uncle Fred got to do with it?'

'University is different to school. It was at university that your Uncle Fred became a rapscallion.'

'A *what*?'

'He . . . he became rather wild. Drinking and gambling and . . . things like that. He fell in with the wrong crowd.'

Roderick had looked at her in wonder. 'How do you *know* all this?'

'How do you *not* know? He was *your* uncle. I thought everybody knew.'

Roderick flicked the end of his cigarette onto the permanent way, began retracing his steps along the platform. So Uncle Fred had been a bit wild, had he? Not quite the paragon Mother painted. One had always had due regard for Uncle Fred but now one felt one might have *liked* him too. There was a certain affinity between them. Not that one was exactly *wild*; not that one was a *rapscallion*. But there had always been moments when one had been rather reckless, whether it was swimming in the canal or taking a tumble with Hobson.

Mother, Dorothea, Eliza had lined up to see him off. There'd been an empty space where Father would once have stood.

Eliza had clung to his hand. 'I wish you needn't go.'

'Don't worry, kiddo. I'll be back in no time.'

He'd passed along the line. 'Well, Doro.'

'Well, Roddy.'

They'd looked at one another and then she'd stepped forward and embraced him. He'd been taken aback. He'd been rather pleased. Finally, as he put his arms round her and hugged her back, he'd begun to feel elated. This was the final proof that everything was back to normal between them. Everything was settled. He could always rely on Dorothea.

Mother had been nonplussed and faintly disapproving of such untoward affection in the stately hallway of Clifton Park. She'd stood tall and straight. 'Well, goodbye, Roderick. *Do* have a good term.' One thing was certain: Mother never changed.

And so he'd taken his leave and here he was, on his way to Gloucester College just like Uncle Fred in the 1870s. Oxford was waiting to welcome him.

If one ever got there. Where was this blasted train?

* * *

Roderick met a chap on the stairs whom he recognised instantly as *one of us*, as Westaway would have it. Like Marchant, this chap had a complacent air about him, as if the entire world had been summoned into existence for his benefit alone.

'I say, hello! I keep seeing you around. We share this staircase, I think. Gosse is the name. My rooms are just here.'

Roderick shook hands warmly and introduced himself. Gosse might be a useful chap to know. There was something aristocratic about him. Might he even be an Honourable?

'Jolly nice to meet you, Brannan. How do you like your rooms?'

'Er . . . nice rooms.'

'But small. Don't you find them small?'

'Rather small, yes.'

Gosse grinned. 'Glad you think so. Thought it was just me. I say, isn't it all a frightful rush! I haven't stopped since I got here.'

'Me too. I've an interview now — a don, I think — and then I'm to be measured for my OTC uniform.'

'What about your cap and gown?'

'I have them somewhere — at the bottom of my trunk, I expect. I haven't had time to unpack properly.'

'I rather like my cap. Don't you like yours? I say, do you want some pictures?'

'Pictures?'

'For your rooms. To hang on your walls. I found this jolly little shop, only I seem to have bought rather more pictures than I needed. They've just been delivered. I wish you'd take some. Why not come later and look them over? I'm just here, this door. If you don't want the pictures, I've some rather excellent port, a present from the pater.'

'Well, thanks, old chap, that's very civil of you. I'll be sure to call by. But I must dash. The don will be waiting.'

'Oh, yes, do go. One mustn't upset the dons, what!'

As he swung down the narrow stairs, Roderick decided that Gosse's mother would definitely not have warned *her* son about spending beyond his means.

* * *

After being measured for his uniform, Roderick sauntered back along the High in the autumnal sunshine feeling very pleased with life. Being a fresher was rather jolly. One was treated with respect. The dons talked to one as an equal. And a chap of the stature of Gosse invited one for port. It was all very civilised. Nothing like being a new boy at school.

He waited at the kerb to cross the street. The High at this time of day was busy, very different to the staid town of Downfield, still less like sleepy Lawham where nothing ever happened. A man up a ladder was whistling a tune as he cleaned windows. Shop awnings flapped in the breeze. Bicycles skimmed back and forth. Horses plodded, pulling laden carts. A lordly motor coasted past.

Roderick's eye was caught by four people on the far pavement, a shy-looking boy and a frosty-faced girl, and two others who were engaged in an animated conversation: a slim blond young man and an earnest girl waving her arms about as she made some forceful point, wisps of dark hair escaping from under her hat. Roderick's gaze lingered on the girls. Were they perhaps examples of those fabled curiosities, bluestockings? Here was a whole new category of women. His interest was aroused. But as he stepped off the kerb, the ground trembled and a tram trundled across his line of sight, an advert for Van Houten's cocoa emblazoned on its side. He waited impatiently, watching the horses straining between the shafts. The tram slid slowly away. The far pavement came back into view. But the four young people had vanished.

As he sprinted across the road, Roderick wondered if perhaps they'd gone down one of the side streets. He could take a look. But then he shook his head. There was too much to do to bother with a wild goose chase. His study of bluestockings could wait for another time.

Putting the incident out of his mind, he hurried on his way.

* * *

Sitting to dinner in Hall, Roderick found he had Gosse on one side and a chap called Kitson on the other. Hall was a large, gloomy, wood-panelled room with a wooden floor. There were long tables decked out with white tablecloths and benches packed with undergraduates. The dons sat in splendid isolation up on a dais, beneath a large portrait of the founder.

Kitson looked up from his soup. 'And what does your father do, Brannan?'

'Actually, he's dead.'

'Oh, bad luck.' Kitson sipped soup, unperturbed.

'Kitson judges a chap by what the chap's father does,' Gosse said. 'Kitson's a Harrovian,' he added, as if one ought to make allowances.

'It's a rather good method of mine,' said Kitson. 'One gets to know all the right people.'

'What about that chap over there? Is he the right sort?' Roderick nodded in the direction of a boy he'd recognised earlier as they took their places for dinner, none other than the rather shy-looking and least conspicuous of the four people he'd seen on the High that afternoon.

'His name is Milton,' said Kitson. 'His father also is dead, but his grandfather is a millionaire. Coal. Or is it iron? I forget which.' Kitson raised his voice. 'I say, Milton. Was it coal or iron that your grandfather made his fortune in?'

Milton looked rather startled at being hailed across the table in so unceremonious a manner. Roderick caught his eye. 'Don't mind Kitson. He's a Harrovian. Didn't I see you on the High this afternoon? You were with two girls.'

'Oh . . . er . . . yes. That would be my cousin, Miss Ward.'

'The dark-haired girl?'

'No. The dark-haired girl is my cousin's friend, Miss Halsted. They are both students at Somerville.'

'I've heard,' said Gosse, slowly stirring his soup, 'that it's impossible to meet girls from Somerville. They are chaperoned.'

'Why would anyone want to meet girls of *that* sort?' said Roderick.

Gosse didn't answer, merely smiled and began stirring his soup in the opposite direction.

* * *

It did not take Kitson long to ferret out some facts about Roderick's father. They were in Gosse's rooms drinking port. There was quite a crowd, Gosse's port being rather popular. Kitson was lounging in an armchair.

'A little bird tells me, Brannan, that your father was the son of a watchmaker and that he ran a small business in Coventry.'

'*Two* businesses, actually, Kitson. Two *large* businesses. You've probably heard of the BFS Motor Company. One sees BFS motors everywhere.'

'I say!' cried Gosse. 'I do believe my pater owns one of those BFS machines! He's something of a motor fiend, my pater. Just wait till I tell him I'm acquainted with the family that makes them!'

'My Uncle Giles is a motor fiend too,' said Milton. 'He races BFS motors, and he runs the BFS showroom in town.'

'Then you must be one of the Darvell Hall Miltons!' said Roderick. 'There are so many of you, one loses track.'

'Milton actually *lives* at Darvell Hall,' said Kitson reverentially.

'Well, yes, I do. My father died when I was a kid and Grandpa took us in. I remember, about a year or so after we'd moved in, there was some sort of fête at the Hall with a competition for motor cars. Uncle Giles drove a BFS machine. He didn't win but one of the other BFS machines did.'

'Do you know, Milton,' said Gosse, 'now that you mention it, I believe I've seen your uncle racing BFS motors at Brooklands.'

Roderick — who only knew of the BFS victory at Darvell Hall from what Father and Dorothea had told him long ago, and who'd never taken much interest in motor racing — now found that his half-remembered anecdotes stood him in good stead, strengthening his ties with Gosse and Milton. Kitson looked put out. This was clearly *not* what he'd intended.

By the end of the evening, Gosse had become George and Milton Gerry. Kitson was still Kitson.

As they were leaving, Gerry Milton took Roderick shyly aside. 'I say, I don't suppose you could help me out. I have to go to tea at my aunt's tomorrow and I'd like to take someone along. I wouldn't ask, only one tends to feel rather outnumbered.'

'I'd like to, old chap, I really would, but there's this logic bumf I ought to get started.' Roderick reached for any excuse. Who in their right mind would want to go to tea with someone's aunt?

Milton looked crestfallen. 'I see. I understand. Thanks awfully, anyway.'

'What's so terrible about your aunt?'

'It's more my cousin than my aunt. Maggie can be rather . . . domineering. She's sure to have invited Miss Halsted, too.'

'Miss Halsted, did you say?' It was not a name one would easily forget: an unusual sort of name. But the girl herself, seen so briefly on the High, was also lodged in Roderick's head. 'Do you know, Gerry, I think I could put off that bumf for one more day.'

'Would you? That's jolly decent of you! You'd get me out of an awful bind.'

'Anything to oblige. After all, we are more or less neighbours back in Northamptonshire. Does . . . does your cousin often invite Miss Halsted?'

'Yes, I'm afraid she does. Maggie and Miss Halsted are great friends. Miss Halsted has a brilliant mind, Maggie says.'

Climbing the narrow stairs up to his rooms, Roderick had doubts about his rash decision to help Milton out. He felt sure that he was bound to dislike any girl who had a 'brilliant mind'. But perhaps an opportunity to examine bluestockings at close range was exactly what he needed. It would surely satisfy his unhealthy curiosity once and for all.

* * *

Gerry Milton's widowed aunt, Mrs Cordelia Ward, lived on the Banbury Road. She was recognisably a Milton. She was also something of a sourpuss. Roderick conjectured that she was eaten with bitterness, having come down in the world from the grandeur of Darvell Hall to a poky little villa on the outskirts of Oxford. Her daughter, Miss Maggie Ward, was plain, dull and humourless but very full of herself. She monopolised the conversation to begin with, sermonising about books and politics and history. Miss Halsted was rather quiet. There was no obvious sign of her brilliant mind.

By the second cup of tea things had started to liven up. Miss Halsted joined in, even Mrs Ward had her say. They were spouting the most incredible militant nonsense: women ought to be awarded degrees, women ought to be allowed to vote, women this and women that. One began to wish that women would all go to the Devil. It was like taking tea with the Three Witches, huddled round a tea pot instead of a cauldron.

Roderick smirked. He made a facetious suggestion that there ought to be women MPs and cabinet ministers, maybe even women generals too. To his consternation, his ridiculous statements were taken quite seriously. The two younger women even began a debate as to whether women should condescend to become generals. Would it not be better to make war illegal? What was needed was an international congress of the world's mothers. If mothers had their say, nations would not find it so easy to sacrifice their sons in the name of a so-called 'sacred cause'.

Gerry Milton's timid objections were quashed without mercy. Roderick felt it beholden on him to come to Milton's aid.

'Now look here, this is all very well, but let's talk about the real world for a moment.'

It was no good. They wouldn't listen. They interrupted and talked over him in what he thought was a most rude — not to say unfeminine — manner. He was making sweeping statements, they said, without a shred of evidence. He seemed to assume his point of view was correct simply because it was a man's point of view. In future men might find they would not have things all their own way. Women were slowly waking up to their importance in the world.

One name seemed to crop up in their talk with monotonous regularity: Mr Antipov says this, Mr Antipov thinks that. Mr Antipov was obviously the fountain of all wisdom. Roderick did not like to show his ignorance by asking who this Antipov was. Some foreign writer, perhaps, or maybe a don?

If Miss Halsted had been quiet to start with, she was quiet no longer. She was now just as animated as when Roderick had first seen her on the High. There was a certain horrific fascination in watching her but she could hardly be called a beauty with all that unruly black hair and a rather Italianate complexion. Her dark eyes blazed, her full red lips curled in a disdainful smile, she swept all before her.

As the tea party finally came to an end, Roderick muttered under his breath, 'When shall we three meet again, in thunder, lightning or in rain?'

'I beg your pardon?' said Miss Halsted. 'I didn't quite catch . . . ?'

'Looks like rain, I said.' Roderick smiled at her disingenuously.

'And you've come without your umbrella, I suppose. How very like a man!'

As they walked back to college, Milton said rather feebly, 'Now you see why I don't like going there alone.'

'Are they always like that?'

'Always.'

'Who's this Antipov fellow they keep talking about? Some sort of academic, is he?'

'No, he's a friend of theirs, a student. I believe he's at our college.'

How wonderfully lucky, thought Roderick, to have the Fountain of All Wisdom at Gloucester College. But what a rum sort of chap he must be, this Antipov. The only man in the world that Miss Halsted (and Miss Ward) approved of.

* * *

'I've heard he has some rather queer opinions,' said Gosse. 'But then, he's a Russian. Russians are queer fish all round.'

It was an overcast, autumnal afternoon and they were rowing on the river, a gusting wind raising waves, the water flecked with fallen leaves. Roderick had no interest in the mysterious Mr Antipov, he really didn't. All he'd said was it seemed odd that no one knew much about him. Even Kitson was no help. He could not say what Antipov's father did.

'Why is Antipov here, in England?'

'No good asking me,' said Gosse. 'I expect he's an assassin. Russia is full of assassins. Perhaps he's the one who shot the Russian Prime Minister at the opera — the Prime Minister with the funny name — Stoily-Pin or something.' Gosse was struck by a sudden idea, stopped rowing abruptly, leaving Roderick floundering. 'Do you know, I might have hit on something there! Antipov could have killed Stoily-Pin and then fled to England in disguise. Shall we ask him? Would we dare? I rather think we should! What do you say, Rodders? I could invite him for coffee in my rooms. Shall I? Yes! I shall!'

'Do as you please, George. I couldn't care less about the fellow. But we shall never get back this side of midnight if you don't pick up your oars, you slacker!'

* * *

By now, mid-way through term, Gosse's rooms had taken on the aspect of a London railway terminus, with people coming and going at all hours. Gosse had all the makings of a first-class snob, but he was not fastidious when it came to making friends. He never bothered about what a chap's father did. Perhaps such niceties didn't matter when one was an Honourable.

The Russian came for coffee as planned. He bowed to them all formally, introduced himself as Nikolai Petrovich Antipov. It turned out that he was the blond young man Roderick had seen in deep discussion with Miss Halsted on the High all those weeks ago. There seemed nothing very remarkable about him apart from the novelty of his being foreign. There were moments when he became quite intense and his eyes — a sort of pale bluey-grey — could be penetrating, but his clothes, Roderick noted, were somewhat shabby.

'And what brings you to Oxford, Antipov?' asked Gosse as he served the coffee. 'Did you come here to be educated in a free country?'

'England has more freedom than Russia, is true. But England is not free country.' Antipov's voice was surprisingly resonant for such a slim frame.

'Of course England is free!' cried Gosse jovially. 'We have democracy. We do not have serfs.'

'In Russia, too, are no serfs now, but poor are still oppressed. In England is the same.'

'Really? You think so? Are the poor not poor because they want to be poor? That's my understanding of it.'

'Poor are made poor. Are exploited.'

'Is that so? Well, well. Can't say I've looked at it in that way before. Won't you have some port, Antipov? It's a present from my pater.'

Gosse got on with everyone. Not in the way Dorothea did, seeing the good in people. More like Father, taking people as he found them. Gosse would have charmed the Three Witches, had them eating out of his hand.

Was this a skill anyone could learn?

But why would one want to charm the Three Witches? Milton could go to tea on his own next time. Those bluestockings were simply not worth bothering with.

* * *

It was a Sunday. There had been a frost overnight and the afternoon was cold and overcast, the golden summer a distant memory. Roderick had been with Milton to tea at Mrs Ward's once more. He couldn't for the life of him think why, when he'd promised himself he wouldn't. Today the two girls were walking back with them. They were taking what Roderick felt was an unnecessarily circuitous route back to town along the canal. Gerry and his cousin were lagging behind, deep in discussion about the latest goings-on of the Milton clan, Uncle Crispin did this, Aunt Eleanor said that, Cousin Adam suggested blah-blah-blah.

Winding his scarf closer round his neck, Roderick said irritably, 'I sometimes think there are enough of those Miltons to populate the entire world.'

Miss Halsted, walking beside him, laughed. 'It does seem a rather *large* family.'

She looked different when she laughed, as if there might be another side to her under her starchy exterior, a more playful side. But she did not laugh much. She seemed to take a decidedly serious view of life. She'd been regaling him as they walked with her opinions of Mr Asquith. Mr Asquith was a hypocrite. Mr Asquith opposed the unearned privilege of the House of Lords while upholding the unearned privilege of men. The scornful tone she'd used when speaking the word *men* seemed at odds with her laughter now. If only she wasn't so intractable! If only she'd give men (some men) a chance!

'Why do you hate men so much, Miss Halsted?' he blurted out. 'Why *do* you?'

Before she could answer, they had to move aside to let a bicycle pass. The wheels swished in the damp and dead leaves. As they fell back into step, his question still hung in the air. Why had he asked it? Why? Had he offended her? But what about *her* offending *him* with her constant disparaging comments?

At length she said guardedly, 'You're quite mistaken, Mr Brannan, if you think I hate men. Nothing could be further from the truth. What I hate is the way women are *enslaved* by men. Women should be free: free to be educated to the same standard as men, free to pursue a career—'

'But why would a woman *need* a career?' he asked in some surprise.

She looked at him rather coldly. 'You can be very supercilious, Mr Brannan. I remember how you laughed the first time we met at the idea of women MPs.'

'But it sounds so *incongruous*, to have an MP who's a woman!'

'I pity your sisters — if you have any. You must be *so* condescending towards them.'

'My little sister runs rings round me, I assure you, Miss Halsted. As for my cousin Dorothea — well, I would never get away with being condescending to *her*.'

'Well, good. I'm glad. But have you ever asked yourself why you are at Oxford and your cousin isn't?'

'Perhaps she doesn't *want* to come to Oxford.'

'Did she tell you that? It's not easy, Mr Brannan, for a woman to come to Oxford. My aunts warned me against it. I'd be ruining my chances, they said. Ruining my chances of getting married, that is. As if I care about that!'

'You don't want to get married?'

'I don't want to be shackled to a man. I shall make a living by writing, as a journalist. I will prove to the world that it *can* be done.'

'Is that what marriage is, being shackled?'

'You seem sceptical. But for many women — too many — that is *exactly* what marriage is. Just think! Until 1882, a married woman had no rights at all. Everything she owned became her husband's on marriage. She herself became her husband's property. This was how the law stood less than thirty years ago! The law has changed since then but attitudes, alas, have not.'

They came to a halt as if by mutual consent, waiting for Milton and Miss Ward. Or was it that they'd run out of things to say to each other? Roderick shivered in the damp air, pulling his scarf ever tighter, watching the ducks and geese on the muddy water swimming towards them, eyeing them speculatively. Even a bluestocking, it seemed, was a complex creature, like all women.

A feeling of resentment that he didn't understand took hold of him as he gazed across the canal, realising that he could see through the tangled branches of the leafless trees on the opposite bank the roofs and gables of his own college.

'Does your . . . your friend Antipov share your views on marriage?'

She looked at him circumspectly, the blazing depths of her eyes suddenly veiled. 'Mr Antipov believes in equality — equality for all, whether it's men or women, the rich and the poor.'

'I suppose you talk about such things all the time. I suppose you are always with him.'

'Not so much here. Not in Oxford. The chaperone rules are too strict — unfair to women. In London one is freer. One can meet whoever one likes. We have set up a discussion group, the Thursday Evening Club. We discuss everything under the sun. It is so liberating, to be able to talk!'

Roderick felt a burning curiosity to know about the *we*. In what way was one freer in London? What about her parents? Did she have parents? What about those aunts who disapproved of university? He knew so little about her — only that Antipov had an unfair advantage, meeting her in London as well as Oxford.

'You shouldn't believe *everything* he says, you know!'

'Everything who says?'

'Antipov.' The Fountain of All Wisdom.

She gave him that cold look again. 'I *can* think for myself, Mr Brannan. I don't need a man to tell me what to believe. We happen to agree on a lot of things, Mr Antipov and I, that's all.'

Roderick kicked savagely at the tufts of grass on the canal bank. He'd said the wrong thing. He always said the wrong thing. Why couldn't he be more like Gosse or Father or Dorothea?

Before he could think of a way of putting things right, Milton and Miss Ward finally caught them up. The conversation immediately turned to the endless exploits of the Milton clan.

As they made their way along the narrow path, Roderick found himself at the back of the little group, squeezed out. He glanced over his shoulder at Gloucester College across the water, half hidden by the trees.

His heart quickened. He could feel the blood beating in his veins. What was happening to him? It was this place — the dreaming spires. Was that correct, was that Oxford, the dreaming spires? Westaway would know. But it could make a poet of anyone, being here. Oh, if only—

But the others had moved ahead. He had to run to catch them up.

* * *

'You seem rather taken with this Miss Halsted,' said Gosse as they ate hot buttered toast and buns in his rooms, alone for once.

'That's complete eyewash, George!' cried Roderick, hurriedly swallowing his toast so he could get his rebuttal in. 'I've only seen her half a dozen times so far this term and it's nearly the end of November already!'

'But you talk about her incessantly.'

'I hardly ever talk about her! Never, in fact! I don't even *think* about her! You do exaggerate!'

'The fresher doth protest too much, methinks.'

'Stop ragging me and pass those buns over, you glutton.'

Gosse passed the buns, licking butter off his fingers. 'I've heard she's a suffragette.'

'Who's a suffragette?' asked Roderick, breaking a bun in half.

'Miss Halsted, of course.'

'I do wish you wouldn't talk about her so *incessantly*, George. She's not a suffragette, anyway. She's . . . she's *modern*, that's all.'

Gosse looked at him sidelong. 'Is free love one of her things? Is that *modern*?'

'I've no idea. Why don't you ask her? I don't believe in love, if you must know. It's all rot.'

'Love is not exactly where the danger lies.'

'What danger? What in Hades are you talking about, George?'

'My elder brother gave me one of his pep talks before I came up. He warned me against the sins of the flesh. One gets clap, apparently. Or syphilis.' Gosse bit into yet another bun with relish. 'Syphilis is rather hateful, my brother said: pustules, seizures, madness.'

'I say, George, are you suggesting that Miss Halsted—?'

'I am merely making conversation.' Gosse gave a bland smile.

Roderick shifted uneasily in his chair. What exactly *was* clap? And syphilis? Gosse was a positive menace with his casual asides, tripping one up. It was all very well for him with his older brother. What about a chap who didn't have a brother, a chap whose father was dead?

But Gosse was mistaken if he thought Miss Halsted was *that* sort of girl. She wasn't, nothing like it. She had pride in herself, she had principles. One might not agree with her on everything but one did . . . well, *respect* her, in a funny sort of way. A chap would have to be blind not to see it. Perhaps Gosse wasn't so clever — wasn't so worldly wise — as he liked to think.

Oxford was full of new experiences, but that had been one of the first, seeing Miss Halsted on the High. It seemed now like fate, a finger pointing.

But if it was fate, then fate had a wry sense of humour, for even that first time Antipov had been with her. She idolised Antipov. No one could match him.

'I say Roddy, you've gone off in a brown study! What are you thinking about?'

'I was thinking . . .' Roderick stirred, sat up. 'I was thinking what a quantity of pictures you have on your walls,

George — if there *are* any walls under that lot.' And with that, Roderick reached forward and swiped the last bun before Gosse could get his hands on it.

* * *

Sitting up late trying to catch up on some work — there was so much going on at Oxford, one was apt to forget about work, and time was ticking on, the end of term looming — Roderick was irritated by the interruption of a knock on his door. Irritation turned to annoyance when he found that it was Kitson who had knocked. Kitson had a habit of paying calls. He liked to keep track of people.

'What do you want, Kitson? I'm rather busy, as you see.'

Kitson was all affability, inviting himself in, plumping himself in the best arm chair. 'Brannan, Brannan, the watch-maker's grandson. How are you this fine evening?'

Roderick returned to his desk which was littered with books and half-finished essays. 'I'm all the better for seeing you, Kitson. Did you know, by the way, that my great-great grandfather was a baronet, and my uncle married an earl's daughter?' It didn't hurt to bring this up now and again. There were no baronets in Kitson's family.

'Funny you should mention your uncle, Brannan. I heard an interesting story about him the other day. It was Milton who told me. You know Milton. You can't get a word out of him most of the time, but when he's been on Gosse's port . . .' Kitson crossed his legs, wiped a speck of dirt off his trousers, smiled in a way that Roderick thought of as calculating.

'What are you blithering on about, Kitson?'

'Milton was telling me about his own uncle — or one of them. There are dozens, apparently. This particular uncle — Uncle Philip — was something of a black sheep. Lived a profligate life. Was the despair of his family.'

'Do get to the point.'

'It turns out, Brannan, that Uncle Philip was a great chum of *your* uncle — your much-vaunted uncle who married an earl's daughter. Frederick Rycroft. That was the name, wasn't it? The same Frederick Rycroft who, after his wife died unexpectedly young in the 1890s, was so beside himself that he took his shotgun and blew his brains out in the library at Clifton Park.' A puzzled look came over Kitson's face. 'At least, I *think* that was what Milton told me. Or was it . . . no, wait, I have it now. It was an *accident.* The gun went off by *accident.* Of course it did!'

'That's complete hogwash, Kitson! Uncle Fred didn't kill himself! He—' But how *had* Uncle Fred died? It had never been made clear.

A chill went up Roderick's spine. He thought of Mother, who never went into the library at home, who never talked about her brother's death. It all seemed to fit. His mind revolted against it but somehow he *knew* it was true.

'What do you *want,* Kitson? Why are you *here*?'

But Kitson seemed to think he'd achieved whatever it was he'd come for. 'I'll let you get back to your work, Brannan. It looks like you need to. I'm up to date with all my essays, of course. Night-night!'

Roderick closed the door. He sank down into the chair that Kitson had just vacated. The fire glowed in the grate. The curtains shut out the night. The little room was silent.

Kitson was a lickspittle. But he was also Machiavellian. No doubt he'd seen the shock he'd caused. He now knew that Roderick had been ignorant of his uncle's fate. Kitson would go running with this story to Gosse and anyone else who would listen. It would make him feel important. It would also tarnish Roderick's reputation. Brannan, Brannan, the watchmaker's grandson, the nephew of a suicide.

. . . after his wife died . . . he was beside himself . . . Roderick frowned. A conversation came back to him out of the mists of the past. He'd just got home from another term at prep school. Dorothea had accosted him. What did *uxorious* mean? Richard's papa (Uncle Fred, in other words) had been *uxorious,* but she didn't know what it meant. 'If you don't know,' he'd said in a lofty tone of voice, looking down his nose at

her, 'then I'm certainly not going to tell you.' Afterwards, at the earliest opportunity, he'd hurried down to the library and looked up the word for himself. *Uxorious: inordinately fond of or submissive to a wife.* He'd not been able to believe that it was a word that applied to Uncle Fred. But now this long-buried memory was like another piece of the puzzle. The picture was becoming clear.

Roderick jumped up. He couldn't bear to sit in this stuffy little room a minute longer. It still reeked of Kitson's nauseating smugness.

He swung down the narrow, timeworn stairs and out into the shadows of the cloister. Breathing in the sharp night air, he patted his pockets for cigarettes as he looked round the quad. There were one or two lights opposite but most of the windows were dark. The sunken lawn was lit by a thin, cold moonlight. All was still and quiet.

He struck a match, shielding the flame with his shaking hand. As he drew on his cigarette, he heard footsteps behind him.

'Good evening.' A low-pitched voice, foreign-accented.

'Antipov! You made me jump! What are you doing here?'

Antipov, of all people. The Fountain of All Wisdom, Miss Halsted's mentor. Roderick flung the used match aside, face-to-face with his adversary. But here, in the hushed environs of Gloucester College, it was impossible to be anything other than magnanimous and enlightened.

'Care for a smoke?'

'A cigarette? Thank you.'

Antipov took the proffered packet of cigarettes and the matches, lit up, breathed out smoke. His eyes glinted palely. The moonlight gave him a famished look.

Passing back the packets, Antipov said, 'You ask what I do. I look at moon and think about cosmos. And you?'

'Nothing, I'm doing nothing.' Roderick took a feverish pull on his cigarette, then burst out, 'I've just found out that my uncle killed himself. I don't mean that he's *just* killed himself. It all happened years ago. But I never knew until now. Why would a chap *do* that?'

'Perhaps he had good reason.'

'I beg your pardon?'

'A man would need good reason to give up most precious gift, life.'

'His wife died, there is that. But it's no excuse. To kill oneself over a woman! It's damned weakness. Tainted blood. A mortal sin. Reflects badly on the whole family.'

Tossing his cigarette away, Roderick swayed, put his hand on a pillar to steady himself. He felt light-headed suddenly. But it was nothing. He'd smoked his cigarette too quickly, that was all.

He lowered himself down onto the top step of the shallow flight that led down to the sunken lawn.

After a moment, the Russian joined him. 'Is not tainted blood. Is not sin, either. That is old-fashioned attitude. One should have — what is word? — *compassion*.'

Compassion, thought Roderick. For Uncle Fred? But what did he know of Uncle Fred? Uncle Fred was a complete stranger. And these were the footsteps he'd be following for so long, the footsteps of a stranger! He felt cheated. He felt as if he'd been lied to. As if he'd been led astray by a *will*-o'-the-*wisp*. How would he find his way back? Whose footsteps could he follow now?

He frowned, lit another cigarette. Antipov, bent over his knees, was still smoking his first. The tips of their cigarettes glowed. The moon hung in the sky, cold, white, remote.

Glancing at the Russian, Roderick said, 'Gosse thinks you're an assassin. He thinks you're the one who murdered the Prime Minister at the Kiev Opera.'

Antipov laughed, exhaling great puffs of smoke. 'Was not me, sorry. I was in England already when Stolypin was shot.'

'You said that a man needs good reason to kill himself. What about killing others? Does one need a good reason for that?'

'Perhaps there was good reason in this case. Stolypin too was a killer. He sent many people to their deaths. In Russia we call the gallows *Stolypin's neck tie*.'

'But weren't they criminals, the people he sent to the gallows?'

'What is crime and what is not?'

'That is self-evident, I would have thought. The law of the land—'

'Laws exist to protect property, to protect those in power. Laws do not benefit ordinary people.'

Roderick curled his lip. Was this the sort of talk that impressed Miss Halsted? And yet, sitting here in the moonlight, Roderick could not feel any animosity towards the Russian. Antipov was not a lickspittle like Kitson. He was not Machiavellian. He presented an open face to the world.

'Are you like this with everybody, Antipov, all this radical talk?'

Antipov shrugged. 'I say what I believe — what I feel *here*.' He placed a hand on his heart, solemn, but then he laughed. 'Sometimes what I say gets me into trouble!'

'Only sometimes?' Roderick found himself laughing too. 'But what to you hope to *achieve*? What can *you* do to change things — what can any man do, alone?'

Antipov didn't answer for a moment, stubbing out his cigarette on the stone step. At length he said, 'Do you know Emelyan Pugachev? He led great peasant revolt in reign of Ekaterina Velikaya — how do you say? — *Catherine the Great*? In Petersburg, Catherine discuss freedom with Diderot, but only talk, talk, talk. Pugachev was man of action. In England you say *actions speak louder than words*, yes?'

'What happened to him in the end, this chap Pugachev?'

'After many months he was captured, he was beheaded.'

'And that's the man whose footsteps you want to follow — the man you want to emulate?'

'Pugachev is inspiration, yes. He showed what one man can do. But I do not follow footsteps. I make my own footsteps. I am my own man, free. Do you see?'

'Yes. Yes. I think perhaps I do.' They would have called Antipov an *individual* at school, that old term of abuse. 'Do you know, Antipov, you remind me of a chap I know, a friend of mine, a man called Westaway.'

'Is he socialist also?'

'No, he's an artist. But he too lives in a world of his own.'

'We all live in same world. That is why is important to make it best world we can.'

'You could be on to something there.' Roderick got to his feet, pocketing the cigarettes and matches. 'Well, good-night, old chap.'

The Russian, still seated, gave a little nod. 'Good night. And *spasibo* — thank you. I like to talk, to improve my English. Is still very bad, but I practise.'

Roderick headed for the stairs but at the last moment turned aside. He wasn't ready to go back to his room just yet. He wanted space and silence. He wanted to walk in the moonlight.

Departing the hallowed portals of the age-old college, he struck out into the empty streets. He felt almost weightless, still a little light-headed, as if his feet were barely touching the ground. It was icy cold. He shivered inside his jacket. He wished he'd brought a coat. But it didn't matter. The cold couldn't hurt him. Nothing could hurt him for now.

Flurries of snow began to drift down as he walked along the High. He turned up the collar of his jacket, shoved his hands deep in his pockets, hunched against the freezing blasts of a sudden, gusting wind. He thought of Antipov's words: *I make my own footsteps*. The thought gave him a feeling of being alone, adrift, unwritten. It was terrifying. Or was it exhilarating? Maybe both. He wasn't sure. He liked not being sure. He liked to think there still things to discover. All he knew was that he wasn't the new Wellington or the next Nelson; he wasn't Uncle Fred or Raynes or even Father; nor was he the heir to the venerable Massinghams, for the Massinghams were all dead and gone, mouldering away in their crypt. He was none of these. He was nobody except himself. The first, the only, Roderick Henry Brannan.

He picked up the pace, striding along the street, puffing and blowing in the cold, smiling too, because he knew despite everything that he would go on trying to *be someone*, to *do something*. He couldn't help it. It was the way he was made. But he'd do it for himself. Not to impress anyone. Not to live up to some long-dead uncle. For himself.

He thought of Mother, Dorothea, Eliza, tucked up in their beds in far-off Clifton Park. He thought of his friends: old friends, new friends, half-forgotten friends, and all the casual acquaintances he'd made on his long journey to this moment — to here and now, Oxford on this winter's night, 1911. There were some unlikely friends amongst them, unexpected friends. Westaway, for instance, and Billy Turner. And — who could say? — maybe even Nikolai Antipov. Why shouldn't he be friends with a Russian and a rival? He could do anything he liked!

And what about Miss Halsted? Was he in love, as Gosse in his roundabout way had suggested? What *was* love? Did it matter when he wasn't sure if Miss Halsted even liked him? But there was plenty of time to find out. There was plenty of time to win her round — if that was what he wanted. Nothing need be decided yet.

He began at last to retrace his steps. He walked quicker and quicker, finally breaking into a run. His footsteps echoed in the silent street. Snow was falling. Frost glittered on the cobblestones. Roofs and chimneys were etched in Gothic lines against clouds silvered by the half-hidden moon. Roderick laughed as he ran. He couldn't stop laughing. What an adventure it was, Oxford, friendship, life, everything! What a supreme adventure! And this was just the beginning.

He ran and he laughed. And the thought of his room, waiting to welcome him back into warmth and light, filled him to the brim with unfettered joy.

THE END

ALSO BY DOMINIC LUKE

THE BRANNANS FAMILY TRILOGY
Book 1: AUTUMN SOFTLY FELL
Book 2: NOTHING UNDONE REMAINED
Book 3: DREAMS THAT VEIL

Thank you for reading this book.

If you enjoyed it please leave feedback on Amazon or Goodreads, and if there is anything we missed or you have a question about, then please get in touch. We appreciate you choosing our book.

Founded in 2014 in Shoreditch, London, we at Joffe Books pride ourselves on our history of innovative publishing. We were thrilled to be shortlisted for Independent Publisher of the Year at the British Book Awards.

www.joffebooks.com

We're very grateful to eagle-eyed readers who take the time to contact us. Please send any errors you find to corrections@joffebooks.com. We'll get them fixed ASAP.

Printed in Great Britain
by Amazon

66711331R00158